D0481784

SC90

THIRSTY

THIRSTY

Andrew Dequasie

WALKER AND COMPANY
NEW YORK

PROLOGUE

THERE ain't no ghost town out in Idaho sadder than what's left of Thirsty. Nobody grew old there because it didn't last that long. Thirsty didn't go much according to eastern laws and had no tradition to live up to. Common sense, horse sense: that was the law in Thirsty.

A sort of western Camelot it was. Dull, unimaginative people, the cowardly and the timid—they never made it as far west as Thirsty.

Thirsty hit its golden age in that last year before it all ended. People like Downwind, Doc Crane, Lillian Hoffman, Sam Ibsen, Sheriffs Johnson and Jones, Shifty, the Dutchman, Hammerin' Harry, Frypan, Chief Many Tongues, and Reverend John—they were all special. And when they left Thirsty, they were like dandelion seeds scattering all over the West, planting little pieces of Thirsty a hundred times over.

Thirsty was a gold-mining town. The men who came there were thirsty for gold and all it could buy. And most of 'em had a special thirst for the stuff the Thirsty Saloon had to offer. But that wasn't how the town got its name. The first gold found in the area was kicked up by old Pete Olsen's mule, Thirsty. Pete was one to give credit where due, and he named the place for his mule.

When Grandpa was very old and I was in my prime, we drove a battered truck as far as we could go on what was left of the road out to the place where Crystal Creek flowed out of a broad valley west of the Bitterroot Mountains. We had to walk the last mile, but Grandpa set quite a pace in his eagerness to stand once again where the town of Thirsty had been.

I stood there with him, gazing at the empty, weathered row of buildings that lined both sides of the main street.

The Thirsty Saloon, at three stories the tallest building in town, still had all of its porch bannisters and most of its gingerbread intact. Momma Rose's place, a squat, rambling, two-story wooden monster, crouched at the bend where the street curved to follow the bench of level land between Crystal Creek and the hills above it. A wide two-story building across from the Thirsty Saloon had a simple sign above the door saying "Food." It had to be the Dutchman's place. Next to it, the modest building with the front door missing, had to be Doc Crane's place. And we had passed a small church, a blacksmith shop, and a livery stable on our way up the street. Grandpa had known Thirsty when it was alive, and I knew it from years of hearing Grandpa speak of it.

Standing there in the weed-grown main street of Thirsty, I saw that Grandpa was lost in memories, and I could no more intrude on his thoughts than I'd interrupt a man at prayer. So I fell to thinking about all those wonderful days in Thirsty that Grandpa spoke of. I could see the place as Grandpa was seeing it, alive and full of the people he'd known there. I sat down on the porch of the Thirsty Saloon and imagined I could see Hank Jones riding into Thirsty for the first time.

CHAPTER 1

THE NEW SHERIFF

HANK Jones never forgot his first day in Thirsty. He had ridden five hundred miles in answer to a letter, mostly sleeping in a bed roll and eating his own cooking, which was a diet nobody would get fat on. He woke up early that morning—cold, stiff, dirty, unshaven, and maybe two hours' ride from Thirsty. So he decided to go on into Thirsty, get washed, shaved, have breakfast, take a nap, and call on the man that wrote the letter.

It was maybe seven o'clock when he rode in. The town looked deserted and the doors of the livery stable were closed, so he walked around back, looking for signs of life. He was back there when he heard a wagon rumbling down the main street at a furious pace. He trotted out front in time to see the wagon scoot past. The driver was laying a whip on the horses, and six rough-looking men were sitting in the wagon bed, laughing fit to bust. Hank stood and watched the wagon disappear up the street with its tailgate flapping behind.

Then, looking up the street from whence the wagon had come, he saw what looked like a large wooden box lying in the street. It was kind of odd, to say the least, seeing the big, barefooted character crawl out from the bottom of the box and come stomping toward him in long johns.

Hank sauntered out to meet the guy. "Excuse me, sir; could you tell me—"

That's as far as he got. The other guy laid a fist like a sledgehammer on him, and Hank went flat out in the street and stayed there.

When Hank came to, he found himself on the floor of the saloon, ignored by the small group of patrons who were having a back-slapping good time. Hank sat up and felt his jaw to see if it was still in one piece, then crawled up on a chair.

One of the other patrons noticed him and came over. "Have a beer, my friend," he said, handing him a mug. "I'm Sam Ibsen. The general store down the street is my place."

"Hank Jones," said Hank, shaking hands. "And thanks for the beer."

"I suppose you're wondering what all happened out there in the street?" Sam asked.

"That's a fact," Hank agreed.

"Well, sir, I know it all because I got some hints yesterday about it," Sam said, drawing up a chair. "That feller that hit you, that's Calvin Cluett, the roughest, meanest critter you ever want to meet. Old Cal built himself an outhouse hanging out over a little stream that runs into Crystal Creek. He built it that way so's the creek would wash things away and he'd never have to move his outhouse. But the miners downstream didn't like it one bit. They'd be panning for gold and come up with the wrong color. Some of the boys asked Cal, politelike, would he please move his outhouse, and Cal just told them outhouses was built that way over to Gilmore and Tendoy, and that's the way his was going to stay. Then he chased everyone off.

"That's when the boys got their heads together and decided what they ought to do about it. When Cal went out to his outhouse this morning and closed the door, they snuck up on the place and nailed two stout poles to it, one in front blockin' the door, and the other in back. Then they just picked up the whole thing with Cal locked in it, rantin' and ravin' like a penned bull." Sam broke off the tale as he erupted into laughter, tears streaming down his cheeks; the boys at the bar joined in, and it took hold of Hank, too.

"They hustled him down to a wagon, drove it straight into town, and dumped outhouse and all right where you saw it." Sam struggled with a belly laugh that wanted out. "I ain't never seen anything so funny as old Cal crawling out through the bottom hole of that outhouse right on the main street in his drawers!"

Tale done, Sam let himself go, laughing fit to bust, along with everyone else in the room. When, at long last, Sam had about gotten hold of himself again, Hank said, "Crawled out through the bottom hole, did he?" and the whole room broke up again. They'd hardly gotten their breath back when Jason, the bartender, said, "Imagine an outhouse giving birth to something that big and ugly!"

Hank Jones was sitting there, sore-jawed, teary-eyed, weak from laughing, and still wearing all the dirt and unshaven beard he'd brought into town that morning, when Sheriff Johnson came in, looked him over, and said, "That is you under all that dirt, ain't it, Hank?"

"Yeah, Mike, it's me," Hank agreed, rising to shake hands.

"Well, let's take a little walk," Sheriff Johnson said. "Why don't you come along, too, Sam."

When they were outside, Sam said, "I reckon you're the feller Mike said he was gonna send for, Hank. Is that so?"

"Mike sent for me," Hank agreed.

"Let's go on down to the jail where we can talk private," Sheriff Johnson said. "I haven't got any customers in there just now."

What they discussed when they got down to it was the fact that Hank Jones had come to take over the sheriff's job. Ordinarily that would have called for an election, but Sam Ibsen, who was mayor of Thirsty, had agreed with Mike that the job could be handed over direct as an emergency thing if they pretended that Mike was just going away for a little while. The real problem was that Mike's eyes were going bad, and they'd kept it a secret because certain people in town were sure to have gotten out of line if they'd known just how bad the sheriff's eyes were.

Sam Ibsen and Doc Crane were the only people in Thirsty who knew Sheriff Johnson's problem, and they'd taken turns staying close to him to serve as seeing-eye dogs when needed. They'd tell him who all was across the street and hail people along the walk by name so's Mike would know. This had been going on for four nervous months, but they'd gotten away with it.

"You're sure you can handle the job?" Sam was asking Hank.

"Hell, don't ask the man to brag on himself!" Mike said.

"He's the best damned shot I know, and we both know there's nobody else in Thirsty fit for the job."

"Did you tell him about Durango, Lucky, and Notches yet?" Sam asked.

Sheriff Johnson hesitated. "Well, no, I haven't. I suppose maybe I should have, but I figured it'd keep."

"Now's the time, then," Sam said. "The way it is, Hank, we've got us a fairly peaceable town. There's a lot of roughnecks here, but they generally abide by the law and don't often go out of their way to be ornery."

"Like that Calvin Cluett feller that laid me out this morning?" Hank asked.

"He was provoked some, Hank. What I'd call ornery is the sort of feller that comes at you without you provoke him."

"And you've got some of those ornery ones around here?"

"Yes, we have. I'd say so, wouldn't you, Mike?"

"Yep!" The sheriff agreed. "About three of 'em to be exact. Durango, Notches, and Lucky. They've got themselves a claim and a cabin up the creek a ways, but they do most of their gold mining at a poker table over in the Thirsty Saloon."

"Couldn't you run 'em out of town?" Hank asked.

"Maybe, maybe not," Sheriff Johnson said. "It would take some shooting, and it looked like a poor bet to me, even when my eyes were good."

"By God! You're getting cautious in your old age, ain'tcha, Mike?" Hank asked, grinning ear to ear.

Mike turned red and swung sharply to face Hank, but Sam spoke for him. "Those three were here before Mike got here, and he's held 'em in line pretty well. Fact is, every time they pushed Mike here into a showdown, they was the ones that backed down. They're the kind of pack rats that'll draw on a fuzzy-cheeked greenhorn, but they back off from a good gun. Don't be judging Mike until you're facing three fast guns and know there ain't a damn soul in town that dares to help you!"

"No offense intended," Hank said.

"None taken," Mike lied. "We'll be pointing those three out to you this evening. Durango is the meanest of the three. He kills for fun. Picks on people too slow on the draw and too dumb or prideful to back down.''

"He misses sometimes?" Hank asked.

"Not really," Mike explained. "Sometimes he don't hit 'em square, and Doc Crane pulls 'em through."

"Notches is almost as bad," Sam said. "He don't draw on a man unless he's provoked, but he provokes damned easy. And the killing don't bother him none. They call him Notches because he puts a notch on his gun butt for each man he kills. He's dumb, and he'll do anything Durango or Lucky tells him to."

"Of the three," Mike said, "Lucky is the smartest and fastest. He shows off his shooting at targets now and then, but he ain't known to have killed anybody. Fact is, he never will so long as Durango and Notches are around. If Lucky wanted anyone shot, he'd have one of those two do it and, like as not, they wouldn't even know Lucky had put 'em up to it. Other than that, he makes it easier for the other two just by being here and having people know he'll back the other two if they need backing."

"Right peaceable little town you've got here!" Hank said. "That's how you described it, ain't it, Sam?"

"Mostly, it is a peaceable little town," Sam insisted. "There ain't no town that's perfect."

"Tell me one thing more," Hank said. "You two were talking a while back as if some people might not cotton to my being sheriff unless it was put up as an emergency thing. Just who is there that wouldn't go along with it?"

"Lucky!" Mike and Sam said it together as one word, then Sam continued, "He'd like to be sheriff, and no one else wants the job. With Durango and Notches to back him, it ain't likely anyone else would even go in nomination for the job. It ain't hard to win an election if you're the only one in the runnin'."

Hank could see that the job wasn't the lazy man's prize he'd mistaken it for, but he'd come five hundred miles for it and Mike was counting on him. That was the clincher. He owed Mike something more than money could pay. It was Captain Johnson of the Union Army who had saved Hank's folks and their neighbors from the thieving carpetbaggers after the War Between the

States. Mike had set a standard of justice even Robert E. Lee could have approved. Hank would have just gone on his way except for that.

Sam took him over to meet Doc Crane and got busy drawing up a formal-looking notice giving Sheriff Johnson an emergency medical leave and accepting the appointment of Deputy Hank Jones as acting sheriff in his absence or for the unexpired portion of Sheriff Johnson's term, whichever was shorter.

Sam would spend the rest of the day sneaking this notice around to the other members of the town council for their marks or signatures. It would be best to keep the whole thing quiet until the next morning, when certain nasty people would be snoozing while Sheriff Johnson left on the stage and Sheriff Jones took over. But Sam did feel obliged to have the town council in on the thing.

Hank managed to get free long enough to get a shave, but he never did catch that nap he'd been planning on when he rode into town. Doc, Sam, and Sheriff Johnson took turns bending his ear all day long. And they maneuvered things so's neither Durango, Notches, nor Lucky got a direct close-on look at Hank that might have prompted one of 'em to ask who the stranger was.

The day went by in a busy but uneventful way, and Hank excused himself about sundown to go catch up on his sleep. Sheriff Johnson, too, decided to lay low, locking the door of his office and stretching out on his bunk with a tired feeling that was more than physical. Now that he had found a sheriff for Thirsty, he had time to brood about his own future. He worried about whether he'd be able to see at all when his malady had run its course. Doc Crane was sending him back east to a doctor who was the top man on eye problems. But Doc Crane wasn't promising a cure.

What would he be without eyes? It was such a terrible question. To be capable of all things but seeing was to be capable of so little. It would be like being reborn, a helpless babe in a world far more fearsome than that first one he'd been born into.

Every time he talked to Doc Crane about it, he fished for encouragement; some words of promise like, "It's going to be all right," or, "It won't get any worse"—or even, "You'll keep enough sight to get by." But Doc Crane had promised no such thing. And, since Doc was a man who kept his promises, it meant, at best, that Doc just didn't know.

Sheriff Johnson was lying on his bunk, wide awake, when he heard Notches and Lucky pass by out front on their way home. That was usually the way of it; Notches and Lucky nearly always left the Thirsty Saloon ahead of Durango. And Durango would announce that his buddies were going home for their beauty sleep. It was a macho thing with Durango to drink more and stay up later than the others. Fact is, Durango always started his drinking later than the others. Early in the evening he liked to stay sober and keep a sharp eye for trouble, which usually originated with him. Later on, when he had everyone sized up and no strangers were likely to show, he'd get to feeling comfortable and start drinking to make up for lost time.

It was a shame to let a good friend like Hank inherit Durango and his buddies. It wasn't fair, but it wasn't fair for a man to go blind, either.

Or was there more to it than that? Maybe there were some unfair things that a man ought to feel obliged to change. Mike got up, walked to the front window, and peered out for a while. Sometimes, at night, he almost believed his eyes were okay. The soft shadows and indistinct outlines of things weren't much fuzzier to him now than they might have been when his eyes were sharp. There was one thing more he ought to do while there was still time.

He buckled on his gun belt and closed the door gently as he went out. The night was quiet, and his footsteps sounded louder than he liked on the boardwalk, so he walked in the dust of the street, turning in at the door of the Thirsty Saloon.

"Evening, Sheriff," Jason greeted him. "What brings you out so late?"

"Nothing much," he answered. "I'll have a beer, if you please."

Mike stood at the bar awhile, sipping the beer and sizing up the voices of the blurry figures at the tables so's to make out who was where. He missed not having Doc or Sam to clue him in. There were only four other customers left. He knew the two playing cards with Durango, but couldn't tell who had fallen asleep at the table across the room. No matter; there would never be a better time to do what he had in mind.

"You know something, Jason," Mike said in tones loud enough to carry to Durango, "one of the few things I won't miss about this town is that ungodly ugly face of Durango's."

"Are you going somewhere?" Jason asked immediately, trying to erase the insult.

"Yessir!" Mike continued. "I don't know that I've ever met a more cowardly, hateful, lying, cheating, bastard than Durango. I sure won't miss seeing that ugly face again!"

The two who were playing cards with Durango had turned a wary eye on the sheriff at the first insult. Now they dropped their cards face down and left the table. Durango himself was caught off-guard by the sudden attack and sat open-mouthed while he considered his choices. Jason grabbed a few bottles and moved to the other end of the bar.

Durango didn't have to hold a very long conference with himself. There was only one proper answer he knew of for a case like this. He stood slowly, pushing his chair back. Speaking deliberately in that menacing voice he'd used so effectively on such occasions, he said, "Maybe you'd like to take back what you just said?"

"Nope!" Mike said cheerfully, moving clear of the bar. "I meant every word of it."

Durango and the sheriff were pretty close on speed. No one could say right away who fired first, but it must have been the sheriff. Durango lay dead with a bullet right square in the heart, but the sheriff was only hit in the shoulder. There had only been the three witnesses. The man who had fallen asleep at one of the tables claimed afterwards to have seen the whole thing, but the others said he had awakened at the crash of the guns and asked if it was closing time already.

Someone went and got Doc Crane to take care of the sheriff, and someone else went and got Joe Turner, the barber, sexton, and undertaker, to take care of Durango. Nobody wanted to go tell Notches and Lucky about it. That could keep.

As soon as Doc Crane had a moment to spare, he sent for Sam Ibsen, and as soon as Sam heard what had happened, he went and woke up Hank Jones. Hank didn't awaken easily, as he'd slept through the gunfight which was just downstairs from his room. Sheriff Johnson was bandaged up and in a drugged sleep by the time Hank arrived.

"He said he didn't think it would be right to go off and leave you alone with all three of his old problems," Doc explained to Hank.

"And him damn near blind?" Hank said. "He's got a damned sight more nerve than I have, and I hope you remember that!"

"Nerve ain't exactly in my line either," Doc said. "That's why I want you two here to back me if Notches and Lucky come calling."

"It's near midnight," Sam said. "We'd better get some sleep here in the office if we can."

Sam and Hank sacked out on the padded benches in Doc's waiting room. Doc had put Sheriff Johnson in his own bed, then chosen the padded chair at his desk since long experience had taught him that it was impossible to stay awake in that chair on a quiet afternoon.

After Doc had blown out the lantern, Hank's voice came out of the darkness asking, "Sam, would you mind telling me where you were born and raised?"

"'Tain't no secret," Sam said. "I come from Harper's Corners. It's west of Richmond, Virginia, a ways. What makes you ask?"

"Considering all that's happened to me since I got into Thirsty this morning," Hank drawled, "and considering that you reckon Thirsty to be a quiet, peaceable little town, I don't never want to set foot in whatever town you're comparing it to!"

Hank and Sam were awake at daybreak the next morning. Sam went across the street to his place to rustle up some breakfast for everybody, leaving Hank to his thoughts—if thoughts were possible in a room with Doc's snoring. Hank tiptoed in for a peek at Sheriff Johnson, who was sleeping quietly, then wandered around looking the place over for a few minutes before settling back on the padded bench to consider what a brand-new sheriff ought to be doing.

Sam came back in with his breakfast fixings in a bushel basket and began setting things out on Doc's desk with enough rattle and thump to wake Doc. It was a fair breakfast: pancakes, bacon, eggs, and coffee. "You know, Hank," Doc said, "Sam has been known to fix pancakes for me, and he's been known to fix bacon and eggs for me, but never all three things at once. Since he wouldn't do all this for me, that makes you a special guest of honor."

"Much obliged, Sam," Hank said. "You didn't have to do all that for me."

"Truth is, I didn't," Sam answered. "I just thought Sheriff Johnson might be awake."

"A man don't stand very long in a place of honor around here, does he?" Hank wondered out loud.

They set aside a plate of breakfast for Mike and dug into the rest in an efficient way that took care of everything but the second cup of coffee in a few minutes.

Hank sat there, blowing gently on his coffee awhile, then turned to Sam and said, "There's a favor I'd like to ask of you."

"No harm in asking," Sam answered.

"I think it might be useful if Notches and Lucky got the word that I'm a real fast gun. Naturally, it won't count if I say it, and maybe they won't believe you either. But, if you sort of mention it around town this morning, maybe it'll spread enough before Notches and Lucky blow in."

"I believe you've got the right idea," Doc agreed. "Those two won't push a fast gun the way they do most people."

"I'll drop these dishes off at my place then get out and do a little talking," said Sam.

"Make it kind of general so's it can't be checked too good," Hank said, walking to the door with Sam. "Tell 'em I don't talk about it much, but I've been a sheriff and a bounty hunter and a Pinkerton man at one time and another."

"Really?" Sam asked. "You been all them things?"

"I don't talk about it much, friend," Hank said, as grim-voiced and straight-faced as you please, then winked at Sam.

"Right!" Sam said, returning the wink. "I get your meaning."

Sam spent an hour or so spreading his message before returning to the office to announce that he'd found a feller who was going out by George Gatlin's place and he'd asked him to send George into town to help out. Not that George, a young miner with dreams of being a doctor one day, would amount to much of a reinforcement, but every little bit helps.

Sheriff Johnson came out of his long sleep after Sam got back. He allowed as how his arm didn't hurt much and he was in generally good spirits. He seemed to find great satisfaction in the good deed he'd done for Hank. "There's just two of 'em left now, Hank. If you have to choose between 'em, be sure you plug Lucky! Notches is too dumb to survive long without Lucky."

"What do you figure on them doing when they hear about Durango?" Hank asked.

"They'll come straight over here and call me out! No doubt about that! Now, if you'll stand with me, we've got them for sure! Like as not, they'll both try to hit me first. If both of us go for Lucky first and Notches second, that'll be the end of 'em! How about it?"

"I didn't come here to watch you commit suicide," Hank drawled. "I'm putting you on the stage out of here this afternoon. How about it, Doc; is he fit to travel?"

"I expect so," Doc agreed, "so long as he visits a doctor every day or two along the way to get his bandages changed."

"That's the way it'll be then," Hank said. "No more gunfighting for you. You're leaving on today's stage."

Mike grinned. "Lucky and Notches have agreed to that, have they?"

"About ten minutes after they go into the Thirsty Saloon, I'll go over there and explain it to them," Hank said in an offhand way.

"Speak of the devils," Sam said. "There they are now!"

Lucky and Notches were walking across the saloon porch,

checking the feel of their guns and gun belts as they approached, then entering with gun hands hanging close to their holsters.

"Do you suppose they've heard about Durango already?" Sam asked.

"They know he didn't come home last night," Hank said. "Like as not, that's all they know. I'll give 'em ten minutes, then I'll go over and talk to 'em."

"Where in hell's my gun?" Mike asked, getting up from the bed.

"You get no gun unless you give your word to stay put right here," Hank ordered.

"The hell you say!" Mike fumed. "And just who in hell do you think you are?"

"I'm the new sheriff here, that's who I am! And I can handle things a damn sight better over at the saloon if you stay here."

Mike sat down on the bed. "It's come to that?" he asked. "I'm not good enough to back you?"

"These are your shoes I'm standing in, Mike. Tell me how you'd want it if you were me."

"Yeah, you're right," Mike admitted finally. "Go on. It's your play."

"Give him his gun, Doc," Hank said. "What kind of artillery have you got, Sam?"

"One rifle, one shotgun, and one pistol," Sam answered.

"Know how to use 'em?" Hank asked.

"Hell, yes!" Sam laughed. "I did my share of hunting and prospecting before I got lazy and opened that store."

"I can make fair use of the rifle if I have to," Doc volunteered.

"Nothin' doin'!" Hank barked. "You just stay alive. There ain't another doctor in thirty miles of here! Who's going to work on my hangnails if you get killed?"

Hank took a last look around the room and said, "We're as ready as we'll ever be. Sam, you sit well back from that window and keep a rifle pointed at the saloon door. If there's any shooting before I reach that door, you fire at the gun flashes while I drop and go off to the right. If there ain't any shooting before I reach that door, like as not there won't be any at all."

Sam hustled to take up his position as Hank opened the door and went out. Not at all to Hank's liking, the sun was blazing bright, casting a golden glare on the dust of the street. He'd be going into the dark shade of the saloon while his eyes were halfway adjusted to that outdoor glare—if nothing happened before he got across the street.

He walked quickly. No point in giving Lucky and Notches extra time to think. He pushed through the swinging doors slowly and walked in as casually as he could.

Lucky and Notches were leaning against the bar, facing him. Hank glanced around the room. Several men were getting settled at tables toward the rear, having cleared away from the bar when they saw him coming with Mike's old sheriff's badge glimmering on his left shirt pocket.

"Mornin', gents," Hank said, stepping up to the bar. "A beer if you please, Jason."

"Where's Mike?" Lucky asked in a flat, angry voice.

"Resting," Hank said. "He got shot up some last night."

"He bushwhacked Durango, that's what he did!" Lucky said, spitting the words and being parroted by Notches, who said, "Yeah! Bushwhacked him!"

"Sounded like a fair fight the way I heard it," Hank said, glancing at the beer he couldn't touch till the question of gunplay was settled.

"Fair!" Lucky barked. "He jumped Durango when he knew Durango'd be full of likker. That what you call fair?"

"Considering that Mike's damn near blind, I'd say it was an even fight," Hank countered.

"Blind!" Lucky roared.

"Ain't you noticed the way Sam Ibsen and Doc Crane have been walking him around town the last few months?" Hank asked.

Lucky thought it over, then said, "Son of a bitch!" in the soft, emphatic tones of a gambler who'd just missed out on a good bet.

"Yuh think it's true, Lucky?" Notches asked.

"Yeah, most likely," Lucky said. "But that doesn't give him any call to gun down Durango!"

"Let's go teach him a thing or two!" Notches said.

"That's just what we'll do," Lucky decided.

"I wish you wouldn't do that," Hank said, straightening up and shifting just a little distance from the bar.

"You expect to stop us?" Lucky asked.

"That's right."

Lucky looked him over. Soft-spoken as Hank was, there wasn't any softness in his eyes. The eyes were ready and the gun hands were ready. And Lucky had already heard the word that this sheriff was a fast gun. Lucky hadn't made up his mind to back down or call the man when Joe Turner blundered right in without seeing what was going on.

Joe had a pad and pencil in his paws and was busy scribbling as he walked in. "Mister Lucky," he said, "I got to talk to you about the funeral. Durango being your close friend the way he was, you'll want to see to a fittin' funeral, won't you?"

"Yeah," Lucky agreed.

"Then, sir, it's my sad duty to tell you that the deceased only had two dollars an' sixty cents on him at the time of his demise, an' that don't buy much of a funeral with the way prices are these days. Matter o' fact, it just about covers a plain pine box."

"Okay," Lucky said. "Notches and me, we'll each kick in ten dollars. Won't we, Notches?"

"Yeah, I guess so," Notches answered somewhat hesitantly.

"Let's see," Joe said, "twenty-two dollars and sixty cents. That'll buy some flowers an' put some varnish and lining in the box. 'Course, Reverend John ought to get paid, and the hearse wagon ought to be cleaned and polished some, and it really makes for an extra fine funeral if we can get some hymn singers."

"That sounds like a whole lot of money," Lucky said.

"Another thirty dollars would cover all of it. Just fifteen more each from you and Notches."

"Get the hell out of here!" Lucky stormed.

"Twenty dollars is final then?" Joe asked, backing away.

"As final as death!" Lucky assured him.

"Yes, sir! Will do just fine," Joe said, then turned and made good his escape.

"Damned vulture!" Lucky muttered. Then, seeing Sheriff Jones still standing on ready alert, Lucky remembered that he'd been considering going to war over Durango's demise before that fool undertaker butted in. Now he had to ask himself another question; if Durango didn't rate more'n a twenty-dollar funeral, was he worth maybe getting killed in a shoot-out? Hell no! Lucky glared at Sheriff Jones awhile, then broke into a grin as he thought of a proper way to back down.

"Sheriff Jones," he said, "you tell Mike Johnson for Notches and me that we hope he lives to be a hundred. Tell him we also hope he goes blind as a bat and has to beg and crawl for everything for the rest of his life!"

"Hell, I wouldn't put him out of his misery for anything!" Notches agreed.

"I wouldn't wish that on anybody," Sheriff Jones answered, and picked up his beer, feeling as if he'd earned it.

Back at Doc's office, he announced that the crisis was over and explained as gently as he could that Lucky and Notches had to agree it was a fair fight, what with Mike's eyesight as poor as it was.

"You told 'em?" Mike asked.

"They'da known sooner or later," Hank said.

"I don't want their damned pity," Mike said, slumping dejectedly on the bed.

"Don't worry, they ain't wishing you anything but the worst!" Hank said, and Mike got the message.

Mike left on the stage that day, heading east in search of a cure. He went as cheerfully as he could, if only to spite Lucky and Notches. The dozen or so friends who came around to see him off made it easier than it might have been, but he saw Lucky and Notches come to the door of the saloon and turn back in. No hooting or jeering. No thumbing of the nose. And that was what hurt. He had their pity!

Things were fairly quiet in Thirsty for a while after that. Hank had to lock up a drunk now and then, but such things were to be expected. He kept a wary eye on Lucky and Notches, and they did likewise. Hank was beginning to wonder what his old friend Mike Johnson had done to relieve the boredom.

But one night, while he was sitting in the jailhouse playing checkers with Doc Crane instead of prowling the streets, a young stranger rode into town and stopped at the Thirsty Saloon. He was a fancy dude, wearing silver-spangled clothes that didn't show much wear, and he was clean-shaven except for a red mustache that was supposed to make him look older but didn't much succeed. He wore two guns, which looked sort of oversized on his slim frame. It takes a close friend to criticize such a thing, and the kid was alone. He probably wanted to look dangerous—and he might have succeeded at that if he'd had a craggy face or sinister eyes, but he had a round face, ordinary nose, and the most innocent-looking eyes you ever saw.

He went into the saloon, had a couple shots of whiskey, and then started talking, which was a big mistake.

"You got no piano or stage for dancing girls?" he asked.

"No, sir," Jason answered cheerfully, "but there's some girls that'll be in later."

"Can't be much to look at, I expect, or they'd move on to a bigger town," the kid said.

"They're as pretty as you'll find anywheres," Jason assured him.

"I guess you ain't been down to Abilene or Laredo," the kid said. "That's where they've got pretty girls!"

Jason let it pass. He had an instinct for avoiding arguments, especially with paying customers. The kid had his third whiskey—which was too much, too soon—then started to talk again.

"Sure ain't what I'd call a lively town," he said.

"It picks up some later in the evening when more of the miners get in from their diggings," Jason said.

"I heard there was gold mining up this way," the kid said, "but there must be a hell of a lot more dirt than pay dirt around here!"

Notches and Lucky were playing their usual game of poker at a nearby table. Notches had given the kid the once-over when he first came in, but hadn't looked his way since. Still, Jason knew that Notches was listening to everything the kid said. It was something you could tell by watching the poker game. Notches might deal while the kid was talking, but he wouldn't make a move that took any thinking. If a raise, call, or draw was up to Notches while the kid was talking, Notches would just sit there and pretend to be thinking about his cards. Jason knew the kid was in as much mortal danger as a fly stomping on a frog's nose, and he tried to save the kid's life.

"Friend," Jason said, "if you really want the pick of the girls, the thing to do is to go on up to Momma Rose's place and meet the girls before they come down here."

The kid looked around the saloon and laughed. "Hell, I'll have my pick right here! There ain't no girl would choose any other man in the place if she could have me! This here's the worst bunch of broken-down old tumbleweeds I've ever seen!"

The kid said it too loud because he was drunk, and if he hadn't been drunk, maybe he wouldn't have said it at all. Notches laid his cards face down and slowly stood up. The other customers, who knew the signs as well as Jason did, shifted out of the line of fire. The kid, totally ignorant of the trouble he was in, ordered another drink.

"You won't need it, son," Jason said, and scooted for the other end of the bar.

"Hey! Loud Mouth!" Notches roared.

The kid turned and looked up and down the bar before asking, "You talking to me?"

"Yeah, Loud Mouth! I'm just a broken-down old tumbleweed living in a dirt town where there ain't any pretty girls and I'm a-talkin' to you! I think you stink! I've smelled polecats what smelled better! I know donkeys what have more brains than you do, toads more handsome than you, an' dogs with better manners!"

"Mister," the kid said, "I'm gonna give you to the count of ten to take that back!"

"Make it three," Notches said. "I'm in a hurry!"

By then, the kid knew he was in deeper than he wanted to be. He'd bluffed his way through a lot of small towns where folks would eat crow rather than risk a shoot-out with a stranger. He could see that Notches wasn't drunk, wasn't bluffing, and wasn't in his first shoot-out. But the kid didn't see any way to back down and had the foolish notion that beginner's luck might be on his side, since it was his first shoot-out.

"One!" the kid said, paused, then got a bright idea and said, "two-three!" real fast and right together that way, starting his draw as he said it. It really was a clever idea, even if Notches did get off two shots before the kid could level either gun.

The roar of Notches' gun brought Sheriff Jones on the run while Doc detoured over to his office for his medical bag. Doc had no more hankering to get to a shoot-out before it was done with than he had to lie under a grave marker proclaiming him an innocent bystander. Leave the glory to the eager participants, he figured. Despite the respect accorded him in Thirsty, he was still a young man in his early thirties with no desire to die young. Leastwise, not foolishly.

Doc found the kid lying on the floor in a pool of blood while Sheriff Jones was being assured from all sides that it was a fair fight in which the kid had gotten no more'n he'd asked for.

Ripping the kid's shirt away, Doc found the two bullet holes and slowed the bleeding. "How is he?" Hank asked.

"Fair," Doc answered. "One slug in his arm, another just below the shoulder."

"Right where I aimed 'em!" Notches lied. "No need to kill him just because he's got no brains nor manners."

They got the kid over to Doc's office, where he fished out the bullets and dressed the wounds properly.

Doc said, "My job's done, how about yours, Hank?"

"Done, I reckon," Hank said. "Mike told me before he left that I ought to go according to the consensus in these things, and the consensus of the people of Thirsty is that your patient there needed shooting!"

"I'd have to argue that," Doc said, "but not till we finish that checkers game I was beating you in. Bring the board on over here, will you?"

Sheriff Jones brought the checkerboard down to Doc's office

and got a demonstration of Doc's fabulous memory of where the checkers had been and just exactly how they'd arrived there. It was like being beaten twice in the same game. Hank lost two more games before he lost faith in his luck and quit for the night.

After breakfast the next morning, Hank was back at Doc's office to see the kid, who was weak and ghostly pale, but able to work on the fried eggs and bacon Doc had brought him.

"Where's my guns?" he asked as soon as he saw the sheriff.

"All things considered," Hank drawled, "you don't get the guns back till you're ready to leave town."

"Why in hell not?" the kid demanded.

"Three reasons," Hank explained. "First off, I don't like shoot-outs in my town. Second, I aim to see that you pay the doctor here even if your guns has to be sold to do it. Third, it's because I'm sheriff here and I say so and I don't give a damn if you like it or not."

The kid blinked as if he'd just been slapped in the face, even though Hank said it all in pleased-to-meet-you tones.

"I'll sure as hell be glad to see the last of this town!" the kid blurted.

"Good," Hank said in that same pleasant voice. "Then everybody can be pleased when you leave."

The kid was still smoldering over the loss of his guns several days later when he was able to get over to the Thirsty Saloon on his own feet. His first visit to the saloon had taught him not to be critical of the town or its womenfolk or its population in general, but he found that it was safe to grouse about the sheriff, provided the sheriff wasn't there at the time.

Notches kept a distrustful eye on the kid for a few days and slowly became convinced that the kid had learned a lesson in the shoot-out. Then Lucky got Notches to thinking about the kid's grudge against the sheriff for taking away his guns. It was a reasonable enough grudge; the sheriff had confiscated the kid's manhood, whereas Notches had only tried to take his life.

Lucky decided that the grudge could be a useful thing, and he told Notches what he ought to do about it. Accordingly, Notches bought the kid a whiskey early the next evening and the two became bosom buddies in the span of three or four drinks. Then the kid was invited to join the poker game, where he appeared to be wallowing in beginner's luck. "Never saw such a run of cards!" Lucky complained good-naturedly. "You sure you haven't got your arm sling stuffed with aces?"

Things went along that way for a few days, then, shortly after the kid got rid of the arm sling, Lucky told Notches it was about time to collect on their investment. So Notches saw to it that the kid got an early start on the day's drinking, then he sold the kid a gun and holster he'd won at poker a few months back.

It wasn't any prize as guns go. The cylinder mounting was so worn and wobbly that you couldn't expect the chambers to line up with the barrel quite as well as they ought to, the front sight was bent, the rear sight was nothing but a notch in the hammer, and the butt looked as if it'd seen considerable use in driving nails and cracking walnuts.

But the kid strapped it on and found that it made him feel just as big as any other gun would have. Now he felt more normal and natural. That naked feeling of being a fly in spider country was suddenly gone.

"Feels good, don't it?" Notches asked.

"Feels right!" the kid agreed.

"That calls for a drink," Notches declared, and they went to the bar for a few rounds while Lucky drifted over to a window and sat there with his chair tilted back and his feet up on a table, watching the slow-motion world out on the street.

Early in the third round of drinks, Notches saw Lucky take off his hat and throw it on the table. It was the signal Notches was waiting for, and Jason probably would have recognized it as a signal too if he hadn't been so annoyed at Lucky's feet being on the table. Most folks in Thirsty knew better than to put their damned dirty boots up on the table. Lucky, being a man of clean and neat habits and rumored good upbringing, ought to know not to put his boots up on the table. But Jason wasn't going to tell him so. Jason could only be thankful that Lucky wore the cleanest boots in Thirsty.

"Let's step outside for a breath of air, buddy," Notches suggested, and the kid sloshed down his drink and went tagging along.

Out on the porch, Notches nodded toward Sheriff Jones, who was striding along the boardwalk on the other side of the street. "Look at him. Don't he just think he's some kind of big Who-I-Am!"

"Yeah!" the kid said. "Too big for his britches is what he is!"

"Do you suppose he'd give back your guns if you asked him real polite and said 'please' and such-like?" Notches asked.

"Ain't no reason to say 'please' to get back what's mine," the kid said, and set off across the street on a collision course with Sheriff Jones.

"Hey! You there! Sheriff! I want my guns back, and I want them back now!"

Hank stopped and looked him over. " 'Pears to me like you've got one gun too many right now."

"You gonna give back my guns or ain'tcha?" the kid demanded.

"You ready to leave town right now?"

"Hell, no! I'll stay as long as I please."

"Then I'll be taking that gun you're wearing."

Right then, without further warning, the kid went for his gun, but he never fired a shot. Sheriff Jones's bullet slammed into the kid's arm just as he got his gun clear of the holster.

The kid was standing there, gritting his teeth and groaning as blood oozed down his right shirt-sleeve. Hank walked over to him, picked up the kid's gun, and said, "Get yourself on over to the doctor's office. You know where it is."

Notches walked back into the saloon and sat down next to Lucky. "Did you see it?" he asked.

"Yeah. He's fast, all right," Lucky said.

"No faster'n me," Notches countered. "I beat the kid's draw as much as he did, and the kid wasn't gettin' over somebody else's bullets at the time."

"It ain't just exactly that simple," Lucky said. "You drew and fired. Jones there, he drew, waited for the kid's gun to clear the holster, then fired."

"I didn't see all that!" Notches said.

"You weren't looking for it," Lucky said. "The only thing I watched was Jones's gun action. He could of fired a lot sooner than he did."

"Could you take him?" Notches asked, accepting his own defeat in the shoot-out-by-proxy he'd arranged.

Lucky thought it over at such great length that Notches was beginning to wonder if he'd heard the question before Lucky finally answered, "It's a mighty close thing! Mighty close. I ain't even sure whether that man's right-handed or left-handed. He used his left today, but when we faced up over Durango, it seemed his right hand was the one he'd use. Like as not, he could use both if he felt the need of it."

Only then could it be truly said that Sheriff Jones had replaced Sheriff Johnson. The law-abiding citizens of Thirsty had accepted Sheriff Jones from the beginning; the rest had put him on probation. Now the probation was over.

CHAPTER 2

DOWNWIND

DOWNWIND was the most gentle, friendly fellow you'd ever want to meet. I suppose you could say he was the way he was because of his handicap, but I've seen a handicap work just the opposite way, too, making a man as mean and miserable as a January wind.

Downwind was completely inoffensive in every way but one. But that one exception was mighty offensive. This good man had a big, bad body odor that just wouldn't quit.

His old grammar school teacher back in Ohio first noticed the problem when she found herself drifting from "swim, swam, swum" and "good, better, best" to "stink, stank, stunk" and "smelly, smellier, smelliest." Being a direct and practical lady, she soon realized the cause of it and had Downwind spend a dinner hour sitting in the swimming hole, neck-deep, his overalls stuffed with chunks of lye soap. It was a point of great controversy for years afterward as to whether it was the soap or Downwind's odor that killed the fish. As for the battle between the lye soap and the odor, the soap lost.

Shortly afterward, Downwind headed west, urged ever onward by those he met along the way. That is, the polite ones urged him onward. There were others who urged him to do all sorts of things, and some of these were inclined to add injury to insult.

That's how Downwind got his name. People who knew him would maneuver themselves upwind of him or insist that he get downwind. The barked command, "Downwind!" remained as his name long after he'd gotten in the habit of moving to the leeward without being asked.

Friendly though he was by nature, Downwind's odor forced him to be something of a loner. Prospecting for gold was a good way to spend a lot of time alone, and Downwind had spent some time at that. But prospecting didn't fit the friendly side of his nature, so he set out to be a farmer instead. After several years of desperately hard work, he had a few milk cows, chickens, corn, vegetables, a house, and a barn. With everybody around Thirsty mucking around after gold, Downwind had the farm market all to himself. He'd come into town every third day and sell out everything he had in less than a half hour. Then he'd go stand in the shade by the livery stable or the blacksmith's shop and talk to people from a respectful distance. Someone would fetch him a beer or two, and after a time, he might saunter over toward the General Store, and Sam Ibsen would pop out to speak to him at the front door and see what he might be needing. After that was taken care of, Downwind would get back on his wagon and head for home.

Downwind was double-damned when it came to women. He never much talked about it, but it stood to reason that if a man couldn't stand the smell of him, female friends were nothing but a forlorn hope.

Most of the men around Thirsty were lonesome for women, but a miner without a wife is still a miner. A farmer without a wife is something different. Take any farmer, and the one crop he wants to raise first and foremost is a bunch of kids. The miner lives for the day when he can strike it rich, pick up his cash, and do whatever it is that he really wants to do. The farmer is already doing what he really wants to do, and he needs kids to help with it and keep it going after he's gone.

The only single girls in Thirsty were the ones at Momma Rose's place. They'd come out to buy things from Downwind's wagon every time he came to town, and he was known to save the best for them and throw in a little extra besides. The girls liked Downwind well enough—from a distance. That's the way things stood, and there was no prospect of change in sight.

Then, one day in early June, the stagecoach came in maybe just a little faster than usual. The driver spotted Doc Crane coming out of the barber shop and called out, "Doc! Get on over here! I've got a customer for you!"

Doc and the driver climbed into the coach, and everyone else on the street came hustling over to gawk, expecting that someone had got shot in a holdup. Then the driver poked his head out and yelled, "Get Momma Rose! It's one of her girls!"

Momma Rose, all 250 pounds of her, soon came churning over and called out, "I'm expecting a girl called Betty Lee. Is that her?"

The identity was confirmed, and Momma Rose launched into one of her famous peeves. "Well, get her on over to my place! Couldn't any of you figure that out for yourselves? Why in the world do I have to come all the way down here just to tell you that?"

Doc answered that one. "She's got a high fever. Might be contagious. Can I quarantine her at your place?"

"Quarantine!" Momma Rose exploded. "Kill my business! It's only money. Doc, if you shut me down, I'm gonna knock you down and stomp on you till you're flat as a rug!"

"Well, she's got to be quarantined someplace," Doc insisted. "You tell me where."

The talk of contagion and quarantine had moved the crowd back a few paces. These were people who would face up to wild Indians and grizzly bears, but disease was something else. You couldn't fight it with a six-gun or an axe.

"I'll give twenty dollars a day for taking care of her!" Momma Rose offered in exasperation. There were still no takers, then someone called out, "I'll do it for free!"

Downwind came forward as people cleared out of his way. "I'm fixing to go home now. If'n the wagon ride ain't too much for her, I'll take her along."

"Now, in the first place, I just don't know if that's proper, sending a lady out to a bachelor place," Doc argued. "Especially with her in no condition to give her say-so."

"Doc!" Momma Rose barked. "She's one of my girls! Don't talk any of your damn-fool Boston nonsense about what's proper! The wagon's okay for her, ain't it?"

"Put some blankets, quilting, and pillows in the back so's it doesn't shake her bones loose," Doc said. "I'll ride alongside and get her settled out there."

So Betty Lee was installed in the back of Downwind's wagon with a generous supply of blankets and enough pillows to prop her into a half-sitting position, and off they went.

All eyes had followed Betty Lee during the transition from the stage to the wagon, so it was natural that Downwind's reaction to his first sight of Betty Lee went unnoticed. His jaw dropped and he stared at her as if she were something totally unbelievable. Despite her distressed condition and the fever flush in her face, Betty Lee was absolutely the most beautiful thing Downwind had ever seen. He had been double-damned with women before; now he was triple-damned. Here was the farmer who wanted a wife and couldn't have one, looking at the one woman he absolutely had to have.

Downwind drove his wagon as if it were loaded with eggs, swinging clear of every rock and chuck-hole he could possibly miss and using the brakes to ease it through the spots that couldn't be missed. The pace was too slow for Doc, and he tried to urge Downwind along, but Downwind wasn't listening. He wasn't talking either, and that was much too unusual to go unnoticed. With a captive audience, Downwind ordinarily would not have allowed any more silence than might have been necessary to listen to the chirp of a bird or two. Downwind had seemed normal enough that morning. Doc had heard him down by the livery stable spouting glad tidings of a good farm year coming along with perfect weather for early spring planting and no winter kill on his fruit trees. On a subject like that, Downwind couldn't have run dry in one morning.

By watching Downwind out of the corner of his eye, Doc found that Downwind was taking a furtive peek at his passenger about as often as the road would allow. No need to puzzle over Downwind's silence any longer; Doc knew exactly where his mind was.

Still, Betty Lee was safe. If there was any man in creation who could be trusted to do right by her, Downwind was that man. Doc resolved to stop by every day to be sure of it, but, meanwhile, it didn't seem proper to be playing Peeping Tom on Downwind, so Doc announced that he'd ride on ahead and light a fire at the cabin.

Downwind's farm was probably the best-tended place in the territory. There wasn't a board, shingle, or rock loose or out of place in anything he'd built, and his animals always looked as if they were about to go to a grange fair. The cabin was small and sparsely furnished, but it was clean and had more windows than most.

By the time Downwind arrived, a plume of blue smoke was spiraling from the chimney and there was a pot of water boiling. Downwind lifted Betty Lee from the wagon without asking whether she might want to walk. Doc grabbed the pillows and such and followed along into the cabin.

After the initial flurry of getting the girl settled and checking her temperature, Downwind put together some soup and coffee while Doc sprinkled his ears with advice on what to do, depending on whether the fever broke or got worse.

Betty Lee fell asleep shortly after taking some of the soup, and Doc allowed as how he might as well get back to town, promising to return early in the morning. After all, there was no getting upwind of Downwind in a cabin and even Doc's nose, professional as it was, could only take so much.

Downwind followed him outside and finally asked, "Doc, what do I do if'n she cain't get to the outhouse when she has to?"

"Ain't you got no chamber pot?" Doc asked. "No, of course you don't. Well, you better build one. Put a wooden seat on a bucket or some such thing. And another thing: you ain't got no door on that bedroom. You better hang a blanket over it. And don't just barge through it without warning. She'll rest better if she don't have to worry about privacy."

"Yessir, I'll do them things right away," Downwind promised, and started digging out some tools as Doc left.

When Doc came back the next day, he was still worried about Betty Lee. A high fever could mean anything from female trouble to typhoid. The sooner he knew, the better he'd feel.

He found Downwind mending harness outside the barn. "How's my patient?" Doc asked.

"Up and around!" Downwind answered with a huge grin on his face that said, 'I did it! I pulled her through!'

Doc was too professional to let it go at that. "Downwind," he said, "there's times when you mustn't rush a recovery, and the day after a fever is one of 'em. Fever takes a lot out of a person. You let her do too much today and you could be looking at a relapse tomorrow."

"Gosh, I'm sorry, Doc," Downwind said. "She was just so eager to be up, it didn't seem right to say no. She ain't got nothing more'n a head cold now."

"A head cold, eh? That's your professional opinion, is it?"

"Maybe you'd better see for yourself," Downwind answered, realizing he had no business trying to diagnose Betty Lee or any other patient.

Doc stomped the mud off his feet as noisily as possible on the porch before going in. Betty Lee was stirring a pot on the stove, and the cabin was agreeably filled with cooking aromas.

"Well, now! Smells like you're quite a cook!" Doc said.

"Doth it?" she asked. "By dothe ith plugged with thith dard code. You the doctor?"

"Yes, ma'am. Doctor Crane at your service. You don't remember me from yesterday?"

"Not much. That trip wath awful! Being tired, hundry, thirthty, an' worried wath bad enough. When I thtarted to feel hot an thick, thigs got confuthed. You got anythig for a dothe code?"

"Yes, I expect I do, but in your particular case, ma'am, it's best we leave that nose cold run its course. Does your natural immunity good to let it win its own battles sometimes."

"Oh," she answered, with such dejection in her voice that Doc was tempted to whip out his whole medical arsenal against her cold. But that would only expose her to Downwind's problem, so he resisted temptation. The next best thing was to change the subject.

"Worried, you said? If it's none of my business, you just say so.

But I can generally do better by my patients if I know the whole problem," Doc coaxed.

"About Momba Rothe; she'th—well, she'th not a lady, ith she?"

"Momma Rose? No, ma'am, she's no lady! But I wouldn't say that to her face, mind you."

"I never worked for anyone like that. I alwathe tried to be a lady."

"Succeeded so far, have you?"

"Yeth!" she answered as if she were throwing down the gauntlet of challenge.

"No offense intended," Doc soothed. "How'd you happen to come to work for Momma Rose?"

"No mondy. No job. No plathe to thtay. I athked around. A feller thaid Momba Rothe would have a job for me. He paid the thtage fare."

"What do you want to do about it now?" Doc asked.

"Don't know," she answered, wiped her ever-running nose disconsolately, then blurted out, "Momba told me not to leaf Pitthburgh!" She started to cry.

"Now, now," Doc said as gently as possible. "It's not as bad as all that. We all have to learn some things for ourselves. I'll tell Momma Rose you've got a contagion. I'm sure Downwind will welcome your company, and maybe we'll think of something before we run out of time."

"Oh, thank you!" she said, looking happy despite a face all sloppy with tears and dribblings.

"I'll tell Downwind you'll be staying," Doc said, heading for the door.

"Doctor?"

"Yes?"

"He'th a nithe man, ithn't he? Downwind, I mean."

"Salt of the earth!" Doc confirmed, and went out.

Doc confided Betty Lee's situation to Downwind, who was only too happy to make room for her and support the contagion story.

When Doc got back to Thirsty, it wasn't long before Momma Rose tracked him down and demanded a report on Betty Lee.

"She's one mighty sick girl," Doc lied. "Symptoms look something like typhoid."

"Typhoid! Why ain't you out there doctoring her? I paid good money getting her up here! You lose her, and I'm liable to take it out of your hide!"

"Ain't no point in my hanging around out there and catching the contagion. Downwind's taking care of her just fine. If you think you can do better, you go on out there!"

"Me! You miserable pill-roller! You'd like to put me out of business, wouldn't you? Me go out to Downwind's place? That'll be the day!" she fumed, and went steaming back to her place.

"Misbegotten old battle-axe," Doc grumbled. "Ain't any horse could carry her out there. Maybe ain't any buggy could do it either."

On the third day of the quarantine, Doc found Betty Lee and Downwind outside, waiting to meet him. "Doc," Downwind began right off, "Betty Lee and me has decided to get hitched!"

"You have?" Doc said. "Well, now, that's—that's really something!"

The happy couple stood there with eyes agleam, and Doc felt an almost overpowering urge to cool them down with words of caution and delay. He resisted that impulse. After all, who was he to play God? Who was to say this wouldn't be a union made in heaven? So he resisted the words of caution that welled up in his throat. He resisted them for nigh onto twenty seconds before they came tumbling out.

"Yes, sir!" he said. "That's really something! 'Course, you'll want to wait a few months so's to get to know each other better. No point in getting hitched in haste and repenting it forevermore."

"We're jutht ath thure ath we'll eber be, Doctor," Betty Lee said, taking another swipe at her still-dribbling nose.

"Doc, could you ride back into town and bring Reverend John out here?" Downwind pleaded. "We aim to get hitched right here, today!"

If it were anyone else asking, Doc would have shot back a thundering no, but Downwind wasn't just anybody, and he was so puppy-earnest that Doc held his fire. And it would get Betty Lee out of Momma Rose's clutches, though it was obvious enough that Betty Lee hadn't yet gotten wind of Downwind's problem.

"Ain't anyone going to offer me a cup of coffee before I go for the preacher?" Doc asked.

"I'll fetch it!" Betty Lee responded, and hurried toward the cabin. As soon as she was out of earshot, Downwind said, "Doc, please don't you say anything to her about why I'm called Downwind!"

"No," Doc said slowly. "I don't reckon that's my affair. But you've got to tell her, you know. It ain't like as if you can hide it."

"I cain't, Doc! I just cain't! I never wanted nothin' more'n I want her! I'm just gonna keep it secret till it cain't be kept secret no more!"

"Then what?" Doc asked.

"I don't know, but we'll get along somehow! Maybe we'll have to live in two houses side by each. Whatever it takes, I'll do it."

Betty Lee came back with the coffee then and handed it up to Doc, who hadn't had a chance to dismount. As she did, her handkerchief fell in the dirt and got stepped on. "Oh dear, thath the latht clean one I had!" she wailed.

"I'll fetch another one, darlin'," Downwind promised, and trotted back to the cabin.

Doc sipped his coffee appreciatively. Betty Lee waited a moment, then said, "It ain't what you might think, Doctor. I ain't jutht doin' thith to get away from Momba Rothe."

"Well then, it wouldn't hurt to wait a few days or so, would it?" Doc asked.

"Yeth, it might. Thupothe Momba Rothe thtarted tellin' lieth about me? Downwind might hear them and change hith mind about me, an' I can't bear to loothe him!"

Doc finished his coffee as Downwind returned with a hanky. Handing the cup back to Betty Lee, he promised, "I'll be back with the preacher today if I have to hog-tie and drag him!"

He was halfway back to Thirsty when he began to picture the day when Betty Lee's nose would clear and she would begin to realize that her wonderful new husband had one strange fault. Doc erupted in spontaneous laughter. The more he thought of it, the more he snickered and chuckled and laughed. Tears of laughter streamed down his cheeks till he looked as if he were drunk, daft, or both.

With considerable effort, he managed to drag his mind away from that subject and resume the appearance of sober, serious professionalism.

He got into town without being much noticed and hitched his horse to a tree behind the church, which was also Reverend John's home. There was no answer to his knock at the back door, so he went around to the front, looking as casual as possible. His knock went unanswered there, too, but the door was unlocked, so he went into the large front parlor that also served as the church meeting room. There was no one there, and the doors leading to the back rooms were locked. He found a small Bible at the preacher's podium and slipped it into his coat pocket.

Leaving the church, he sauntered up the street to the General Store. A checkers game was in progress down by the stove, which hadn't been dismantled for the summer yet, but no other customers were around. Doc went over to the counter and leaned against it sideways. "Slow day, is it?" he asked Sam Ibsen.

"Sure is," Sam agreed. "It gets like this around noon."

"You wouldn't know where the Reverend John is, would you?" Doc asked.

"Be gone for a few days," Sam answered. "Took the stage south yesterday."

"Damn," Doc said softly, losing his casual air for a moment.

"What would you be needing Reverend John for?" Sam asked.

"Oh, it's just—well, do you know anyone else in town that's got any books to read?"

"No," Sam said thoughtfully, as if he'd never considered that question before. "Reckon you and the Reverend are the only book people in town."

Doc considered his predicament at length, then asked, "That mayor's title of yours; is that an honorary thing or is it bona fide official-like?"

"Doc, when mail comes from the capital addressed to the Mayor of Thirsty, who do you suppose it goes to?"

"You?" Doc guessed.

"Absolutely! I got elected fair and square, and that pack of legal experts over to the capital know it, even if you don't!"

"Just something I thought I'd ask," Doc apologized. Then he waited awhile to let the wound heal before saying, "You know, there's a real good fishing hole out on the North Trail. Let's go on out there and catch a few."

"Naw," Sam replied with regret. "Gotta tend the store."

"Hell, you mean to say your checker team there can't watch things awhile?"

"Well, they ain't exactly obliged to stay here, you know," Sam answered.

"So, let 'em lock up and hang out your 'gone to dinner' sign when they leave," Doc insisted.

"Well, no, I'd better not. That's no way to run a business," Sam said, though he was showing definite signs of weakening.

"Sam," Doc said, "who fixed your busted arm when you fell from the ladder last year?"

"You did."

"Do you expect you'll ever need my help again?"

"I might."

"One hand washes the other, Sam," Doc advised.

"Yeah. I reckon it does," Sam agreed, then walked over to the checker table. "You boys lock up for me when you're done. If anyone comes in before you lock up, take notice of what they take and ask 'em to settle up with me later."

A short time later, Doc and Sam were riding out on the North Trail toward Downwind's place with their fishing poles stuffed into Sam's rifle holster. "Let's pick up George Gatlin, too," Doc said.

"George Gatlin!" Sam said. "Are you loco? He ain't no fisherman!"

"No. I don't expect he is," Doc said wistfully. "But there's something else we've got to attend to, and we're gonna need George "

"Just what kind of foolishness are you getting me into?" Sam asked.

"I'll tell you as soon as we've got George," Doc promised. "No use explaining the whole thing twice."

Picking up George was much easier than picking up Sam had been, except that now Doc had to fend off questions from both of them until he could get out on the open trail where a man could be sure of privacy.

"It's like this," Doc began. "Downwind and that girl that came in sick on the stage; they want to get married."

"Downwind? Ole Downwind?!" Sam and George asked almost in unison.

"Yep," Doc answered. "With Reverend John out of town, I figure it's a job for the mayor, and that's you, Sam!"

"You sure I can do a wedding?" Sam asked. "I ain't never done one, and I'm not even sure it's legal."

"It's legal, and I've got the reverend's Bible to make it proper," Doc answered. "And we've got myself and George for witnesses."

"What about the contagion the girl's got?" Sam asked. "I don't want to ketch nothin'."

"Nothing worse'n a head cold now," Doc assured him. "And, in case you're wondering, she can't smell a thing."

"Cain't smell anything?" George asked, then broke up with a big "Haw, haw, haw!" which was promptly joined by Sam's "Hee, hee, hee!" till tears were rolling down their cheeks and they were rocking in their saddles as if they'd fall off at any moment. Doc watched sternly for a while, then caught the infection and fell to laughing with them.

They had almost regained control when George said, "Remember the time that grizzly went chasing after Downwind, got a whiff of his stink, and took off for the high country bawling fit to bust?" That was good for another five minutes of convulsive laughter, then Sam said, "An' remember that Indian what was gonna tomahawk ole Downwind but decided he'd best not open up anything that smelled that bad from the outside?" And when they'd recovered from that one, it was Doc's turn with, "Remember when Hard Rock Hackett wanted to quit the poker game while he was winning and Lucky Martin wouldn't let him? Ole Hard Rock called in Downwind to play his hand and that game busted up right then!'' More laughter, more tears, more back-slapping, and many more remember-whens filled the time, till the three of them were feeling too weak and exhausted to stand another remember-when.

It's possible that all of these Downwind tales were pure fiction, but they'd been told and retold so often around Thirsty that the border between legend and truth was lost.

"Anyways," Doc said when things had settled down, "I promised Downwind we wouldn't say anything to Betty Lee about his problem, and I expect you boys to hold to it."

"How in the world am I gonna keep a straight face?" Sam snickered.

"Just think of all the favors Downwind has done for you," Doc said. "That might help."

"I guess we can do it if we try real hard," George said, "but, for God's sake, let's make it an open-air ceremony!"

They had covered another mile or so of the trail before Sam said, "I can see why Downwind wants a quick, quiet wedding, but how'd he talk the girl inta it?"

"She's afraid of Momma Rose. Took stage fare money from Momma Rose to get here, but never did that kind of work before."

"What's Downwind think of that?" George asked.

"He didn't say," Doc replied. "And I didn't ask."

"You know, Doc," Sam said, "you're the one that ought to be afraid of Momma Rose. You told her the girl was quarantined with a contagion, now here you are setting up a sneak wedding. Momma Rose'll call that stealing. She's gonna kill you!"

"I can walk faster'n her full-steam waddle," Doc answered bravely.

"Rattlesnakes don't have to chase people to bite 'em," Sam persisted. "They just wait. An' with the kind of hammy hands Momma Rose has got, she don't need fangs. One swat an' she'd belt you clean inta kindom come!"

"I reckon she'd like to," Doc admitted, "but there's days when she needs a doctor, and I'm the only one around. If she doesn't catch me before she thinks of that, I'll live."

"And if she does, you won't," George put in solemnly.

The three of them managed to talk of other things during the rest of the ride out to Downwind's place. The wedding was a reasonably nice ceremony, conducted under fair skies with Doc, George, five horses, three cows, and a few dozen chickens for witnesses. Afterwards, Sam took a blank page from Doc's notebook and made out a wedding certificate, which eveybody signed, revealing Downwind's real name—which was not long remembered. There was cake and coffee afterward, then Doc, Sam, and George left, claiming they had to be getting back to town.

About halfway back to Thirsty, Doc announced that he'd be taking the west fork of the trail to go fishing.

"Kinda late in the day for that, ain't it?" Sam asked.

"Not if I stay all night," Doc answered.

"You're lookin' to stay clear of Momma Rose, ain'tcha?"

"If I were," Doc answered, "it might be a good idea for the feller that performed a certain wedding ceremony to do likewise."

"It might at that," Sam agreed. "I reckon I'll go fishing too."

"Mind if I come along?" George asked.

"I was sort of counting on you to deliver the news about Downwind's wedding, George," Doc said. "Just sort of spread it around Thirsty."

"You want it to blow over before you get back, huh?" George asked.

"That's about the size of it," Doc agreed.

"Okay, but next time you go fishing, I go too. Right?"

"Right!" Doc said. "And just one thing more; hold onto the news about Downwind and Betty Lee till sundown, so's to discourage folks from riding out to their place, will you?"

With that, they went their separate ways: two fishing fugitives and a young prospector itching to deliver what could only be classed as a major news bulletin.

It was past noon on the following day when Doc and Sam stopped by George's claim on their way into town.

"Lord Almighty! What happened to you?" Doc asked as soon as he caught sight of George.

"Make a guess," George shot back as he ran his fingers carefully over his swollen right eye.

"Momma Rose?" Sam asked.

"My! Ain't you clever! How did you ever guess?" George asked sarcastically.

"That woman is worse than a mongrel dog!" Doc said. "Why in the world did she have to go and hit you?"

"Maybe it was because I was there," George said. "Oh, she said she was sorry afterward. Said I was a good customer and she didn't mean me no harm and all. A lot of good that did me!"

"All because of Downwind's wedding?" Sam asked. "You didn't do nothing to her?"

"Heck, no! She come storming up to me and sez, 'What's this I hear about Downwind and my Betty Lee?', an I told her they got hitched and was right in the middle of saying what a nice wedding it was when POW! No warning a-tall! She belted me halfway across the street!"

"That's just awful," Doc consoled. "Something ought to be done about that woman. I hope you aren't peeved about me and Sam not being there?"

"No, Doc. Not at all," George answered, smiling for the first time. "I done got mine. Now you're on the way in to get yours."

Doc and Sam were real shifty-eyed cautious when they rode into Thirsty and put their horses up at the livery stable, but Momma Rose was nowhere in sight. Sam opened his store and checked to see that all aisles to the back door were clear. Doc opened his office and sat where he could watch all the approaches.

It was a quiet afternoon. Flies buzzed at windows, sparrows and butterflies fluttered about the streets, and the huffing of the blacksmith's bellows could be heard halfway across town. Doc tried to read a medical journal but kept dozing off. He hadn't slept too well last night. The weather had been good and it was soul-satisfying to sleep under the stars, but a saddle blanket on the ground just doesn't compare to a bed. Still, he couldn't just go lie down. Momma Rose wasn't going to respect the privacy of his bedroom. Dead or alive, he never wanted to be caught in bed by or with Momma Rose.

Doc stuck it out all afternoon, then decided he'd rather go looking for trouble than hide in some damn fool place where trouble would find him anyway. He got up and walked over to Sam's store.

"She hasn't been in, has she, Sam?"

"Nope. I think I'd of noticed if she had," Sam answered with a weak smile.

"Well, if she comes looking for me, I'll be over to The Dutchman's getting a bite to eat," Doc said, in a show of bravery that fooled no one.

The Dutchman's was the best and only restaurant in town. It was still possible to get speared with a splinter from the rough and unpainted furniture if you were careless, but the worst of the splinters had worn off in use. The brief menu was chalked on a slate and seldom changed. It wasn't much, but the Dutchman tended it with pride. The dishes were clean and the food was safe.

Doc took a seat where he could watch the door, but, when the Dutchman delivered his order, he forgot about Momma Rose and dug in with gusto. There were a half-dozen other patrons in the place, and the first warning Doc had that something was wrong came when he noticed that all chatter of knives and forks had ceased. He looked up at the massive form of Momma Rose and froze in mid-chew.

"Doctor Crane," Momma Rose began in a soft and sweet tone that was totally unexpected under the circumstances, "it's nice to see you back in town. You were too busy to see us yesterday, weren't you?"

Doc gulped some water and cleared his throat. "What can I do for you, Momma Rose?" he asked.

"Oh, you've done plenty for me already, you have," Momma Rose answered in that same soft tone. "You took my Betty Lee, cleared up her contagion, and got her married, in just two days, didn't you?"

"Three days," Doc corrected. "And she's still got a mighty bad head cold."

"That's all you care about, isn't it, Mr. Doctor Man from Boston? It doesn't matter that all my time and trouble and expense of bringing her here was wasted, does it?"

"I expect that Downwind will repay your stage fare," Doc answered, still flinching inwardly at the explosion he expected at any moment.

"Oh, he'll pay, he will," Momma Rose assured him, "and you're going to pay something, too."

Doc scrooched back on his bench and prepared to duck, but Momma Rose continued in that same soft, mocking tone. "You've never been over to my place for anything but doctoring business, have you? Think you're too good for my girls, don't you? We're sinful and you're not. Ain't that so?"

"I never said any such thing," Doc defended.

"You don't have to," Momma Rose said. "You could live here the rest of your life and you'd still be a Boston man, with all your sinning done sneaky and private-like."

Doc deeply resented that. Not the part about the sneaky sinning. An accusation like that, coming from Momma Rose, meant nothing to Doc or anyone else who knew him. But Doc loved the West and thought of himself as part of it. He'd worked hard to lose his Boston grammar. He'd accepted 'hell,' 'damn,' and 'ain't' as everyday words, to be used freely as his western friends used them. He still wasn't sure what Momma Rose's game was, but he wasn't about to sit still for all her blather about him being a Boston Man. "Momma Rose, get to the point if there is any, my dinner's getting cold."

The unnatural quiet that had fallen over The Dutchman's when Momma Rose first entered still prevailed. All ears had been tuned to the quiet conversation between her and Doc. Now Momma Rose moved back a pace and raised her voice a notch to deliver a prophecy. "I know men, Doc! Even such as you! I know there'll come a time when you'll want one of my girls more than anything else in the world! And when that time comes," she hissed, pausing for effect, "I'll see to it that you can't have her!"

She turned and left as triumphantly as if she'd just demolished her worst enemy. Doc sat there, open-mouthed and totally mystified. Most any man in Thirsty would tell you that Momma Rose's place was elegant in every way. But Doc didn't see it like that; he saw only the squalor and degradation of womenfolk reduced to sin. And Momma Rose wasn't going to let him have any of her girls? That had to be the most ridiculous threat he'd ever heard!

"She's not going to let me have any of her girls! Haw, haw haw! Hee, hee, hee!" He sat there shaking with laughter, which some of the customers joined and some did not, according to whether they understood Doc's view or were just thankful that no such threat had been leveled at themselves.

CHAPTER 3

A BIT OF FINERY

IN the days following Momma Rose's threat to Doc, it became clear that she was determined to punish him exactly as she said she would. But her way of going about it was as ridiculous as the threat itself.

Doc would be sitting in the Thirsty Saloon, having a beer or two and a bit of quiet conversation. Momma Rose would come in, park at a nearby table, order a beer, and just sit there, knitting or crocheting. Then her girls would start parading in and out on trivial errands.

Whenever the detour wasn't too obvious, they'd head straight for the sleeping hound dog, Ole Shiftless, just to have an excuse to lift their skirts high and giggle a bit as they stepped over him. Then they'd go over to Momma Rose and deliver their lines in baby-sweet voices, just loud enough for Doc to hear. "Momma, where are the sewing needles?" or, "Here's your yarn, Momma," or, "Momma, should we have corn or potatoes or both at dinner tonight?"

And they'd always bend down at Momma's table so's to reveal something of what was under their dresses, fore or aft. Doc tried hard not to look, but every now and then a voice within him would ask, "What's the harm in looking?" and he'd look. Just casually and professionally, of course. After all, a doctor sees all sorts of stuff like that, along with a lot of other stuff he'd rather not see.

The girls knew their business, though, and, whether Doc would admit it or not, there was a difference between the things he saw in a medically professional way and those same things when they were flaunted, held available, and offered with a teasing smile.

Poker-faced though he remained, his blood pressure and pulse rate told a different tale. There were a couple of those girls that could really put Doc in a quarrel with himself, between his animal instincts and his Boston-bred disgust at their tainted profession. It was a torment, as Momma Rose meant that it should be, but he'd be damned if he'd let her know.

Momma Rose arranged the same sort of show at the livery stable, The Dutchman's, and wherever else she could catch Doc for a few minutes.

Another thing that made it tough on Doc was that the whole town knew what was going on. It got so's everybody took special notice of Doc's comings and goings and whether Momma Rose was there, too. Sometimes she guessed where he might go, and he'd find her sitting there like a monstrous spider. He couldn't just turn and walk out again because she was there. That would be admitting defeat.

In his time of torment, Doc heard no voices raised in his defense. Why should Jason, over at the Thirsty Saloon, complain? His business boomed with all those people who came in to watch the show. Likewise at The Dutchman's: business was great when the kibitzers followed Doc in. If any of the spectators complained, it was only for lack of a good view. Most galling of all, the tease that was aimed at Doc found many a mark among the spectators, and Momma Rose's business prospered as never before!

Doc often wondered if he might reason with Momma Rose, but he dared not try. After all, you don't chase away the devil with a cry of pain.

Near the end of the first week, he hit upon a neat defensive strategy, quite by accident. He had decided that he had no choice but to hole up in his office till the whole thing blew over. George Gatlin had agreed to stay with him, play checkers, and fetch food and drinks as needed. It would be the life of a prisoner, but it would defeat Momma Rose's attack.

Not so. When it became apparent that Doc would not come out, Momma Rose sent her girls in. Doc had never seen such an avalanche of female trouble in all his life, and it may well have been the highest concentration of such complaints in medical history. It was an epidemic of breast pains, abdominal pains, and moles in private places needing inspection. The girls always presented their allegedly ailing parts in the sexiest possible way, and some of the old spectator group had the gall to traipse into Doc's waiting room with their fictitious complaints too. But now Doc was getting paid in cash for his torment, and the business boom had abruptly died for the others.

He knew it wouldn't last. Momma Rose wasn't going to let him get rich at her expense. But what did he care? He had found the perfect defense. And he had even done the girls a favor. Not that he would have gone much out of his way to do any favor for that sinful bunch, but he bore them no real malice and the favor would be at Momma Rose's expense, not his. It was Cindy, one of Momma's girls, who told him about it.

"Golly, Doctor, I sure am glad you got Momma Rose mad at you."

"Why should that be?" he asked.

"Well, Momma says she knows all us girls worked on you real hard, and it ain't our fault you ain't coming around. And she says that's because you're a Boston man."

"More to the point, Cindy, I'm a God-fearing man," Doc said, and he was sorely tempted to lecture on that point, but decided it would be a waste of breath. This girl was too young, too sensual, and too foolish. He'd gotten in enough trouble for his part in taking Betty Lee away from Momma Rose and didn't really want to risk steering another of her girls into the straight and narrow.

"Momma says Boston men choose women by their clothes, and she's gonna get us all some fancy new dresses straight from Saint Looey. She ain't gonna charge us but half price," Cindy said.

"Cindy," Doc said, kind of disgusted-like, "Momma Rose is plumb ready for the looney bin, but if that's what it takes to get some nice clothes on you girls, more power to her. Run along now. There's nothing medical about you that needs fixing, and I'll thank you to pay me two dollars for saying so."

Cindy paid the two dollars and went swivel-hipping out through the waiting room. Doc was strongly tempted to give her a slap on the fanny, but that would have been unprofessional. The only rumps he ever patted were on horses and babies.

So Momma Rose was going to sink some money into dresses to impress him. He smiled a broad smile. Good! Let her squander her money. The girls' 'half' of the cost was more likely to be eighty or ninety percent of the total, but that was their affair. All dressed up, the girls might not look much like what they were. Maybe a few strangers would even mistake the town for a civilized place.

Cindy was the last of Momma's girls to come in that day, and none came at all the next day. So, on the third day, Doc decided to step outside and stroll over to the saloon for a beer.

No Momma Rose, no girls; just a nice restful beer. The siege seemed to be over.

Days passed, and normalcy reigned supreme. Doc tended his business and everyone else tended theirs.

Doc was sleeping in his back room the day the stage came in from Gilmore by way of Smithville. He didn't see the elegant young lady who climbed down and looked around as if she must surely be in the wrong place. Her impression of being in the wrong place was intensified by the stares of local people that indicated she was an uncommon sight in this town.

The stage driver popped into the Thirsty Saloon for a beer, which he took sixty seconds to swallow. Returning to the stage, he found that there was the young lady's luggage to take care of.

"Where will I put your luggage, ma'am? Will you be staying in town, or are you meeting someone here?"

"I'm really not sure," the lady answered. "Where is Mrs. Rose's School for Young Ladies?"

"Mrs. Rose's School for Young Ladies?" the driver echoed with a frown, thoughtfully scratching his head. "Never heard of it, ma'am."

The lady stared at him. "Are you sure?" she asked. "This is Thirsty, isn't it?"

"Yes, ma'am! I know it pretty well, too. If there were a Mrs. Rose's School for Young Ladies here, I'd know it. Tell you what, though, there's a Momma Rose here. Maybe she's some relation."

"That's possible," the lady answered with renewed hope. "Shall we ask her?"

"You wait right here, ma'am. I'll go ask." He started off quickly without giving the lady a chance to respond. He went into the big house at the bend in the street and soon came out again with Momma Rose huffing along beside him.

"Miss Hoffman!" she called out as she approached. "My goodness, I should have been out here to meet you, and I would have if this stage had a schedule a body could trust!"

The stage driver scowled and said, "There's people what set their watches by this stage, and you know that to be a fact."

"Them ain't watches they're a settin, them's calendars!" Momma Rose said with a careless wave of her hand. "Why don't you do something useful and take Miss Hoffman's luggage over to my place?"

Momma Rose hooked her right arm through Miss Hoffman's left and started toward her house. Miss Hoffman offered no resistance, but there was a pained look on her face that said Momma Rose wasn't the sort of lady she had been expecting.

"Any of the people hereabouts been stuffing your ears with nonsense about me?" Momma Rose asked, turning a sharp eye on Miss Hoffman.

"Heavens, no; I've only just gotten here. Why? What would they be saying?"

"Oh, nothing in particular," said Momma Rose. "You know how idle people gossip. Some of 'em might say most anything."

"Yes, I suppose so," Miss Hoffman agreed. "Tell me, how did you ever choose this town as a location for a young ladies' school?"

"That's a long story," Momma Rose hedged. "Suppose we save it for later? Did you bring the dresses?"

"Yes, indeed! And a very fine selection at that. I'm sure you'll be pleased with them. They're in my luggage."

"I suppose you'll have to freshen up or rest a bit, but would you mind if my girls try the dresses on right away?"

"Not at all. But please leave the fitting to me. I'm sure your young ladies are no strangers to the sewing arts, but some of these fabrics are quite special, and my company couldn't possibly take them back if they were damaged by the customer."

They went up the stairway to the porch, and Momma Rose let Miss Hoffman in the front door, which was wide enough for two people if one of the two was not Momma Rose.

Miss Hoffman's luggage was lined up in the entrance way, and Momma Rose's girls were milling around them like kids at ice cream time.

Miss Hoffman stood at attention, waiting for introductions, but Momma Rose said, "Well, dig in, girls! Miss Hoffman says it's okay so long as you don't change or damage anything."

"They're all locked," Cindy pouted. "The trunks are all locked."

"Sorry!" Miss Hoffman said, and dug into her handbag for a key ring. She was going to unlock the trunks herself, but, as soon as the key ring appeared, Momma Rose snatched it and flung it to the girls. Many hands grabbed for the keys, but Cindy got them. The second key she tried worked the lock of the first trunk, and one of the other girls grabbed the keys as Cindy opened it.

Not very ladylike at all. Miss Hoffman watched the proceedings with a look of disapproval that went unnoticed. "Not that one, that's mine!" she commanded as one of the girls pounced on the last trunk, which was smaller than the others. "Oh, damn!" the girl said, and tossed the keys back to Miss Hoffman.

"Lookee me!" Cindy cried, holding a pink dress against herself. "Ain't I gonna be a swell one!"

"Just don't you button all them buttons! Some of the fellers around here ain't gonna give you all that much time to undress," one of the girls answered. This brought a chorus of laughter, followed by the appearance of a disheveled-looking man at the head of the stairs.

"Lordy! You all make enough noise to wake the dead!" he groused as he descended the stairs.

"You all paid up?" Momma Rose asked as he headed for the door.

"Yes, ma'am, he paid," one of the girls answered.

"Come again," Momma Rose called after him as he left.

"Mrs. Rose!" Miss Hoffman cried in obvious horror. "What kind of ladies are these?"

"They're the only girls in town," said Momma Rose. "That's what kind of girls they are!"

"Merciful heavens! You're running a house of ill repute?"

"Ill repute? Hell, no, honey! We got the best reputation in the business!" Momma Rose laughed herself out of breath at her own joke.

"Oh! Oh! Oh!" Miss Hoffman stuttered in rising pitch, looking from one to another of these iniquitous girls. Then she bolted for the door. The door slammed behind her. Momma Rose, chortling at Miss Hoffman's distress, came out to watch her run down the street. Miss Hoffman ran back to the only place in town she knew, the stage stop in front of the Thirsty Saloon. She grabbed onto a hitching post, turned to look back at Momma Rose's place, then collapsed in the dust.

Watching the performance, Momma Rose muttered, "Huh! Not strong enough to work for me, she ain't!" Then she lumbered back into her house to see that the girls didn't damage the goods.

Several men ran over to Miss Hoffman. "What do you reckon Momma Rose done to her?" one asked.

"Mebbe she jest swooned er fainted er sumpthin like 'at," another said.

"Go fetch Doc Crane. I'll fan her with my hat," said another. He was still fanning when Doc Crane came trotting over, coatless and sleepy-eyed.

"I'm fanning her," the one with the hat explained.

"Yes, I can see that," Doc answered. "I wonder if you couldn't have found something more smelly than that sweaty old hat to do it with."

Doc knelt down, pushed back an eyelid, and checked her pulse. "Nothing too serious," he said, straightening up. "Carry her over to my office. She'll come around in a while."

The blacksmith scooped her up and headed for Doc's office. Doc tarried in the street a moment to find out who his patient was, but learned only that she'd come in on the stage with a lot of luggage, had gone over to Momma Rose's, and had come running back like the devil was after her. Probably another case like Betty Lee, Doc thought. Alone, flat-busted broke, and no one to look after her. Maybe this one didn't know what Momma Rose's place was. It seemed safe to diagnose the lady's complaint as shock.

Doc hustled back to his office and wafted some smelling salts under his patient's nose. Miss Hoffman responded with a twitch and a sneeze. Her eyes opened, she uttered a startled "Oh, my goodness!" and sat bolt upright, casting wild glances about the room.

"It's all right, ma'am. I'm a doctor."

She stared at him a moment, and then her eyes puddled over. "What am I to do, what in the world am I to do?" she asked in a voice heavy with worry, then buried her face in her hands.

"About what, ma'am?"

"That dreadful Mrs. Rose!" she answered.

"Momma Rose?" Doc asked. "Most people who come out here to work for her know what to expect. You didn't?"

"No! She claimed to be running a school for young ladies!"

"Truthfulness is one of the many virtues Momma Rose is lacking," Doc commented.

"How on earth can I fulfill my contract with her?" Miss Hoffman wailed.

"Forget it. She can't hold you to a contract based on lies."

"I accepted the contract, and I'll honor it in full."

"You'll work for Momma Rose?"

"Yes."

"You've done that work before?"

"Ever since I was a little girl."

Doc's eyebrows went up a notch, and he stared at her a moment before he said, somewhat coldly, "Then you don't have any problem, do you?"

Now it was Miss Hoffman's turn to look puzzled. "But she's running a house of—a *house*!" she stammered.

"True," Doc answered. "And you're going to work for her."

Miss Hoffman turned a bright pink. "Oh, merciful heavens!

How could you think that? I'm a dressmaker; *that's* what I've done since I was a little girl. You didn't really think—"

"No, no. Not really," Doc lied. "You're obviously not that sort. Somehow, we've misunderstood each other."

"We certainly have," Miss Hoffman agreed. "The Hoffmans of Saint Louis and the dress company that bears our name are completely above scandal or dishonor!"

"Of course. It's a pleasure to have you in town, ma'am. Some people around here need reminding of the virtues of a true lady."

"Thank you," Miss Hoffman said with satisfaction. "Perhaps you could advise me as to where I might stay until the stage returns. I had intended to stay at Mrs. Rose's, but of course that's out of the question now." She smiled for the first time.

"A place to stay," Doc repeated thoughtfully, as if to himself.

"Surely there is a hotel or boardinghouse?"

"Yes, and no," Doc answered. "The Thirsty Saloon has rooms, and The Dutchman has a room or two, but I wouldn't recommend them to a lady. No, ma'am, not to a lady."

"Oh dear!" Miss Hoffman said.

"The man who runs the General Store, Sam Ibsen, he's the mayor of Thirsty. He's got decent living quarters over his store. Maybe he'd agree to bunk with me awhile and let you use his rooms."

"I hate to be such a bother."

"No trouble at all," Doc assured her.

"There's one thing more."

"What's that?"

"I'll need a place to do the fitting and alterations on the dresses Mrs. Rose ordered. As you can appreciate, doing it where the girls live is quite out of the question."

"Well, let's see what Sam says about it," Doc said.

Pretty as she was, Doc had the feeling that he'd best get her moving rather than let her sit and think up more work for him. Doc knew damn well that he wasn't going to say no to anything this lady wanted.

Sam Ibsen was just as vulnerable. He surrendered his living space, volunteered to fetch all the water she'd need, and insisted on setting up a fitting room any way she wanted it. Doc could see that he'd unloaded his problem right enough, but she was the first real lady he'd seen since he'd come to Thirsty, and he wasn't all that anxious to part with her company.

Doc hung around awhile, unsure of his next move. Miss Hoffman was very busy telling Sam just what she'd need, and Doc couldn't think up a way to catch her attention without catching some of that work she was unloading on Sam. Finally he said, "Well, I guess I'll be running along. Got some things that need tending to," and headed for the door.

"Oh, Doctor?" Miss Hoffman called.

"Yes?" Doc answered.

"Could I possibly impose on you and Sam to escort me to dinner? I know I'm probably being silly, but I really haven't the courage to dine alone in such a frontier town as this."

"No trouble at all, my pleasure!" Doc said, echoed by Sam. Doc agreed to return in due time and went on his way, feeling like a card shark who'd played his cards right.

Not that Doc considered taking Miss Hoffman to dinner an event of importance, but it just so happened that he felt like washing, shaving, and getting spruced up for dinner that night. He probably would have done that many times in the past several years if he'd felt like it.

Sam Ibsen apparently had the same notion that day. It was the first time Doc could remember seeing Sam without a glistening sheen of silver beard stubble by evening. A fool thing for Sam to be getting slicked up for the lady, him being sixty years old. Doc fancied that he knew a thing or two about stages of life and, whereas Doc's thirty-two was the prime, sixty was definitely over the hill.

The dinner was one of the most enjoyable in Doc's memory, even though it was at The Dutchman's, and he wouldn't long remember for sure what he'd eaten, in spite of having paid for Sam's dinner as well as Miss Hoffman's. The thing about it was that Miss Hoffman was such a good listener. She wanted to know all about Thirsty and Doc and Sam, and all the western lore that only got to Saint Louis secondhand.

After dinner they took a brief stroll that didn't cover more than a hundred yards since the far end of town that trailed off beyond Momma Rose's place wasn't fit for a lady. They ended up back at Sam's store and soon realized that Miss Hoffman hadn't gone unnoticed by the rest of the town. Sam's store started to get crowded when the word got around that Doc and Miss Hoffman were playing checkers there. The kibitzers didn't bother Doc's checker playing, but they did cramp his overall style. How in the world could he say anything meaningful under these circumstances?

Meanwhile, Sam was trapped behind his counter by the trickle of business that came in with his flood of visitors. In an effort to regain some of Miss Hoffman's attention, Sam launched into a sales talk on a new type of gold pouch he had in stock. The inside was smoother, the seams were tighter, and the double drawstring was safer than any other pouch he'd ever seen, he declared, showing each of these features in detail.

It was just the sort of diversion Doc needed. He leaned across the table and whispered to Miss Hoffman, "Why don't I go get a horse and buggy and pick you up at the back door? There's lots of countryside to see." Miss Hoffman smiled and nodded. Doc headed for the front door, and Miss Hoffman went to the back room. It was done so smoothly that some of those who had turned momentarily to watch Sam had the distinct impression that Doc and the lady had vanished before their eyes.

Nothing outwardly dramatic happened during that buggy ride. No stolen kisses, no furtive embraces, no binding promises, not so much as an endearing word. But Doc was hooked, and he knew it and didn't care. And Miss Hoffman knew he was hooked but, in the style of the times for proper eastern ladies, pretended that she didn't know and couldn't imagine that any such thing was on Doc's mind. And this was as Doc expected, for he knew that the heart of a proper eastern lady had to be won slowly and ever so gently.

Doc was up much earlier than usual the next day. He wanted some extra time for washing and shaving, just in case Miss Hoffman also proved to be an early riser. Having completed his grooming, he got to casting a critical eye on his office and waiting room. Why had he never noticed its shabbiness before? Such an office would be an absolute disgrace in Boston, and it wasn't exactly a western showpiece either. He got a damp rag and wiped off some of the heavier dust layers, promising it would be cleaned up properly the next morning before he got himself all ready.

There ought to be a proper shingle hanging over his door, too. That faded old board with 'Doctor' painted on it in black square block letters just wouldn't do. The Reverend John was known to do carpentry for hire, and he was a whiz with Old English lettering. Doc sat down and sketched out a sign proclaiming 'Edward E. Crane, Medical Doctor.' With raised gilt letters on a black background, that would do it! It wouldn't come cheap, coming from Reverend John, and it was hard to haggle with him on price, him being a man of the cloth. The only other carpenter for hire in town was Joe Turner, but there was no artistry in Joe Turner at all. He was strictly a pine box and outhouse carpenter. So, hang the expense; let Reverend John earn his daily bread.

The bare shelves that held all his medical supplies simply wouldn't do. Glass doors were needed to keep the flies and dust out, with key locks to lend that official touch. Maybe, between the sign and the glass doors, he could haggle price with Reverend John.

Doc bustled down the street with the sketch for his new sign, went around to the back of the church, and knocked on the reverend's door.

Reverend John was slow in coming to the door, and it was only when he appeared in slippers and nightshirt that Doc remembered it was quite early in the morning.

"Someone's dying?" the reverend asked.

"No sir, Reverend. If I'm too early, I'll just come back later," Doc said.

"Too early for what? Good lord, have I forgotten an appointment with you? Come in, come in! I'll be ready in a moment," the reverend said, looking flustered and apologetic and not pausing to give Doc a chance to explain.

Doc went in and had a seat while the reverend rushed about,

getting dressed, profusely denouncing his bad memory. After five minutes, the reverend popped out of the side room, hat in one hand, Bible in the other. "Lead on, my good doctor," he invited.

Doc squirmed in his chair and said, "I don't know where you're going, Reverend, but I'm right where I set out to be!"

"Oh, really? What brings you out so early?" he asked, with a hint of peeve in his voice.

"Well, it's about some glass doors and this here sign," Doc said, prattling on about the glass doors he needed while the reverend looked over the sketch.

The reverend kept silent until Doc had run out of words. Then he said, "It's Miss Hoffman, isn't it, all this sudden concern with appearances?"

"I wouldn't say it is, and I wouldn't say it isn't," Doc answered.

"I don't mean to be too direct," the reverend continued. "It's just that I don't want to miss another wedding like I did with Downwind and Betty Lee."

"That was an emergency, Reverend. It couldn't be helped!"

"Yes. Quite so, quite so," the reverend agreed, "but we'll try to hold our next emergency wedding in the church, won't we?"

"We'll do that! We certainly will, Reverend," Doc agreed. "Now, about that sign and the glass doors—"

"Consider it done! You'll have a sign that would be the envy of Boston and the best glass doors this side of the Mississippi!"

"And how soon could—"

"You'll have the sign tomorrow. The doors will take a few days. It's the glass; it's got to come quite a distance."

"That's first-rate, Reverend! Now, about the price—"

"No problem at all, Doctor Crane! I'll do the job and you can pay me whatever you think it's worth!"

"But I should have some idea—"

"It's a labor of love, my friend," the reverend insisted. "To do it well will refresh my soul. Monetary reward in any amount is a trivial thing in comparison, don't you think?"

"Well, yes, but—"

"It's been a pleasure seeing you again, my friend. You will be in church Sunday, won't you?'' the reverend asked, rising and opening the door to usher Doc out.

"Yes, sir! I'll be there!" Doc agreed, leaving with the feeling that he'd just gotten the bum's rush. It just wasn't possible to dicker price with Reverend John. So the price would be whatever Doc thought the job was worth. That was no bargain at all. Anything less than top dollar would be a criticism of the job and Reverend John. In return, one could only hope to have Reverend John bargaining in his behalf at the Pearly Gates when the time came.

Worse still, the reverend seemed to be expecting a wedding, and Doc had only met the lady yesterday. That thought hadn't crossed his own mind yet, but now that the thought was there, it wasn't all that preposterous. He just didn't like the notion of Reverend John perching on his pew like a vulture waiting for Doc's bachelor spirit to die.

For the next three days, Doc Crane escorted Miss Hoffman to every meal and went with her on short walks and long buggy rides. Sam Ibsen or some other damned fool often invited himself along, but Doc and Miss Hoffman still managed to exchange some confidences. The intruders even added romance to the thing by forcing Doc and Miss Hoffman to adopt an 'us against them' posture. By the fourth day, Doc had Miss Hoffman to himself most of the time and was addressing her as Lillian when they were alone. The more pesty intruders had gotten fed up with Miss Hoffman's way of sending them on fool's errands. Take Jake Perkins, the livery stable man, for instance. He invited himself to ride his saddle horse alongside the buggy once; claimed the buggy wasn't quite right and he'd better be there to fix it if need be. Anyway, Miss Hoffman spotted a little blue flower clinging to a crevice in a high, overhanging gravel bank and asked Jake if he'd fetch it for her. He went scrambling up that gravel wall like Sir Lancelot after the Holy Grail; clawed and scratched his way to the flower and felt the whole damned side of the bank collapse as he picked it, just as if that had been the only thing holding that part of the world together. Jake went flopping and sprawling to the bottom of the bank in the midst of a great cloud of rocks and dust. His hands were cut, his lip was bleeding, and his pants were torn, but the little blue flower was intact. Proud as a rooster, he trotted over to Miss Hoffman with it and found her holding a whole bouquet of those little blue flowers that she and Doc had just picked in the shade of the buggy.

Those fool's errands of Miss Hoffman's were all like that. When a feller came back from one, he knew exactly who the fool was.

During all this, Doc worried about Momma Rose. Her girls were putting on a fashion parade in their new dresses at every opportunity, and the effect was about the same as if a tribe of trained monkeys were doing the modeling. Miss Hoffman did an industrious, nit-picking perfect job of fitting the girls, but you had to see the result right away to appreciate her skill. Give any of those girls twenty minutes with a newly fitted dress and they'd snag it on a nail, slop coffee on it, or swap dresses with someone two sizes larger or smaller. Momma Rose was not happy. She had wrapped her girls in expensive wrappings and what had happened? Doc had taken up with that prudish seamstress in such a way that he scarcely noticed them, and the girls were so busy with their finery that business had fallen off. As a matter of fact, some of her girls seemed to have gotten the notion that they might be too good for some of the regular customers.

Momma Rose was in a foul mood, so Doc kept a weather eye on her, but he was too taken up with Miss Hoffman to really give it much thought. That was before Sunday.

Doc was looking so presentable that Sunday that he'd have drawn admiring glances even in Boston. He was feeling especially good about his mustache. No more the dour, drooping thing of times past; he had trained it into a sprightly upward curl. Now he had an adornment, not just a soup strainer.

Miss Hoffman had taken to serving meals in Sam's kitchen for herself and Doc and Sam. It was her way of paying him for the use of his quarters, and Doc paid for the groceries as his share of the deal. The result was a damned sight better than the Dutchman's cooking. Sam garnished every meal with lavish praise, and Doc carried the courting burden of trying to outdo Sam's praise. Doc was impressed with that lady's cooking, and maybe that was part of what the lady had in mind, too.

On that particular Sunday, Miss Hoffman had prepared the most perfect breakfast ever to grace a table in Thirsty, and they took their time over it. Finally it got close to church time, so Doc and Sam actually volunteered to clean up the dishes while Miss Hoffman got ready for church. Going to church was something Doc and Sam normally did only when it couldn't really be avoided, like washing dishes. They were feeling extra Christian when they sallied to church after cleaning up.

Churchgoing wasn't done too regular in Thirsty. There were maybe five people who went every Sunday, and about fifteen like Doc and Sam who might show up about once a month. The rest went only on special occasions. So it was an astonishing thing to find all of Momma Rose's girls in church that morning.

"What in the world do you make of that, Sam?" Doc whispered.

"Beats me," Sam whispered back. "Momma Rose must've put 'em up to it."

"Indeed she did not!" Miss Hoffman whispered. "It was my idea!"

"Really?" Doc whispered.

"Of course!" Miss Hoffman whispered. "I've been giving those girls a good talking-to during their fittings."

"Oh good, they need that!" Doc said, casting a worried glance at Sam, who rolled his eyes upward as if to say, "God help us now!"

Reverend John delivered a hell-fire sermon on sins of the flesh that morning, and Doc remembered it as one the reverend had cut loose with about a year ago. Had the reverend originally planned to deliver this one, or had he resurrected it especially for the girls? Either way, it was right on target; tears of repentance could be seen flowing down cheeks that hadn't known such tears in years.

Doc, Sam, and Miss Hoffman were still standing on the church steps talking to Reverend John after the service when Momma Rose came boiling out of her front door, still buttoning a huge floral-print dress that billowed around her like a sagging gas bag.

The girls were still thirty yards away when Momma Rose cut loose on them.

"You been to church, ain'tcha? Getting your ears stuffed with Bible talk that don't earn your keep, nor buy your clothes, nor do nothing but confuse ya! What did I tell you girls about that stuff? Hell on earth is what it is. Damned if you do and damned if you don't! It don't do nothing for nobody! Don't you all listen to nothing I tell ya?"

When Momma Rose paused to catch her breath, Cindy took foolish advantage of the pause to answer. "Miss Hoffman says ladies go to church and we ain't never gonna be ladies if we don't, so we're gonna go ever' Sunday from now on!"

"What!" Momma Rose screamed, laying a hammy paw on each of Cindy's shoulders and drawing her close before screaming a second "What!" and shaking Cindy till she looked like a rag doll.

"That Cindy," Sam said, shaking his head sadly. "I think she'd stick her finger in a buzz saw just to see how sharp the teeth were."

"Git on home, all of you!" Momma Rose barked at her girls, and gave Cindy a fling in the right direction. Fixing a glaring eye on the church, Momma Rose spotted the enemy gathered there and proceeded to the attack, arms akimbo and fists clenched for battle. "You all stay right there!" she shouted, well aware that they were nimble enough to elude her all day long if she didn't catch them now.

"Good morning, Mrs. Rose," Reverend John greeted her as she came to a puffing halt as the foot of the church steps. "You're a trifle late for the regular service, but you're more than welcome to come in."

"Don't talk foolish!" she snapped. "You all bin confusin' my girls and I want a stop to it. They're already thinkin' they're too good for the men folks around here, an' if that keeps up, they'll be good for nuthin'!"

"They'll be ladies, Mrs. Rose," Miss Hoffman objected. "Ladies with the clothes, manners, and virtues that good men everywhere admire."

"Ladies!" Momma Rose exploded. "Just one the likes of you is too many for this town! You just get your tail on Tuesday's stage and don't never come back, that's my advice to you!"

"She'll stay as long as she damn well pleases!" Doc growled, throwing caution to the winds.

"No need to argue the point," Miss Hoffman broke in. "If Mrs. Rose pays for the dresses in full by Tuesday, my business here will be at an end and I will have to be getting home, much as I have enjoyed my stay here."

"You're gonna have to knock a few dollars off of that bill for the flimsy nature of the goods," Momma Rose advised.

"More likely I'll have to add to it to cover the extra repairs for all the damage your girls did," Miss Hoffman replied.

"Huh!" Momma Rose snorted. "We'll call it square at the original price! It'll be worth it just to be rid of you!"

Momma Rose waddled over to the saloon for a beer, and the others took a slow walk around town before splitting up to attend to various chores, which in every case included a nap. The day had been badly damaged for Doc, though. Miss Hoffman, his Lillian, would be leaving on Tuesday. He'd known that from the start, but had managed not to think about it.

What if he proposed? Would she accept? And if she accepted, would he be sorry he proposed? The very thought of proposing was uncomfortable. As uncomfortable as losing Lillian's company. Thirsty was not her kind of town, and that was a big part of the problem. Even if she did accept a proposal, it would mean he'd have to leave Thirsty; she wouldn't be happy there. It was a damned tough decision.

The rest of Sunday and all of Monday went by on eagle's wings as far as Doc was concerned. Then it was Tuesday, and he was helping Miss Hoffman into the stage.

"We're going to miss you more than I can say," Doc said.

"We?" Miss Hoffman teased. "Won't you miss me just a little more than the others?"

"More than all the others put together."

"You'll write, won't you?"

"There'll be a letter on every stage," Doc promised.

"You really must visit Saint Louis someday. There's so much to see and do! And, Lord knows, there's always room for a good doctor!"

"I'll come. I can't say just when, but I'll come!"

Doc waited till the stage was out of sight before going back to his office. Sam Ibsen had moved back to his own quarters, and Doc had the whole place to himself again. He moved things back to where they had been before he made room for Sam. Then he mixed up some salves, ground some medicinal roots, and pressed a few pills. Not that all these things would be needed soon, but he felt a desperate need to keep busy just now.

Two hours went by before Doc ran out of sensible things to do, but he didn't let that stop him. He had a pouch full of lead buckshot that a cashless patient had used to pay his bill. Setting a small-mouthed bottle in one corner of his office, he took a seat in the opposite corner and began trying to pitch the buckshot, one by one, into the bottle. By the time he had a dozen pellets in the bottle and several hundred scattered around the floor, the door opened and Reverend John came in.

"Don't you knock, Reverend?" Doc asked.

"Neither the Lord nor the devil knocks," Reverend John answered. "Am I not between them?"

"All of the rest of us are, and we knock," Doc said.

"Even if I had knocked, you wouldn't have had time to pick up your toys there," Reverend John said matter-of-factly.

"I could have said I'm busy and please come back in an hour," Doc countered.

"But you invited me," the reverend persisted.

Doc thought about it a moment. "I don't remember that!" he said.

"You did, last week. To make some glass doors!"

"That—yes, I did, didn't I?" Doc turned to look at the open shelves that had seemed so badly in need of improvement last week. He had done some talking to Lillian about his plans for fixing up his office, but now he wondered if she'd ever see the result. And that miserably depressed feeling he'd been trying to avoid came crashing down on him.

"The wood and the glass are on order and ought to come on the next freight wagon," the reverend said, sensing that Doc might back out if he thought he could.

"Finish your measuring then," Doc said with a careless wave toward the shelves. "I've got to go out for a while."

Try as he might, Doc couldn't work his way out of the vacuum left by Lillian's departure. Not that day, nor the next, nor the next. Come Friday, he started writing the letter that was to go out on next Tuesday's stage. By Saturday, he was making his third try at writing that letter, having carefully burned the first two. It was a problem of saying enough without saying too much, of being warmly aloof, of capturing Lillian's heart without surrendering his own.

By Sunday he realized that the captured heart was his, and he'd better get himself on a stage for Saint Louis to make the final surrender. A letter just couldn't do the job. On Monday he told Sam and George that he had to make a trip on professional business and officially appointed George as acting doctor in his absence. On Tuesday he was on the stage, feeling like an evangelist on a pilgrimage to the holy land.

Two weeks later, when the stage came into Thirsty, the driver went over to the General Store and asked Sam to come on out to the stage. Sam went along under protest, claiming he didn't have time to play games. The driver didn't argue, just flung the stage door open and said, "We gotta get him on over to his office."

Sam peered intently into the stage. "My Gawd, is that Doc Crane?"

"Yep! That's him!" the driver said. "Found him in the dirt behind a saloon down in Gilmore! Sure is a mess, ain't he?"

"I think we've buried people that didn't look any worse than that," Sam said.

"Well, let's get him out," the driver said, climbing in and pulling Doc forward. Doc made some grumbling sounds, but the driver pulled him to his feet and pushed him to the door, where Sam laid hold of him and helped to ease him down. And there he teetered, face covered with stubble and dirt, clothes rumpled and torn and smelling of whiskey and sweat.

They had started across the street with Doc stumbling along between them when Momma Rose came barging along and blocked their path. "Hello, Mr. Boston Man, sir!" she cooed. "Been out visiting your Lady Love, have you? Hee! Hee! Hee! Hee!" she laughed. "I told you you'd want one of my girls someday, didn't I? And you can't have her, can you, Mr. Boston Man?"

Doc opened a pair of the most godawful bloodshot eyes, lurched forward, and puked on her feet, then passed out cold and hung limp between Sam and the driver.

"Damn!" Momma Rose cursed, looking at her messy shoes. "Damn!" She turned and went stomping back toward her place.

"Now what in hell do you suppose she meant about Doc wanting one of her girls?" Sam asked.

"Ask Doc when he sobers up," the driver advised. "Let's get moving; I gotta see to my horses yet."

George Gatlin was snoozing peacefully in Doc's swivel chair when they carried Doc in. Sam sent him over to tend to the General Store and settled down to tend to Doc himself. The coffee had boiled down to mud by the time Doc began showing some life, but coffee wasn't what Doc wanted anyway.

"Whiskey. Fetch me a bottle of whiskey, Sam," Doc pleaded.

"No, sir! Coffee is what you're gonna get!"

"You're my friend, ain't you?" Doc insisted.

"Right! That's why you're getting coffee!"

Doc suffered through a cup of coffee, declared it pure poison, and fell asleep again.

Sam grabbed one of Doc's pots, went over to The Dutchman's, got it filled with soup, and was back long before Doc woke up again. Getting it into Doc wasn't as easy, but the mule in Sam was stronger than the mule in Doc that day.

"Is there anything else you want?" Sam asked.

"I sure as hell wouldn't tell *you* if there was!" Doc answered. "You force coffee and soup into me when I tell you I don't want it; you flat-out refuse to get me a real drink, which was the one and only thing I did ask for—"

"Doc," Sam said, "We'll have a drink together, just one, if you'll tell me what in hell happened to you."

Doc mulled it over a bit. "Momma Rose'll tell you and the whole blessed town soon enough, if she ain't done it already."

"She said something about you wanting one of her girls," Sam prompted.

"You got a drink or ain't you?" Doc asked.

Sam pulled a pint bottle from his jacket, poured two small glasses, and handed one to Doc, who promptly downed half of it. There he sat, a dirty, unshaven wreck. He just stared at the floor and said nothing.

"Well?" Sam prodded.

"That business trip," Doc began. "It wasn't business. I went to see—" and he paused, struggling for control before he could get out the name—"Miss Lillian Hoffman."

"Well, sure, we all figured that," Sam said.

"I was gonna propose. Gonna do whatever I had to to marry that lady and make her happy," Doc said, wiping at his eyes. "I went to the address she gave and found her. She's the proprietor of Miss Hoffman's School for Young Ladies—the biggest damn cathouse you ever saw! She's a madam, just like Momma Rose!"

"Lord almighty!"

"Momma Rose set her up in business. What she did here was just a favor for Momma Rose."

Sam and Doc finished their drinks, and Sam poured again without being asked to. "She thought it was funny, did she?"

"Well," Doc hesitated, "she didn't laugh. I think I'd of hung myself if she had."

"That's the meanest, lowest, most contemptible, low-down, two-faced trick I ever heard of!" Sam declared.

"Momma Rose said I'd want one of her girls one day, and she'd see to it that I couldn't have her. And that's exactly what she's done," Doc said, the tears beginning to flow. "I still want what Lillian seemed to be so bad I could cry for her, but she's a bitch, Sam. Oh God, she's a bitch!"

CHAPTER 4

MURDER AT THE MANSION

IN the weeks that followed Doc Crane's retreat from Saint Louis, he made a slow and steady recovery to his old self, though it was really the murder at the mansion that finally ended his melancholy and brought his self-esteem back.

A lone rider had come pounding down the main street of Thirsty early one morning and gone straight to Sheriff Jones's office. The sheriff came out a few minutes later, borrowed his visitor's horse, and went galloping back up the street.

The horse's owner went trotting over to Doc's place and barged right into his bedroom to wake him up. "Come on, Doc!" he urged. "We gotta git a couple o' hosses and git ourselves out to Slim Barlow's mansion!"

"What for?" Doc asked. "Has Slim been hurt?"

"Yessir, he's got a huntin' knife slammed in his back! That must've hurt real bad before he died."

Doc grabbed his pants and started dressing. "Who put the knife in him?" he asked.

"Dunno fer sure. Some folks think it was Isrul Douglass. His claim is right next to Slim's, you know. There was a quarrel between 'em. Slim said someone was stealin' from his sluice. Never named Isrul flat-out, but he slanted the suspicion that way and Isrul was real peeved about it!"

They had to saddle their own horses, what with Jake, the livery stable man, being too slow to suit them. They took Doc's horse and Sheriff Jones's horse and got on their way.

Everyone in Thirsty knew Slim Barlow's mansion. It was a local architectural highlight. About two years back, Slim had hit a rich pocket in his claim not more'n three weeks after he started digging. He decided to build himself a genuine, first-class mansion on a little knoll just beyond the gold-bearing dirt. He ordered lumber, framed windows, and an especially fine entrance way with elegant framing and stained glass windows above and on both sides of the door. Naturally, special stuff like that took some time to deliver, and Slim threw a few parties in Thirsty while he was waiting. Meanwhile, the rich ore suddenly petered out and Slim found that he'd spent beyond his means. He found other buyers for the lumber and the framed windows he'd ordered, but that entrance way was something else. Slim couldn't find anyone who needed a front door for a mansion. Undaunted, he decided his fortunes would surely change for the better again, so he took delivery on that fine entrance way and built a modest log cabin around it. Absurd as it may have seemed, it struck a responsive note among the other miners. The log cabin was reality, but that fine doorway set into it expressed the dreams and hopes of nearly every miner there. Folks didn't laugh at Slim Barlow's mansion. They admired it. And Slim took great pride in showing it and describing what it would be when he hit rich dirt again.

But it was obvious now that he wasn't going to hit rich dirt again. He was still lying on the ground by his sluice when Doc got out to his claim. A couple dozen miners were milling around the place, discussing poor Slim's demise. Sheriff Jones came forward to greet Doc. "Look him over, Doc, and tell me anything you can about it that I can't see for myself, will you?"

"Do my best," Doc promised, and knelt beside the body. Slim was face down, and Doc looked him over carefully before reaching over to pull the knife from his back. It was wedged tight and took a fierce pull to work loose. "It took a powerful man to drive that knife home!" Doc remarked. "A tall man, too, judging by the way it was slanted!" Then Doc rolled Slim over, revealing an expression of surprise and pain frozen on the dead face. Slim's eyes were wide open and his mouth agape. "I'd guess he's been dead at least eight hours," Doc announced.

"Anything else?" the sheriff asked.

"He died just about as quick as that knife hit him," Doc said. "Were there any footprints near him?"

"Yessir, dozens of 'em!" Sheriff Jones answered ruefully. "Seems like everybody roundabout got here before I did and took turns stomping their feet all over the place."

Cougar Ledbetter, who had a claim upstream from Slim's, broke in. "Aw, Sheriff, I tole you there warn't no other footprints but Slim's here when I got here, an' I was the one what found him!"

"Sure, Cougar," the sheriff answered, "Slim put that knife in his own back, didn't he?"

" 'Course not!" Cougar answered. "That knife was thrown! A killer don't leave no close footprints when he throws his knife. And you know as well as I do that Isrul Douglass is a man what kin throw a knife that way."

"Slim's knife's gone from the scabbard on his belt," Doc observed. "Like as not, that's his own knife in his back. Seems like the killer had to leave footprints to put that knife where it was. And the slant of it tells us for sure certain that it wasn't thrown."

"Most everybody around here has a knife like that," Cougar insisted. "That's the killer's knife in Slim's back, all right. The killer just took Slim's knife afterward so's his own empty scabbard wouldn't give him away."

"Then the killer would have left footprints when he came for the knife, don't you think?" Sheriff Jones asked.

"Okay, okay!" Cougar blurted. "So the killer wrastled with Slim somewheres and got his knife, then when Slim was runnin' fer a gun, the killer threw the knife and hit Slim square in the back. An I still say Isrul Douglass done it!"

"You're the only one that got a decent look at the footprints— did they look like Slim had been running?" the sheriff asked.

"No. Now that you call it to mind, he warn't. An that's wuss. It means Slim was walkin' away, trustin' like, not expectin' any trouble when Isrul Douglass flung the knife in him."

"You got no call to be blaming this on Israel Douglass, Cougar!" the sheriff growled. "I'll find out soon enough who did it! Till then, don't you be throwing knife words at anyone. You keep on about Israel Douglass, and you'll have me thinking a feller named Cougar is trying to get rid of his neighbors; one by murder and another by lynch mob.''

Cougar backed off and turned away. Sheriff Jones turned his attention back to Doc. ''You through with Slim?'' he asked.

''Reckon so.''

''I'll turn him over to Joe Turner, then. And I'd be obliged if you'd come over to Israel Douglass's claim with me, sort of like an extra pair of eyes and ears. Maybe you'll see something I won't.''

They walked their horses over to Israel's claim, the distance being hardly enough to make it worthwhile to mount. Israel was sitting on his front step puffing a pipe. A shotgun leaned against the cabin beside him, and a lanky, red-haired boy of twelve years or so was sitting on a sawhorse sharpening an axe with a whetstone.

''Mornin', Sheriff, mornin', Doc!'' Israel greeted them.

''Have you heard the ruckus over to Slim Barlow's this morning, Israel?'' the sheriff asked.

''Yessir. My boy's been telling me about it,'' Israel answered. ''Skeeter an' me, we ain't set foot on Slim Barlow's claim in over two months. Not since he started talkin' like as if I was stealin' from him.''

''Some folks think you killed Slim Barlow,'' the sheriff said.

''So I heard,'' Israel answered. ''What's your thinkin' on it?''

''Don't know yet. I'd like to see your knife, though.''

Israel pulled the knife from its sheath and handed it over.

''Folks say you're mighty good at throwing a knife, Israel.''

''Ain't nobody better!''

''Israel, I'm thinking you'd best come into town with me,'' the sheriff said.

''You arrestin' me?''

''Wouldn't be giving your knife back if I were,'' the sheriff answered, handing back the knife. ''It just seems like it's best for you and Skeeter and everyone else.''

''You worried about a lynchin', Sheriff?''

''Could be.''

''Sheriff, somebody slammed a knife in Slim Barlow's back. I ain't the one what done it, an' whoever did do it is still runnin' loose out here. That there's what you ought to be worried about.''

''I ain't forgot that,'' the sheriff answered. ''Fact is, if the killer kills again, it's best you be in Thirsty so's everybody knows you ain't the killer.''

''Ain't they liable to get that notion when they see me sittin' in jail?''

''You could stay in one of Jason's rooms over to the Thirsty Saloon.''

''Cain't afford that.''

Doc considered whether he shouldn't volunteer to put Israel and Skeeter up at his place, but he knew that would be crowding things more than reasonable. Besides, Israel wasn't much in the habit of washing. He was definitely a man who was more admirable from a distance than close up. The upshot was that he volunteered for half the package. ''I've got room for Skeeter,'' he said. ''Maybe it's best and safest that Israel bunk in the jail.''

''So long as I ain't under arrest, the jail will do fer me,'' Israel agreed.

Sheriff Jones got back to Thirsty late in the afternoon and found his jail empty. Skeeter was sitting at the edge of Doc's porch, tossing pebbles into pockets of powdery dust at the edge of the street.

''Where's your pa?'' the sheriff asked.

''He went over to the saloon for a beer,'' Skeeter answered, pointing across the street. The sheriff was hungry and thirsty. Now he decided he had a reasonable and professional excuse to take care of the thirst first, so he went over to the saloon.

Israel was sitting alone at a table along the wall, nursing a mug of beer. All the other customers were lined up along the bar or parked at the tables nearest the bar. Sheriff Jones moved up to the bar and ordered a mug of beer. Jason poured it right away, slid it across the bar, and leaned over to whisper, ''Israel paid for his drink with dust!'' The sheriff nodded politely, and sipped his beer. Jason leaned over the bar again and whispered, ''Dust just like Slim Barlow used to bring in!''

The sheriff hadn't hardly gotten back to his beer when Cougar

Ledbetter approached and asked, "Well sir, are you still the only man in Thirsty that don't know who killed Slim Barlow?"

"You still figure you can steal Israel's claim by getting him lynched, do you?" the sheriff shot back.

"Damn you!" Cougar shouted, swinging a massive fist at the sheriff. Sheriff Jones ducked, sloshed his beer in Cougar's face, then slammed his left into Cougar's jaw. Cougar's eyes rolled and then closed as he fell to the floor.

Jason slid a fresh beer over to the sheriff. "Thanks for not hitting him with the mug. Those things are hard to come by out here."

Things were in danger of getting calm and peaceful again when Lucky Martin spoke up. "You missed Slim's funeral, Sheriff."

"Buried already, is he?" the sheriff asked, taking notice that Notches had gotten up from Lucky's table and moved off to the left side of the room.

"Reckon you'll ever figure out who did it?"

"Most likely."

"That's nice," Lucky said in a very bland way. "I'm glad you're likely to do something about it."

"What we aren't going to do is hang the wrong man," the sheriff said.

"Good!" Lucky said. "I'm glad we aren't going to hang the wrong man. Even if we all know there's only one man hereabouts who could have thrown that knife."

"Hell's fire!" the sheriff answered. "From what Doc Crane says, that knife wasn't thrown! It was plunged in on a steep slant, the way any stab knife is!"

"That's exactly so. That knife was plunged in by hand," Doc agreed from the doorway, having just come in.

"Plunged in, eh?" Lucky asked. "I wonder if a friend or enemy did that? Slim had lots of friends, but just one enemy. The whole thing would be easier to figure out if an enemy did it."

"Slim had an enemy all right," the sheriff agreed. "The worst kind: one he didn't know about. That's the kind it takes to put a knife in the back!"

"Sure, Sheriff," Lucky mocked. "Or maybe it was just some

drifter that did it. Some low, no-account drifter that went through here without any of the rest of us seeing him."

"That's something that needs asking," Sheriff Jones said. "Did anyone see any strangers hereabouts yesterday or today?"

The question was greeted with silence until Cindy spoke up. "There was a feller got in late last night. He was camped down by the spring below town!"

"I didn't see no such feller," Momma Rose snorted.

"He didn't come up to the house. Said he was lonely but didn't cotton to crowds, so we was talking for a time down to the livery stable."

"You little cheat!" Momma Rose barked. "You wasn't gonna tell me, was you?"

"I was, too! I just forgot," Cindy said, skipping over behind Lucky's table as Momma Rose came after her. "Here's your money," Cindy said, pulling a folded note from her blouse and flinging it across the table. A flurry of screaming, clawing, and swatting followed, which no man was fool enough to interfere with. Cindy left with a bloody nose and an eye that would soon be swollen.

Doc left, following after Cindy. "Huh!" Momma Rose snorted. "Look at that fool doctor traipsing after that little wench. She ain't no more'n bruised, and here I am scratched and bit fit to get lockjaw. Fat lot he knows about what's important!"

The men were quiet. It pained them to see Cindy treated so. She was the general favorite among Momma Rose's girls. And Momma's stock with the miners had been lower than a snake's belly button ever since that mean trick she and Miss Hoffman had played on Doc. But there were some things a man couldn't interfere with.

Sheriff Jones had taken advantage of the ruckus to walk out unnoticed with Israel.

Doc hustled Cindy over to his office, got the nose bleed stopped and tended to the bruised eye. "You sure put yourself in a bear trap that time, Cindy! It's good what you did, speaking up about that stranger, to protect Israel. But if it should happen that there wasn't any stranger, you ought to let the sheriff know so's he doesn't waste time in that direction.''

Cindy frowned, then said, "You tell him, sort of quiet-like, Doc. If you're done patchin', I gotta go!''

He didn't have long to dwell on Cindy. Skeeter came in right after. "Doctor Crane," he asked, "do you suppose a kid like me could figure out who killed Slim Barlow?''

"So far, you couldn't do any worse than the rest of us," Doc conceded.

Skeeter pulled a chair up close and hunched over with his elbows resting on the desk. "Slim Barlow said someone was stealing from his claim, didn't he?''

"That's what he said."

"With Slim gone to glory, what do you suppose the thief might do?''

"You're thinking the thief will come back?" Doc asked. "You've got a good idea there, but all we've got to do about it is tell the sheriff.''

"No, sir!" Skeeter insisted. "That thief will be keeping track of the sheriff. Sheriff Jones might just as well try sneaking up on that thief wearing cowbells and lanterns.''

"Supposing I agreed to help you, what do you figure we ought to do?" Doc asked.

"Well, sir," Skeeter said, squirming in his seat, but keeping an earnest set of eyes fixed on Doc, "all's we gotta do is hide in Downwind's wagon and drop off in the bushes by Slim Barlow's claim. It'll be dark enough so's we can slip into Slim's cabin an' wait for the thief to show up.''

"Downwind knows about this?" Doc asked.

"Yessir—he's a-waiting for us!''

"Suppose the thief shows up right smack dab in the middle of the night, how do you expect we'll see him?''

"I reckon we need a lantern," Skeeter admitted.

"Not just any lantern, neither," Doc advised. "It has to be shielded so's it can be lit without showing any light till just exactly when we want it to.''

"You got a lantern like that?" Skeeter asked.

"Just so happens I do," Doc admitted with a sidelong glance at Skeeter. "What do you suppose we ought to do when we see this thief? Throw rocks at him?"

"No, sir!" Skeeter said. "Ain't you got a few guns?"

"I reckon I could bring a six-gun if you think I ought to."

"Ain't you got one for me?" Skeeter asked.

"Not likely," Doc said. "If there's any shooting, I want you to cut and run for help, not go slinging lead every which way."

"Aw!"

"No two ways about it," Doc declared. "Do we go, or don't we?"

"Yessir!" Skeeter agreed. "An' we better go right away afore Downwind gets tired of waiting for us."

Doc rummaged around in one of his back rooms, then came forth with the promised lantern and six-gun. "You mosey over to the livery stable with the lantern." Doc said, dumping a few extra cartridges in his coat pocket. "I'll come along directly so's we don't look like a parade."

Separately, Doc and Skeeter climbed into the wagon, Downwind tossed a canvas over them, and they were on their way. A bumpy hour later, they heard the wagon splash through the upper ford on Crystal Creek, then felt it climb the opposite bank. "Guess I'd better light this lantern before we get there," Doc announced softly, fumbling with its shutter, then striking a match to the wick. The light flared briefly under the canvas, then Doc closed the shutter and the light was gone.

"Golly, that works just fine!" Skeeter said.

"Just remember where it is if you don't want to blister yourself on it," Doc warned.

A short time later, Downwind tugged on the canvas and whispered, "This is as close as you'll get." Doc and Skeeter climbed out from under the canvas, Doc whispered, "Thanks, Downwind," and they hopped down over the tailgate.

It was early dusk. Doc and Skeeter moved in close to the nearest bushes and crouched there till the sound of the wagon faded and they could tune their ears to the other sounds of the night. Skeeter whispered, "Foller me," and started off in a creeping crouch that

Doc imitated. Following a rocky path, they soon reached Slim Barlow's mansion, a gloomy mass dimly visible in the fading light. Again they stopped and listened for what seemed like an eternity to Doc. He fished the six-gun out from under his belt and held it with his fingers cupped around the trigger guard.

"Come on," Skeeter whispered and led the way around to the front of the cabin, then crept onto the porch on hands and knees. Doc played rear guard, stopping at the edge of the porch with his gun held in both hands, finger on the trigger and thumb hooked over the hammer. Skeeter crept to the door, turned the knob slowly, and pushed gently, then harder. The door didn't budge. Slowly, Skeeter stood and felt along the edge of the door, then crouched down and crept back to Doc.

"Sheriff's got it padlocked," Skeeter whispered. "Best we just sit here on the porch an' wait." Doc agreed to that, and the two of them settled in side by side with their backs to the wall. It wasn't terribly uncomfortable, and Doc figured a certain amount of discomfort might be useful in keeping them awake.

An hour later Doc got to wishing he'd brought a blanket or two anyway. He leaned over to Skeeter and whispered, "You'd best take a nap now. I'll wake you in an hour or so and take my turn at napping."

Before Skeeter could answer, there was a clattering sound down by the creek, and all thought of sleep vanished. Skeeter took up the lantern, and Doc pointed his gun in the direction of the noise. A few moments later, the clattering repeated, a little closer.

"He's comin'!" Skeeter whispered.

"Wait till he's close," Doc whispered back.

"Let's get over to the edge of the porch," Skeeter whispered.

"Okay. Slow and quiet."

They reached the edge just as a crashing sound came from the sluice. "Close enough?" Skeeter whispered. "Yes!" Doc answered. "Light him up!"

A blaze of light shot from the lantern as Skeeter tripped the shutter. Doc jumped to his feet and shouted, "Hold still, right there!"

A startled raccoon stared back at them from his perch on the sluice, eyes glowing in the lantern beam. Skeeter flicked the beam around to either side of the coon, looking for some other thief.

"Hell!" Doc said, walking stiffly down toward the sluice. "It's only a coon!"

Skeeter came along beside him, keeping the lantern beam on the sluice. The coon dropped something and scampered off. "Let's see what he dropped," Doc said, and Skeeter pointed the beam down below where the coon had been. "Crawdad's claw," Skeeter announced, picking up a half-inch pink and brown claw.

"Guess he came up on the sluice for a crawdad dinner," Doc agreed. "But what in tarnation did he do that made such a racket?"

Skeeter flashed the light around under the sluice and brought it to rest on two melon-sized stones, saying, "Them stones was moved recent. Looks like they fell off the sluice."

"Reckon that's it," Doc agreed. "But they had to be perched up on the edge of the sluice to get knocked down that way. The coon wouldn't move 'em that far if they were just sheltering a crawdad down in the sluice."

"Slim took to settin' rocks on the edge of his sluice that way about the time he started accusin' Paw of stealin'," Skeeter said. "Reckon he figured they'd bust the toes of any thief that bumped 'em in the dark."

"Uh huh," Doc said. "Reckon I did see 'em when I was out here with Sheriff Jones, but I didn't think much on it just then. Guess it shows that no one in the crowd that was out here today trifled with the sluice."

"Honest folks don't fool with another man's sluice, even if he's dead," Skeeter said.

"That coon," Doc mused. "Do you get many of 'em along the creek here?"

"Used to," Skeeter said. "The crawdads got fat on worms and garbage the miners was sloshin' into the creek, and the coons would be down here every night, but folks got to admiring the taste of a coon dinner and the style of a coonskin hat, and pretty soon they wasn't any coons left."

"Except the one we saw tonight?"

"Yessir. First one I seen in about two years."

"Gimme that light a minute," Doc said, tucking the six-gun back under his belt. He flashed the light this way and that. Finally he grunted, "Well, I reckon I know who killed Slim!"

"You do!?" Skeeter exclaimed, eyes agog.

"Let's go on down to your Paw's claim and get settled for the night. I'll tell you the way of it there."

Skeeter jabbered at Doc all the way down to his Paw's cabin, trying to get Doc to let go of what he was thinking, but Doc would only say, "You saw as much as I saw. Now you just see if you can't figure it out the same as I did."

They had a lantern lit and their bunks ready when Skeeter said, "Well, that coon had something to do with it. You're thinking it was the coon messing around in Slim's sluice and Slim thought it was a two-legged thief, same as we did for a while. Ain't that so?"

"That's part of it all right. A man don't know how much rich mud he might have in the riffles of his sluice, so if he sees some of it's been dug out, thieving is the first thing that comes to mind. Anyway, Slim Barlow wasn't noted for deep thinking. He generally took the first idea that popped up and didn't go looking for another without he had to."

"And Slim set up them rocks to help trap or scare off the thief."

"Right," Doc agreed as he pulled off his boots and settled down on a bunk. "Now, don't you think he might have set more traps?"

"A trap what could throw a knife?" Skeeter asked.

"Exactly. And part of it's still out there, plain as day. Slim Barlow banged into his own trap and killed himself. Like as not, he heard that coon and forgot about his trap when he went stomping after it!"

"I didn't see no trap like that," Skeeter protested.

"Blow out the light and get to bed. I'll show you come morning."

"There was a hacked up sapling out there with a rope dangling from the top," Skeeter ventured a little later from the darkness of his bunk.

"There, now," Doc said. "You did see it! You just didn't think about it."

"How did it work?"

"If you noticed the way the top of that sapling was split and laced together, you ought to be able to figure out why that was done."

"You reckon a knife handle was wedged into that split?"

"Absolutely!"

"And the rope was used to bow the sapling down like a cocked spring?" asked Skeeter. "But I didn't see no kind of trigger there."

"There's another sapling there with a nail driven halfway in just above the ground, and there's a rub mark on the bark just below the nail. That's where the rope was brought down to ground and brought around toward the trigger at the sluice."

"I didn't see no trigger," Skeeter persisted.

"What did the loose end of the rope look like?"

Skeeter thought before answering, "Nothing special. Just a little loop with string and tar holding it."

"Sounds pretty special to me," Doc said. "A man could drive a peg straight down in the ground, then pull it up above ground maybe an inch. Then he could pull that sapling down in a tight bow, run the rope over to that peg, and put that little loop over it. There's your trigger. Any man steps on that peg, he gets slammed by the sapling."

"You reckon we'll find that peg?"

"Absolutely! Right in the dirt where Slim was standing last."

There was a long pause, and Doc had almost dozed off when Skeeter asked, "Do you suppose Slim knew what hit him?"

"Go to sleep, dammit!" Doc groused. And, to his surprise, Skeeter did. Or, at least, he quit that chatter-buzzing that had earned him the nickname of Skeeter. Doc was soon asleep too.

But the day was not done. Doc suddenly awoke to the painful realization that someone had just sat down on his arm! "Git the hell off my bed!" he roared.

A voice, much deeper than Skeeter's, barked, "Who in hell's in here?" and a third voice answered, "Varmints! We got us a

bunch of varmints!'' Doc yelled, ''That you, Sheriff?'' ''Yeah,''
the sheriff answered, ''it's me and Israel. Folks in town were
getting in a lynch mood, so I figured Israel would be safer out
here. We tried to find you two before we left town. We figured
that you had heard what was going on and slipped away like Israel
and me was about to. Is that the way of it?''

''No. Not exactly,'' Doc answered. ''Light a lamp and let's figure out where we're all going to sleep.''

''Nothing doing!'' Sheriff Jones said. ''No lights. I ain't inviting trouble!''

''You and Skeeter stay put,'' Israel said. ''I'll dig out blankets
so's me and the sheriff can sleep on the floor.''

''You ain't told me what you're doing here then, if it ain't because of the lynch mob,'' Sheriff Jones reminded Doc.

''Skeeter, you tell 'em what we were doing,'' Doc said. ''I'm
going to sleep!''

Doc lay there, listening, as Skeeter started with his idea about
catching the thief and their ride out in Downwind's wagon. He
meant to stay awake to be sure that Skeeter told it right, but, despite his efforts, was soon asleep.

Doc woke to the sounds of Israel and the sheriff scuffing
around, getting breakfast and such. It was sometime past dawn,
but not nearly so late as he'd like to sleep. ''Kinda early to be
getting up, ain't it?'' he complained.

''You'd be getting up a damned sight earlier if you'd slept on a
dirt floor like we did,'' Sheriff Jones grumbled.

''Well, now,'' Israel chuckled. ''I'm about to fix you fellers a
breakfast worth gettin' up early for! Tain't often I has such good
company, an' I'm gonna make it worth your time!''

That changed the general mood for the better, and they were
soon busy rehashing all that had gone on. They woke Skeeter for
breakfast and let him chatter away while they set to work on Israel's bacon and flapjacks and coffee fit to wake Lazarus.

Breakfast was just decently done when a rifle shot sounded outside, followed by a demand to come on out. Sheriff Jones peeked
out the window and announced, ''We sure do have a lot of com-

pany out there. Mighty glad we don't have to share breakfast with 'em!"

"Let me do the talking," Doc advised. "They ain't figured out a quarrel with me yet."

Sheriff Jones nodded. "Reckon you're right. Poke a white flag out the door ahead of you. Me an' Israel will cover from the windows."

So Doc followed his white flag out the door and stood on the doorstep, blinking in the bright sunshine.

"Send Israel out!" Lucky Martin barked, showing himself at the edge of a tree.

"First thing," Doc yelled, "I'd like to show you all the trap that Slim Barlow set and killed himself with!"

So saying, Doc marched himself up toward Slim Barlow's claim, right past a half-dozen grim-looking miners clutching a goodly assortment of rifles, six-guns, and shotguns. When he was a dozen paces beyond them, Doc turned and glared. "Well, dammit, are you coming, or are you afraid the truth will spoil the murdering you've got in mind?"

"Stand fast!" Lucky shouted. "It's a trick!"

"Yeah!" Notches echoed.

"I'm gonna look!" one miner announced. "Me, too," another agreed, and Doc walked away with most of the miners following him.

When he got them out to Slim's sluice, he gave them a preamble about the coon with the crawdad and about the rocks Slim had perched on the sluice for a trap. Then he showed them the parts of the other trap, which some of the miners recalled seeing when Slim was found. Doc had a couple of miners bend the sapling down while he ran the rope under the nail at the base of the other sapling and then out where Slim had lain. "Now don't let go of that thing while I'm over here!" Doc cautioned as he fished around in the dirt at the far reach of the rope. At last he found what he was searching for and, with some effort, pulled a peg out of the ground a little ways and slipped the loop over it. "Now, ease up on that sapling kind of slow-like," he yelled, and watched as the rope stretched taut and held.

"There's Slim's trap!" he said proudly. "Fetch about three boards from the end of the sluice and we'll see it work."

The boards were eagerly snatched loose and brought up. Doc set two of them up, leaning against each other just beyond the trigger peg. "Now, will somebody wedge a hunting knife in the end of the sapling? Careful now, don't spring it!"

When the knife was fitted in place, Doc said, "Stand clear and watch it now!" And he toppled the third board over onto the trigger peg. The trap sprang with a real whiz-bang, slamming the knife clear through one of the standing boards with a tremendous whack. The sapling rebounded without the knife and stood quivering over the board that lay where Slim Barlow had been found.

Among the many comments from the miners, "Ole Slim sure knew how to fix himself a trap, didn't he?" summed it up.

"Well, my friends," Doc said, "ain't it time to go back to Israel Douglass's and set things right?"

The response was a joy to behold. The miners were now as eager to make amends to Israel as they had been eager to hang him. The whole crowd turned like a swarm of bees and headed for Israel's place.

Lucky Martin saw them coming and mistook their intent. "You got a torch to burn this varmint out?" he asked.

The miners swarmed up to Lucky, who began to read the message in their faces when Calvin Cluett, the biggest, ugliest miner in the territory spoke up for them. "You damn near had us murder one of our buddies for nothin' a-tall! You get your ass back to Thirsty, Mr. Martin, or you ain't never gonna be Lucky again. An' take that bastard Notches with you!"

No doubt about it: Lucky Martin was the loser.

CHAPTER 5

OLD INDIAN REMEDY

ON a slow day, of which there were a great many in Thirsty, the arrival of the stage was a matter of some importance. Folks would speculate on whether the stage was late or would be late, as if it mattered. The question of who or what might be on it, and the news it might be carrying from the other gold camps, allowed boundless room for discussion. If one weren't inclined toward outguessing the future, one could talk about the things, people, and news that actually had arrived on previous stage visits and let the listener's imagination leap to the conclusion that such great happenings could occur again, perhaps that very day.

Three passengers came on the stage that day. There was a whiskey drummer and a hardware salesman. Those two by themselves would have been enough to supply Thirsty's ordinary needs for news from the outside world. But the third passenger provided that rare thunderclap of news that makes a day memorable for years to come.

Miss Hoffman was back!

After what she'd done to Doc Crane, coming back took a lot of brass. Any man having done anything half so ornery wouldn't have shown his face within a hundred miles of the scene of his crime.

Nobody smiled at her or tipped their hat. But that didn't seem to bother her. She looked folks over serenely as if they were nothing more than potatoes on a market shelf. Then, apparently not seeing any potatoes that pleased her, she turned and went down to Sam Ibsen's store.

"Hello, Sam!" she called out as she approached the counter.

"It's Mr. Ibsen to you, Miss Hoffman," Sam answered, not at all surprised to see her, because word of her arrival had flashed through the town at top speed.

"Do you suppose Doctor Crane would see me if I went over to his office?"

"Try Momma Rose," Sam said, not bothering to tell her that Doc was out seeing a patient. "She's your friend."

"No, that won't do," Miss Hoffman answered. "I was hoping you might be able to tell me where I could stay in Thirsty."

"Why don't you just get back on the stage?" Sam said. "You can still catch it if you hurry."

"I'm here to stay," Miss Hoffman said.

It was against his gentlemanly instincts, but knowing what she'd done to Doc, Sam wanted some measure of revenge, so he said it. "Some of the boys might be dumb enough to do business with you, but Momma Rose won't even let you get started. One of her is more'n enough for this town, and even she knows it."

Miss Hoffman flushed angrily but managed a civil reply. "I'm here to bury what's past. That's what most folks come west for, isn't it? A new beginning."

"In your particular case," Sam said, "you ought to start where no one knows you."

"I'm here to stay, Sam," she repeated, then turned and made her way past a group of men who had drifted in to see what was new.

"Miserable Jezebel!" Sam said after she'd left. "There ain't nobody in this town going to forget what she did to Doc!"

"They's all alike, women is," one of the miners said. "As different from a man as a cow is from a horse. An' I'm damned if we don't gotta share the same pasture with 'em sometimes!"

Miss Hoffman went from Sam's store to the Thirsty Saloon and dickered with Jason for a room. "I don't have any rooms for permanent let," Jason explained. "What few rooms I do have are just for people stranded or passing through."

"Stranded. That's me," Miss Hoffman said.

"They're awful bare rooms and hot as an oven on sunny

days," Jason cautioned. "You wouldn't be half-pleased with any of the rooms I've got."

"I'll manage," Miss Hoffman said. "I'm having my trunks sent over."

"Look," Jason said, "you can't run any sort of business from your room. No gentleman callers, nothing like that."

"Good." Miss Hoffman said. "Just the way I want it. Now, which room is mine?"

"First one to the left at the head of the stairs on the third floor," Jason said, handing over the key, a token of surrender.

Doc heard the news long before he got back to town. Somebody had spread the news out through the mining claims within hours after her arrival, and Doc, on his way back to Thirsty, got the word from every miner he met. Most of the men tried to lay the news on him in a casual way, as if it were no big deal. To their surprise, that was exactly how Doc took it.

Doc's wound had healed. He had survived her supreme treachery as one survives a first attack of typhoid. Now he was immune, or so he thought.

Still, Doc was gun-shy about exposing himself to this particular affliction again. Although he felt foolish about it, he kept an eye on Miss Hoffman's comings and goings for several days, seeing to it that they didn't meet. When she went to The Dutchman's, he'd saunter over to the Thirsty Saloon for a beer. Then, when he'd see her leaving the restaurant, he'd amble out the side door, circle around several buildings, and stop in at The Dutchman's.

Of course, Doc had done a lot of thinking about what he'd say if Miss Hoffman were to come barging into his office. He hadn't chosen the exact words from the many possibilities he'd considered, but he wasn't about to tolerate her presence in his office short of dire medical emergency.

Lucky Martin was the only man in town who gave Miss Hoffman friendly encouragement. Several times he invited her over to his table at the saloon, held the chair for her and brought her a beer, just as if she'd never done a thing to Doc. Twice he went over to The Dutchman's with her. When people asked him, casual-like, what they'd talked about, he'd answer that it was none of their damned business.

It was the third or fourth day when word got out that Miss Hoffman had bought the Thompson house, a strange-looking building next to the livery stable. When Jed Thompson had built the place, he'd had in mind to build a three-story hotel but, not being a mathematician, he didn't realize in time that his money didn't match his plans. He'd taken down the second and third story walls that were in place when he ran short and used the lumber to put a roof over the first story, which explains why it ended up as a sprawling one-story building with a couple of three-story chimneys poking through the roof.

Jed Thompson wouldn't have sold the place to Miss Hoffman, but he didn't know that Lucky Martin was only acting as Miss Hoffman's agent when the deal was made.

Doc's only comment was, "Well, now we know what she's been talking to Lucky Martin about, don't we?"

Folks took notice as Miss Hoffman moved into the place, then settled down to watch in earnest when she changed into denim pants and an old shirt to start in cleaning and painting. That would have been pretty fair entertainment, even if Momma Rose hadn't gotten into the act.

Most of the watching was being done from kitty-corner across the street, in the shade of the blacksmith shop. Hammerin' Harry Smith didn't mind the company so long as they stayed out of his way. And they were careful to do that because they had a great deal of respect for any man who might be hustling around with a chunk of hot, heavy iron in his tongs. Hammerin' Harry liked the local folks well enough, but he delighted in meeting strangers since, being a black man, he could greet them with, "Sir, you are looking at a blacksmith who is a *black Smith!*"

Anyhow, the door of Momma Rose's house banged shut way up the street, and you could tell the minute you saw her that Momma Rose was on the warpath. Down the street she came at full-cruise speed, puffing along, red-cheeked and snorting so's you could imagine steam billowing from her nose.

"What d'you make of that?" one of the spectators asked.

"Looks like two tons of trouble on the hoof," another answered.

"If she turns inta here, it's every man for hisself," the first one warned.

But she sailed past like a cannonball bent on someone else's destruction. And the someone else was Miss Hoffman.

"Hey, you there! What the hell do you think you're doin'?" she bawled, stopping just short of Miss Hoffman's porch.

Miss Hoffman looked at her and said, "I don't expect it's any of your business," then went back to her painting.

"I'm makin' it my business, sweetie!" Momma Rose bellowed, and went stomping across the porch at Miss Hoffman. "I warned you not to set foot in Thirsty again the last time you was here, didn't I?" she fumed as she stretched those ponderous arms of hers out to take hold of Miss Hoffman.

Miss Hoffman flicked her loaded paintbrush at Momma Rose's face, then skipped lightly out of her way. A generous splash of red paint blinded Momma Rose, but she made a ferocious lunge at the spot where Miss Hoffman had been, tripped over the paint can, and went sprawling into the big red puddle she'd made.

"Damn you!" she shouted, wiping the paint from her face with a dry corner of her skirt. "I'm gonna paint you with your own blood!" She grabbed onto a porch post and hauled herself to her feet, then went charging down to the other end of the porch, where Miss Hoffman had retreated.

Miss Hoffman just stood there like a kid caught in a stampede, too terrified to move. But, at the last instant, she skipped aside to the lee of a porch post. Momma Rose tried desperately to make a hard left turn, but momentum was against her and she teetered lopsidedly toward the end of the porch. That's when Miss Hoffman wrapped her arms around the friendly post, lifted her feet high in the air, and slammed both heels into Momma Rose's shoulder, dumping her off the porch backwards so that she hit the ground and somersaulted clear over onto her stomach.

"I'll kill you!" Momma Rose screamed, but Miss Hoffman had taken the offensive. Momma Rose was trying to get up in the manner of a cow, with her tail end high in the air and her head down when Miss Hoffman got behind her with a board and smacked her fanny so hard it sounded as if the board had cracked. Momma Rose screamed and flopped forward, then started to get up as before, only to have Miss Hoffman smack her rump again with at least as much vigor as before. This happened three more times before Miss Hoffman was satisfied that Momma Rose had scrambled far enough from her premises.

Miss Hoffman backed off, holding her board like a baseball bat, while Momma Rose, covered with dust and paint, climbed wearily to her feet. Momma Rose stood there awhile, tired and out of breath, then said, "You ain't heard the last of this, dearie!"

"Let's finish it now, then!" Miss Hoffman said, and came at her. Momma Rose turned and fled. "You owe me a bucket of paint!" Miss Hoffman called after her, then chucked her board aside and went to see about cleaning up the mess on the porch.

The ruckus was over. Calm and quiet returned. Hammerin' Harry Smith, the blacksmith, shook his head in admiration and said, "That Miss Hoffman can't be all bad! No, sir! There ain't nobody with that kind of spirit that's all bad!"

He got no argument from the others on that. It had been a good, fair fight. The underdog had won. Big, bad Momma Rose had gotten spanked in spades. It left all the boys at the blacksmith shop with the feeling that God was in his heaven and all was right with the world.

Harry Smith went back to his forge, and the others went off to the Thirsty Saloon to savor the event properly over a drink or headed out toward their claims to spread the good news among those who hadn't been fortunate enough to witness the titanic clash.

Doc Crane had seen Momma Rose go churning by on her way to battle and had watched the fracas from his doorway with severely mixed emotions. On the one hand, he couldn't lose; the arch villains who had plotted so treacherously against him were at each other's throats, and whatever they got served them right. On the other hand, there would be something tragic, something like a loss to the world, if that Dresden-doll face of Miss Hoffman's were disfigured. He didn't want to see that nose broken, the eyes swollen and blackened or any such thing, no matter what she'd done to him. Yet, of the two, Miss Hoffman was the greater villain, wasn't she? Momma Rose made no secret of her soiled profession or her contempt for decency as Miss Hoffman had.

So the outcome of the battle brought no great joy or sorrow to Doc Crane. Satisfied that neither party would need doctoring, he went back into his office and got on with reading a medical journal. George Gatlin burst in a short time later in a great state of enthusiasm. "Did you see that fight?" he asked.

"Yep."

"Well? What do you make of it?"

"No honor among thieves, I reckon."

"That's all?"

"That's all."

"Still mad at her, huh?"

"Mad at who?"

"Miss Hoffman!"

"I'm not mad at Miss Hoffman, and I'm not mad at the devil," Doc answered, looking up from his journal for the first time. "All I ask is that they both go to Hell and leave me be!"

"Oh," George said, backing off. "Well, I've got to be going. Got things to do."

Doc watched him go. What in hell had George expected? A medal for Miss Hoffman for clobbering Momma Rose? They were bad ones, those two, and the one beating the other didn't subtract one iota from the badness of either one.

There was another surprise in store for Thirsty that day, though. Miss Hoffman sprang it when she came out and nailed a big sign board over her porch. It was direct, simple, and to the point. It said "Laundry," and a smaller cardboard sign tacked to the wall next to the door detailed the terms of price, delivery, and extras.

The sign came in for a lot of discussion over at the Thirsty Saloon that afternoon. Jason and Lucky Martin allowed as to how Miss Hoffman might, sure enough, be going to run a laundry there. Doc said he didn't know, or care, what the sign meant. But Jake Bitternut felt sure he knew what the sign meant. "It means

she's open fer business, and you all know what business I mean,''
he proclaimed. ''That's just the way they do it in places like Saint
Looey, where she comes from. They put up a respectable sign to
keep a place looking proper, but one feller soon tells another what
goes on there and pretty soon the sign works just as well as if it said
what it meant.''

Jake stood there at the bar soaking up beer and explaining the
laundry sign at great length to anyone who would listen, until
Lucky got tired of hearing it. ''Tell you what, Jake,'' Lucky said.
''I'll bet you ten dollars that she ain't open for any business but
laundry.''

''Ten dollars?'' Jake asked.

''Ten dollars. Even money.''

''Done!'' Jake said. ''I ain't never won off you before! You just
sit right here till I gets back!''

Jake went out the door with a full beer mug in hand, trying to
sip the stuff as he walked—a sloppy, sloshing effort at best. He
stomped up onto Miss Hoffman's porch, kicking and scraping his
boots as if they were covered with mud. It was just his gentlemanly way of letting the lady know she had a customer. Jake knew
that it wouldn't hardly be polite to sashay up as quiet as a mouse
and startle the poor lady.

Lucky Martin just sat back at the Thirsty Saloon, waiting to
collect on his bet, but several less patient parties had scurried over
to the blacksmith's shop to watch from its dark recesses. They saw
Jake stomp through the doorway to a counter Miss Hoffman had
put in and heard him bang on the little bell on the counter. They
could see Miss Hoffman come to the counter but couldn't make
out what was going on, excepting that it seemed like Jake was
doing a lot of talking and foot shuffling. Then it seemed like Jake
leaned across the counter and grabbed Miss Hoffman. She let out
a squawk, which was followed by a loud yelp from Jake. Then
Jake came tearing out of there, and pretty quick there came the
sharp crack of a rifle and a puff of dust kicked up at Jake's right
heel. Three more shots in quick succession stirred more dust
around Jake's fleeing feet while Jake threw aside the encumbering

beer mug and ran in earnest. A final shot shattered the beer mug, then all was quiet.

Jake bolted into the Thirsty Saloon, cast a wild eye out at the street to see if he were being followed, then sank, panting and puffing, into the nearest chair and examined his boots. "Oh, Lordy!" he complained, putting one foot up on a table for display. "Just look at the big chunk she shot out of that heel! And she pretty near busted my right arm over that counter of hers!"

"Maybe she didn't quite understand what you wanted," Lucky Martin suggested. "Why don't you go back and try again?"

"That ain't funny," Jake pouted. "I coulda got killed!"

"You'da been killed if she wanted you that way," Lucky said. "Those bullets were hitting right where she wanted 'em to. From what I know of women, she might have been flirting with you. Playing hard to get so's you'll appreciate her more when you do get her. A woman like that expects a man to try again. Leastways, she knows a *real* man will try again."

"Yeah? Do you really think so?" Jake asked, studying Lucky's face carefully.

"That's what I believe," Lucky said, as serious and earnest as you please. Then he added, "I also believe in Santa Claus and the Tooth Fairy!" Then he burst out laughing, and everyone joined in except Jake.

"Hell, I got better things to do than fool around here." Jake paid off his bet with Lucky and stomped out.

Sam Ibsen played hooky from his store a while later to drop in on Doc Crane. "Did you see old Jake Bitternut go flying up the street with those bullets biting at his heels?" Sam chuckled.

"Fine mayor you are, laughing at a thing like that!" Doc shot back. "That woman would be under lock and key right now if this town had any kind of law!"

"Aw, it was self-defense, Doc! Jake didn't believe that laundry sign and went over there thinking she was open for another kind of business, if you get my drift."

"Uh huh. Well, she didn't have to bust that beer mug. Somebody's horse is likely to come up lame with broken glass!"

"Aw, she went out there and picked up the glass. Didn't you see that?"

"No. I don't pay attention to everything that fool woman does."

"Aw, Doc, give the devil her due."

"She'll get her due some day, all right! And it won't be anything she'll want."

"Yeah, well, I guess you're right," Sam agreed.

"You know I'm right. That woman ain't to be trusted. Any damned fool around here that gets taken in by her, knowing what she did to me, gets no sympathy from me. Anyone that dumb gets the hoss laugh from me, long and loud!"

"Sez you. You ain't the sort that hoss-laughs your friends!"

"Anybody that has anything to do with that woman ain't no friend of mine."

It was a statement of policy, clear and concise. In the days to come, all of Doc's close friends and sympathizers, who included most of the people in and around Thirsty, took his threat to heart. The new laundry got leper-colony treatment. Among its few customers, Lucky Martin was the only one who'd linger to exchange a few friendly words. And those two tall chimneys standing above the roof came to be known as the devil's horns.

Doc froze her out of his thinking as much as possible, though he still went to some trouble to avoid meetings with her. And there were times when he could truly and completely forget her, such as the time he got involved in the Indian remedy for Downwind's problem.

One day Downwind had come in to see Doc. "Doc, I know I've pestered you about this a hundred times, but I gotta pester you again. Ain't there nothing you can do about my problem?"

"I sure wish there was," Doc said. "It's a problem with Betty Lee now, is it?"

"Sure is," Downwind said disconsolately. "Trouble is, when two people share a misery, they don't each get half, they each get all of it! Doc, did you ever meet Chief Many Tongues?"

"Many Tongues?" Doc puzzled, "Sometimes I wonder if there is such a man. Seems like he's more legend than real. I saw him from a long ways off once. Leastways, people said it was him, but it could've been any Indian."

"I'd like for you to meet him tomorrow out to my place," Downwind said.

"Why should I do that?" Doc hedged.

"He says there's an old Indian remedy for my problem. I asked him if you could watch and see how it's done."

"Agreeable to that, was he?"

"Yessir, Doc. He'd like to meet you. He gets lonely for educated people to talk to."

"You know him pretty well?"

"Yessir. I ain't what *you'd* call educated, nor Chief Many Tongues wouldn't call me educated neither, but I know a lot more book things than his braves do."

"People say he was an English Army officer once. Is that so?"

"A colonel in the Royal Fusileers. An English general took him to England and put him in military school. An experiment it was. Maybe the general was thinking on having Indian allies again. I reckon Many Tongues did good at it, but he got to thinking he owed something to his people, so he came home."

"They tell me that the Wolf Tribe to the north of Many Tongues' people keeps him busy. Tough, warlike, nasty bunch. That so?" Doc asked.

"Yessir. They's tough. And they's warlike. And they's nasty. But they're afraid o' Chief Many Tongues."

"I reckon I've got to meet that man! I'll get out to your place as early as I can tomorrow," Doc promised.

Doc got to Downwind's farm a couple of hours after dawn the next day, happy to be away from Thirsty and that damned Miss Hoffman for a time. Chief Many Tongues, looking every inch an Indian chief, rode in a short time later. He wore a feathered headdress and buckskin clothing. He was tall, lean, bronzed, and had the prominent nose and cheekbones of his people. But he also wore a Victoria Cross on his chest and a pair of six-guns at his waist. He appeared to be about Doc's age. Doc reflected on the thought that this man had been in military school in England while he'd been in medical school in Boston.

Downwind provided effusive introductions that ranked Doc and the Chief each as being his very best friend. Chairs had been placed on the porch, and Betty Lee served tea to the chief and coffee to Downwind and Doc.

"I'm certainly delighted to meet you, Chief Many Tongues," Doc said. "That's a very impressive headdress you're wearing. It's not a war bonnet, I hope?"

"Merely a symbol of rank," the chief said.

"Your name, Chief Many Tongues—were you called by that name before you went to England?"

"No," the Chief answered.

Doc paused to sip his coffee, hoping the chief would do some talking, but the chief just sipped his tea.

"This remedy you have for Downwind's problem," Doc asked, "you're reasonably sure it will work?"

"Yes," the chief answered. "Doctor, what does the phrase, *'Et tu, Brute!'* mean to you?"

"It's a line from Shakespeare's *Julius Caesar* in the scene where Caesar was assassinated."

"Good!" the chief exclaimed. "Then you are an educated man. The first such I have met in many years! Have you read much of Shakespeare?"

"Well, there's *Romeo and Juliet, A Merchant of Venice, As You Like It, Othello, Hamlet, Macbeth, The Tempest, A Midsummer Night's Dream, Richard the Third,* and *Much Ado about Nothing.*"

"Excellent, we have much to talk about! Come, we will ride with Mr. Downwind to my village."

They were soon mounted and on their way, with Doc Crane and Chief Many Tongues jabbering away on things Shakespearean. The talk made little sense to Downwind, but he wasn't much listening anyway. Oh, glorious day! If only he could go home to Betty Lee a cured man. No more that invisible obstacle between them; no longer that confusion and pain in her voice.

Their course led up into the high ground past an invisible boundary which separated the miners' domain from that of Chief Many Tongues and his people. No sane white man came here uninvited, but Downwind had been here many times. He had a standing invitation; he was the only white man who did.

When they were still an hour's ride from the nearest of Chief Many Tongues' villages, Downwind thought of that long ride ahead and got impatient. "Chief," he said, breaking in on the chatter between Doc and the chief, "will your medicine man be ready for me when we get there?"

Chief Many Tongues frowned at the interruption and said, "There will be no medicine man at the village."

"I thought we was riding to him!" Downwind erupted.

"Not riding *to* medicine man," Chief Many Tongues answered, "riding *from* medicine man!"

"Riding from him?" Downwind echoed, and even Doc looked surprised.

"Friend Downwind," the chief said, "you stink and this offends the nose of Betty Lee. Old Indian remedy does not stop stink. It stops the complaint of the nose."

Downwind thought about that for a moment. "You mean the medicine man is at my place working on Betty Lee?"

"Perhaps all done now," the chief confirmed.

"I ought to be there, not here!"

"No," the chief explained. "She scream, you get in way!"

"Scream! Oh Lord, I'm goin' back!" Downwind declared, wheeling his mare about and taking off at a gallop.

Doc and Chief Many Tongues went tearing after him, but there was no catching him. Stinging branches whipped at them as their horses plunged down the trail, pitching and swaying with the uncertain footing. By the time they broke clear of the woods, Downwind was a good hundred yards ahead of the chief, and Doc was another hundred yards behind him. Doc thought he ought to have a pretty good horse for what he'd paid for it and was determined to close the gap, but the horse wasn't up to it. By the time they reached Downwind's place, neither the chief nor Doc had gained an inch on Downwind.

Betty Lee was near the smokehouse with two Indians. Downwind tore into the yard and jumped from his horse on the run. "Betty Lee! Did they hurt you, honey?"

Tears streamed from her eyes, her hair looked like a wet mop, and her breath came in coughs and gasps. Downwind held her close. "Betty Lee, I thought they was gonna fix me. They didn't say they was gonna do anything to you!"

It was a while before Betty Lee could say anything, then she said, "Those savages, don't they know anything? That smoke! It ruined my nose, just ruined it. I may never ever smell anything again!"

"That was their whole idea, honey."

Betty Lee stared open-mouthed at Downwind, then broke into a wild laugh. "Ha, ha, ha! Old Indian remedy! Ha, ha, ha! Old Indian remedy! Ha, ha, ha!"

Things went pretty well from there. Downwind joined in the laugh, the medicine man and his apprentice flashed toothy grins, and Doc and Chief Many Tongues had a few giggles themselves. "It is as your Mr. Shakespeare says," the chief said. "All's well that ends well!"

CHAPTER 6

THE VENISON FEAST

THE man called Frypan used to be a range cook. He'd spent maybe five years cooking for cowpokes on cattle drives and home ranges. He was the last person in the world who should have complained about the Dutchman's cooking. Lord knows, he'd heard his share of bellyaching about grub from those cowpokes. But it was like as if Frypan had stored up all the complaints he'd ever gotten just to unload them on the Dutchman.

Frypan's trouble was that he'd spent two years in New Orleans as apprentice to a French cook. At least Frypan said he was the cook's apprentice. More likely he was the dishwasher. Frypan was under the impression that he and he alone knew the difference between good and bad cooking.

He'd stomp into The Dutchman's once or twice a week, the Dutchman would glare at him and say something like, "Vy you come here? You never like anyting," and Frypan always had an answer ready like, "I figure some day you're gonna make a mistake and cook something right, and I'm feeling lucky today!"

One day early in fall when the wind was cold and a chilling rain was falling, Frypan went stomping into The Dutchman's, traded the usual insults with the proprietor, sat down, and ordered roast beef and baked potatoes. Soon after this was served, Frypan remarked, "Buffalo! A feller shouldn't ought to try passin' off buffalo fer good beef!"

"Beef!" the Dutchman insisted. "Dot iss beef!"

Frypan looked up, noted the sharp carving knife in the Dutchman's hand, and went ahead anyway. "Well, yuh shoulda chased off the buzzards before they got to the best part!"

"Bah, you know nudding! You come here from saloon full mit whiskey, and nudding taste right because you bin full mit whiskey!"

"Antiseptic!" Frypan said. "Tain't safe to eat this stuff without something in me to help kill it."

"Someday I make you cook, then everybody, they see you know nudding about it!" the Dutchman warned.

"Any day, Dutchman!" Frypan answered, "Why, I could whip up a venison feast the fellers around here would call a bargain at three dollars a head. Trouble is, they'd want it every day and I couldn't get my mining done!"

"Yah, sure! Alvays you complain about my food, but alvays you clean your plate."

" 'Course I do! When it's too bad to finish, I take what's left back to my cabin fer rat poison."

"Someday I giff you rat poison for sure!" the Dutchman growled.

Frypan tossed thirty cents on the counter and left. He was always grinning when he left. He enjoyed these arguments with the Dutchman. With the Dutchman on the defensive, most of the fun was bound to be on Frypan's side of the fence.

That was about to change, though. A couple of the Dutchman's customers had pricked up their ears at Frypan's mention of a venison feast. They liked the Dutchman's cooking well enough, but it was only a notch better than what they could cook for themselves, and the monotony of it did wear on them, especially with the prospect of a long, hard winter just ahead. Venison sounded pretty good. Anything would have at that time.

The word drifted from The Dutchman's, to the livery stable, to the Thirsty Saloon, then to Momma Rose's and up to the headwaters of Crystal Creek, and to all points between, that Frypan had offered to cook up a venison feast at three dollars a head. When the first few eager customers approached Frypan, he made the supreme mistake of accepting their money. By the time he realized that everyone within a day's ride of Thirsty would be coming to his feast, the trap had closed.

In the flustered confusion of the thing, he'd said it would take him at least a week to get ready, and that had become the official date: Saturday, a week away. Now, as he considered the size of the job, he knew he needed a month.

He had no kitchen or equipment to speak of, no supplies, no deer. The one thing he did have was lots of money. Three dollars a head! A princely sum! Success would be a prosperous thing; failure could be fatal. Some of those miners expected guarantees with every penny they spent.

The first thing Frypan did was to hire George Gatlin to go out and scout the deer. Don't shoot any just yet, he'd told George; just see where they are so's to pick 'em off later. Then he rented an empty barn down beyond where Miss Hoffman's laundry was and set about cleaning it out. He wasn't quite sure how he was going to cook all that venison. The Dutchman was the only man in town with the right equipment, but Frypan couldn't even bring himself to ask. Hell, the Dutchman would sure enjoy that, wouldn't he? Most likely the venison would have to be roasted over an open fire. There weren't enough pots to cook it any other way. 'Course, if the weather turned miserable, he'd be in real trouble. There wouldn't be room to set up tables in the barn and still do the cooking there.

By the end of the day he'd made a good start on cleaning the barn, and was debating whether it was good enough when George returned.

"How's my deer herd?" Frypan asked.

"I didn't see hide nor hair of any deer. Nor tracks or droppings either."

"Well, you better look some more!" Frypan growled. "We got us some of the best damned deer country in the world hereabouts."

"We did, sure enough," George said, "but that was three or four years ago. Folks have shot an awful lot of deer since then. I couldn't find anyone that's shot a deer in months, and that's because they haven't seen any."

"We'll just have to do our hunting a little farther out from where the miners hunt," Frypan said.

"Most folks think the deer have gone up in the Indian territory, where there's shelter and brush to live on. I value my scalp too much to set foot in there!"

"There's got to be some deer in the flatlands between here and Smithville," Frypan said. "You do your scouting down that way tomorrow. When we're ready, we'll take a wagon down that way and do some real hunting."

"I hope you're right," George said. "I'll get down there early tomorrow."

George left, and Frypan stood there scratching his head. No deer! It didn't seem possible. The thought crossed his mind that maybe he ought to call the whole thing off, but he liked the feel of all that money, so he decided to hang on. There had to be some deer out there.

There was more bad news the next morning. Frypan had gone over to Sam Ibsen's store to stock up on all the accessory stuff he'd need for the feast, and he was doing all right until he got to flour and salt. "I'm fresh out, Frypan," Sam explained. "The Dutchman bought me out yesterday."

Frypan suddenly felt like he'd stepped into a chuck-hole. "Bought a lot of it, did he?"

"Sure did! More than twice what he usually needs! I told him I ought to keep some on hand for other folks, but he said if anyone came in for flour or salt to just send them over to his place."

"When's your next order due in, Sam?" Frypan asked.

"About ten days, I expect. That's if an early snow don't close the trail. You know how the weather can be this time of year."

There was another store of sorts toward the seedy upstream end of Thirsty. It was a dingy, rat-infested place that survived because it was a mile closer to some of the miners than Sam's store. Frypan went there right away and got the same story. The Dutchman had bought out all the flour and salt.

On the way back down the street, Frypan tried to get himself ready to deal with the Dutchman. He had the flour and salt. What would he want for them? A big chunk of revenge for one thing. The price would be cash and humility, probably a lot of both. And suppose the price was too high? There was a limit; if the price was too high, he'd just say, "Okay. You keep that flour and salt till

Hell freezes over, Dutchman! I'm going out and tell the boys they can't have their venison feast because of you!" Yessir. That would loosen things up!

And that's pretty much how it went. Frypan got his flour and salt at a price that left his ears flaming red and a hot little coal in his heart burning for revenge. As soon as he'd gotten his flour and salt stashed away, he went back to the stores and bought all the coffee and spices in sight. Two could play at that game!

George Gatlin came back that evening with more of the same bad news he'd had the day before. There were no deer to be found. All he'd seen down in the flatlands was jackrabbits and some signs that a lone buffalo had been around.

"Well, maybe we can make a deal with the injuns," Frypan said. "It'll serve just as well whether we hunt 'em or buy 'em from the redskins."

George shook his head. "I already asked Downwind about that yesterday—he's sort of cosy with the Indians out there—and he says we won't get any deer from them no way. They've seen how the deer got wiped out around here, and they're keeping a sharp eye on what they've got left."

Frypan mulled it over, looking both tired and defiant, like a horse that had just been broke. Finally, he looked up at George and said, "You done good, George. I know it ain't your fault. But you just keep it quiet. If anyone asks you, tell 'em you seen signs of a herd, but don't tell 'em where. Maybe we're licked and maybe we ain't. I got to think about it some more."

Some time later Frypan went over to Doc Crane's office and, finding the waiting room empty, went on into the inner sanctum where he found Doc snoozing in his leather chair. A few gentle tugs at Doc's shirt-sleeve woke him in short order.

"Oh! Musta dozed off," Doc said, leaning over to pick up a medical journal that had fallen to the floor. "Some awful dull reading in there," he said, tossing the journal on his desk. "What can I do for you, Frypan?"

"Well, first off," Frypan said, "you don't go around blabbin' about people's problems when they come to you professional-like, do you?"

"No, sir! Absolutely not! You're free to talk about your problem in absolute confidence here." Doc paused and waited in vain for Frypan's expected outpouring of hernia, louse, or sex problems, then prodded, "Well, what ails you, Frypan?"

"It might be that I only got one more week to live," Frypan said.

"You let me be the judge of that," Doc cautioned. "Lots of people with an ailment get down in the mouth and think things are a lot worse than they are."

"It's not exactly medical, Doc; it's that venison feast thing."

"Oh yes," Doc said. "That's a great thing you're doing! Wouldn't miss it for the world. They tell me you're expecting nigh onto four hundred people. Is that true?"

"Four hundred and eighty," Frypan said.

"Four hundred and eighty!" Doc repeated. "How many deer do you reckon to have?"

"About none, more or less."

"None!" Doc repeated. "I sure hope you don't mean that. Some of that mining bunch would kill you for a thing like that."

"Well, I told you that it might be that I only got one more week to live," Frypan said.

"You need some kind of help getting the deer?" Doc asked.

"There ain't none to be got," Frypan said.

"None?"

"Oh, the injuns has got some, but the deer is safer in their territory than I would be."

"You'd best start giving folks their money back as quick as you can," Doc said.

"It don't matter none to you if folks don't get a chance to get together and have a good meal and all?" Frypan asked.

"Of course it matters," Doc protested, "but what can't be just can't be."

"I come here because I figured an educated man like you might know something I don't," Frypan said, getting up to go. "Guess I was wrong."

"You come back here and sit down," Doc said. Frypan paused with his hand on the doorknob, then did as he was told. He'd used this trick on Doc before. Doc just couldn't stand the notion that he, with his vast education, could stand as helpless before a problem as some illiterate pup who might never have seen the inside of a schoolhouse. "You're certain there ain't any deer?" he demanded.

"George Gatlin spent two days scoutin' fer 'em and talkin' to a lot of people who ain't seen any," Frypan answered.

"Well, what else is there?" Doc asked. "Ain't there something you could fake to seem like deer meat if you cut it up in little chunks?"

"There's a lot of jackrabbits, and maybe one buffalo if we can catch up to it before the injuns do. But nobody's gonna mistake that tough, stringy stuff for deer meat."

"You can fool 'em on taste if you spice hell out of it, can't you?"

"Yeah, I could fool 'em on taste," Frypan admitted.

"Then it's only the toughness we've got to hide?"

"Sort of."

Doc rocked back in his swivel chair, plunked his feet on his desk, clasped his hands behind his head, and stared at the ceiling. "A nice, big pressure tank would do it."

"Do what?"

"Cook the toughness out of your jackrabbits or buffalo or whatever else you come up with."

"How's it gonna do that?" Frypan asked, pulling his chair closer.

"Ain't you ever noticed that it takes longer to cook stuff in the high country than it does down in the valley?" Doc asked.

"Sort of," Frypan said, "but what's that got to do with cookin' rabbits or buffalo?"

"Everything," Doc said, warming to the subject and blessed with a sure example of the value of his education. "Water can't get any hotter than boiling. If you're on top of a mountain, where the air pressure is low, the water boils at a lower temperature, and it takes longer at that lower temperature to cook anything. Down in the valley, air pressure is higher so the water boils at a higher temperature and things cook faster. Now, that's about as far as

Mother Nature can take us, but we can do better than that, can't we?''

"Oh sure," Frypan said uncertainly, "I reckon we can."

"Exactly," Doc continued. "We can get ourselves a pressure tank, load it up with meat, water, seasoning, and maybe some vegetables, light a fire under it, and let the pressure go right on up to whatever it'll take. The kind of temperature you get that way will cook the toughness out of anything!"

"By Gawd, Doc, that's first-rate!" Frypan said, but after a moment's reflection added, "There ain't no such pressure tank as that closer'n a hundred miles of Thirsty, is there?"

"Well, it's not such a common article in these parts," Doc admitted. "Why don't we go down to see Hammerin' Harry? Maybe he'd know if anyone's got one."

So they went down to see the blacksmith. Hammerin' Harry was flattening the red hot end of an iron bar when Doc and Frypan got there. He kept up his beat till the iron cooled, then stuck it back in the forge and turned to see who his visitors were. "Hi, Doc! Hello there, Frypan! I sure hope it's you that wants something, Frypan, and not Doc! Any time Doc wants something, it's some little bitty thing I ain't never made before and he wants it right now!"

"It's your lucky day, Harry!" Doc said. "We're looking for big stuff today, and we can wait maybe three days for it!"

"Uh huh," Harry grunted.

"What we need, Harry, is a boiler—a good big one that'll hold pressure. Do you know where we can lay hands on one?" Doc asked.

"You're being sly with me, ain't you, Doc?" Harry asked, looking at him sort of sideways. "Just look at him, Frypan, standing there pretending he don't know what I'm saying."

"I wish I was half as sly as you think I am," Doc said. "Maybe I could get people to pay their bills if I were."

"It's real important, Harry," Frypan said. "You do know where there's a boiler, don't you?"

"Sure do!" Harry said. "It's up in my loft. Ain't never even been used."

"Oh hell, yes!" Doc said. "It's the one that Colonel Welling-broke,—Wellingbrooke,—"

"Wellingboor. Colonel Wellingboor," Harry said. "He was gonna build a steam pump and really show folks how sluicing ought to be done. He was gonna sluice more in a week than all the rest of the miners could sluice in a year. Got all the stuff ordered, then went bust in a card game. Just rode out quietly one night without so much as good-bye. The pump never got shipped, and I never got paid."

"Well, Lord almighty!" Doc exclaimed. "Let's have a look at that boiler of yours."

"Go on up there if you like," Harry said, waving toward the ladder to the loft. "I got me some hammerin' to do."

A few moments later Doc and Frypan were warily circling the big riveted iron tank that stood in the loft. "What do you think, Doc?" Frypan asked.

"She's a humdinger!" Doc said. "Looks made-to-order! You can unbolt the whole top, load her up, and bolt it back together again. That thing must hold more than fifty gallons, wouldn't you say?"

"Yessir! That's nigh onto seventy or eighty gallons," Frypan answered.

Hammerin' Harry came into the loft a while later and asked, "What d'y'all think of it?"

"We'd sure like to borrow it, Harry," Doc said.

"Borrow!" Harry exclaimed. "What's wrong with buying? I cain't make no living loaning things."

"We only need it till the end of the week," Doc insisted. "We wouldn't have any more use for it after that than you would."

"I'll rent it to you. How's that?"

"Done!" Frypan said. "Ten dollars for one week. Fair enough?"

"Fair enough!" Harry agreed, and a short time later they were lowering the big tank down to the street with ropes and pulleys attached to the beam that jutted out over the outside door to the loft. That is, Harry and Frypan were doing the lowering while Doc stood in the street doing the directing.

Safely into the street, they tipped it onto its side, rolled it down to the barn Frypan had rented, and set it upright just inside the back door.

When it got down to cleaning the thing out, Doc went back to his office. Dishwashing had never held much interest for Doc. Besides, Frypan's barn was in plain view of Miss Hoffman's laundry, and Doc's determined effort to ignore her presence made it damned near impossible to forget. She was a skunk in his yard, and the sooner she left the happier he'd be. Meanwhile, just avoiding her seemed the best strategy.

But Frypan was back before dark. "I gotta ask another favor of you, Doc," he began. "It's gonna take an awful lot of rabbit to fill that kettle."

"Hold on now," Doc said. "There ain't no way I can make those rabbits any bigger'n God created 'em!"

"I know that much," Frypan said, forcing himself to smile. "What I need is help with the hunt. I cain't just ask anybody, neither. I gotta have helpers what can keep their mouths shut. I done asked George Gatlin to get out to Downwind's place and ask him to help. Between you, me, George, and Downwind, I think we got a chance."

"Do I get a free meal out of this?" Doc asked.

"Sure do! How about it, Doc?"

"Well, that's better pay than I get from some people."

"Now you're talking!" Frypan said. "By Gawd, I knowed you was a regular feller! Quick as it gets dark, you just slip on down to the barn with a bedroll and shotgun. Bring a rifle too if you've got one."

"You're starting tonight?" Doc asked.

"Got to!" Frypan said. "We daren't have any volunteers tagging along! Cain't keep no secret that way."

Doc and Frypan left the barn shortly after dark, driving a wagon drawn by two sturdy horses. Nobody paid much attention to them, and they kept their hats and voices low to keep things that way.

Several hours later they met up with George Gatlin and Downwind and continued on to the edge of the flatlands, where they bedded down for the night.

Doc awoke to the aroma of Frypan's skillet, and after a quick breakfast they were underway again. Frypan was desperately eager to get at least one deer for display purposes, so the plan was to fan out across the grassland, shooting no rabbits until at least ten o'clock. That way they could be quiet and just maybe be lucky enough to come across a deer or two. George went off to the left and Downwind to the right. Frypan drove the wagon straight up the middle, and Doc perched beside him with his rifle at the ready.

There was an abundant crop of rabbits all right, but neither Doc nor Frypan saw anything bigger. Just at ten o'clock they heard a shot far off to the right and Frypan muttered, "Damn! I shoulda said no rabbit shooting till noon. We coulda spared a couple more hours."

Then, off to the left, they heard George open fire. Doc set his rifle aside and picked up the shotgun. "I reckon deer season just closed. Let's do some rabbit hunting!"

For a full hour they rolled forward across the grass, taking turns driving, shooting, and retrieving rabbits.

"I don't believe neither one of us has missed a shot," Frypan remarked at last.

"Don't see how a feller could miss with a shotgun," Doc said.

"I dunno," Frypan said. "I didn't reckon you to be any kind of a shot."

"You didn't!" Doc said. "Why bring me along then?"

"We got ourselves an awful mess of skinning and cleaning to do. I thought, you being a surgeon, you'd be especially good at that."

"Uh huh," Doc said. True, there was a lot of skinning and cleaning to be done. Doc wasn't looking forward to that at all, but he was glad this was a rabbit hunt and not a buffalo hunt.

Just past noon they reached a grove of trees where there was a water hole. Doc and Frypan got there first, and George was close behind with two sacks of rabbits tied across his saddle. Downwind came in a little later with a sack of rabbits and a deer.

A deer! Frypan had never been so happy to see a deer in all his life. "How in the world did you come up with that?" he asked.

"Well, I reckon I know more about staying downwind of critters than you folks do," said Downwind, and they all had a good laugh on it.

"Got him pretty close to ten o'clock," Downwind said. "I didn't have no watch, but there I was, sneaking into range of that critter, knowing it was getting close on to ten o'clock and scared you fellers would cut loose with your artillery and spook him clean out of the territory afore I could get a shot in!"

"I see you got him cleaned good," Frypan said. "Mebbe we could all do part of the skinning, so's we can all say we did our share of deer skinning in case we're asked."

"That sounds like a pretty truthful sort of a lie," Doc said with a wink at George and Downwind.

"When you gotta lie, it helps to have some truth a-hind it," Frypan insisted. "A lie ain't no good a-tall without it sounds convincing. You notice I didn't invite Reverend John on this hunt, don't you? That man can keep a secret and he's a damned good hunter, but he cain't tell a good lie to save his soul! Nossir! There's an art to it."

Having the deer improved all of their spirits and made the cleaning chore less of a chore. They were all in it with Frypan now.

"What about the bones?" George asked. "No matter how you cook it, nobody's gonna mistake jackrabbit for deer when they see jackrabbit bones."

The question jarred Frypan something awful. He'd been so eager to accept Doc's answer to the deer shortage that he hadn't even considered the bones. "Yeah, Doc," he said, "this damn fool idea can't work if folks see the bones."

" 'Course not," Doc answered. "You gotta cook it long enough so's the bones slide right out."

"Gawd, Doc," Frypan lamented. "That could take a long time!"

"No such thing," Doc assured him. "Most things ought to cook about right in maybe fifteen minutes after you get up to pressure. You cook these jacks an hour or so and they won't give you any trouble at all."

Frypan thought it over, then said, "You boys gotta help me with the cooking and serving. We gotta keep the cooker in the barn and everybody else outside so's they don't see what's going on too close. I'll tell 'em they can't come in 'cause my recipe's a secret, and that'll sure enough be the truth!"

"Supposin' the weather turns real miserable?" Doc asked. "Those boys will come through the door with pickaxes if you try to keep 'em out in a blizzard."

"Yeah," Frypan agreed. "They sure would. Well, we'll put the cooker in a clean stall and block the front with a table. Yeah, and I'll hang a blanket between the cooker and the table. If we can't keep 'em out, we'll still get by."

None of it was what you'd call foolproof, but it would do. Foolproof would have been too dull, monotonous, and eastern, anyway.

When all the skinning and cleaning was done, the meat was salted down in pots in the wagon, Downwind took the rabbit fur, Frypan kept the lone deer hide, and the rest was buried. Tomorrow, Frypan would tack the deer hide to the side of the barn, and folks who asked would be told that Downwind had taken the rest of the hides to trade with the Indians. So far as possible, the conspirators would tell the truth and the listeners would create the lie.

They headed back and got the wagon into Thirsty long after dark. Frypan and George bedded down in the barn with the precious cargo and set about putting bars and bolts on all the entrances early the next morning. From then on, they would take turns going out until the big feast was done with.

Downwind came in with a load of potatoes, carrots, butter, milk, and firewood the night before the feast and stayed over to help with the fixings. Doc stopped by to see how things were going and found Frypan about as calm and unconcerned as a bride on the eve of the wedding. He was tripping over everything in sight, cutting his fingers with the peeling knife, jabbing splinters into himself with the firewood, and babbling worry words like a drunken magpie. Doc had never seen the man so discombobulated before. Fortunately, George and Downwind were running a better show. It looked like they'd be in good shape for baked potatoes, stew, and pancakes to serve in place of bread. The fireplaces looked safe enough, and the pressure cooker was about as clean as any cook pot in Thirsty ever was. Doc inspected the leather gasket that would seal the bolted-on top and speculated a bit on whether or not it was moldy, but, what the heck, it was going to see enough heat to kill any mold anyway. He meant to check out some other stuff on the boiler but he got too preoccupied over Frypan's jitters.

It wouldn't do to have Frypan get into a state of nervous exhaustion. Doc went and got a bottle of whiskey, prescribed about a half pint of it for Frypan, then made him lie down on a pile of straw. Doc sat there and gave soothing answers to his babblings until he fell asleep, then stretched out to sleep himself.

When Doc awoke shortly after dawn, Frypan was already up and busy loading the boiler with rabbits, potatoes, carrots, spices, and deer meat. Doc lay still and watched him awhile. There was some improvement. He was still in constant fidgeting motion, but his face looked less haggard and he wasn't falling over things. He would survive until the serving started, then everything would get easier and more natural. Facing up to an enemy, crisis, test, or challenge was usually easier than just thinking about it.

Doc went out for a short walk and found the town as crowded as he'd ever seen it. Everybody he'd ever met in Thirsty was there on this day. And the Dutchman was probably having a good laugh at Frypan since people were lined up outside his place, waiting their turn to get in for breakfast. Hell, the town ought to pin a medal on Frypan for bringing in so much business. Yessir, a medal! Dead or alive!

Doc had intended to have breakfast at The Dutchman's, but there was no point in standing in line there when he could just go back to the barn and make use of some of Frypan's pancake mix. That was easier said than done. Downwind and George Gatlin were busy, so Doc set about making his own pancakes, bedeviled by frequent interruptions from Frypan, who was in the final throes of concocting the recipe for the main course in the big boiler.

"Doc, you gotta help me decide," Frypan pleaded. "I got me more spices than you can shake a stick at: basil, anise, cloves, bay leaf, cinnamon, pepper, mustard—you name it, I got it!"

"Just use whatever they used to use down in New Orleans," Doc suggested, "only double it."

"I cain't!" Frypan said. "That's what I'm trying to tell you! I got lots of spices, but they ain't rightly enough of any one of 'em!"

"Then trust in the good Lord and throw in everything you've got," Doc said, grabbing up a plate to rescue his pancakes, which were in great danger of scorching.

Having tended to his pancakes, Doc took a moment to inspect the spice problem more carefully, but it was too late. Frypan had dumped in the whole works and was stirring it with a big wooden paddle. "I sure hope you know what you're doing, Doc," he said. "It looks a bit much to me."

Doc sat down and ate his pancakes. He had the feeling it would be the only good meal he'd have that day.

Then came the bolting-down ceremony. The boiler lid was heavy, but Frypan, Downwind, and George hefted it into place and began tightening the bolts. That's when Doc remembered what he'd been about to check on when he got preoccupied with Frypan's condition the night before. "What kind of pressure will this thing hold?" he asked.

"The gage goes up to two thousand pounds," Frypan said. "I expect that's what she'll hold."

"Two thousand!" Doc exploded. "You'd better be holding hands with your guardian angel if it ever gets near a hundred pounds!"

"Aw, it'll be all right, Doc," Frypan said. "She's got a safety blow-off valve on her."

"The hell it will!" Doc said. "That blow-off valve probably came from wherever that gage did. It's no more likely to belong to that tank than the gage does! You unscrew that blow-off valve, and I'll show Downwind how to make a pressure control to go on that pipe."

"I ain't got no time to lose, Doc!" Frypan complained.

"Then don't lose it," Doc said. "Get that valve off there, then go ahead and light your fire. We'll have the pressure control ready by the time she boils.''

Doc took Downwind over to Reverend John's woodworking shed and fished out a small round stick and a piece of smooth board about eight inches square. Doc whittled a taper on the round stick so it came to a point at one end. Then he got a screw and fastened the blunt end of the dowel perpendicular to the middle of one of the flat faces of the board. Doc held it up for Downwind to see as he explained, ''You put this pointed stick straight down into the pipe that blow-off valve was on. Then you twist it around a bit so's the pipe digs into the board a little bit and so's you're sure it's not wedged tight. Then you get a brick and set it on the board for a weight. Just one brick, mind you! You want this thing setting in there so's the steam pressure can raise it up if the pressure gets too high. And you don't want to make any damn fool mistakes like getting it wedged on there too tight. Matter of fact, you'd best lift it every now and then and let some steam out just to be sure the steam doesn't swell the wood and get it stuck fast. Now, you got all this? You understand it?''

''Sure, Doc! I wiggle it on there to a good fit, set one brick on it, make sure it's loose, and check it again ever so often,'' Downwind answered.

''Good! That's exactly it!'' Doc said, thumping Downwind on the back. ''You get on back to the barn with it while I hunt up Hammerin' Harry and find out something more about that boiler.''

Doc was on his second pass through town before he found Harry in the livery stable. ''Oh, there you are!'' he called out.

''Seems as though,'' Harry agreed.

''It's about that boiler Frypan rented from you,'' Doc began. ''How much pressure can it take?''

''I don't rightly know,'' Harry said. ''Colonel Wellingboor, he done all the figuring.''

''How about the pressure gage and blow-off valve on it, where'd they come from?''

''Colonel Wellingboor said he got 'em off some old mining equipment.''

"Uh huh," Doc said, and paused awhile to mull things over before saying, "I sort of feel like Colonel Wellingboor didn't know much about what he was doing."

"You and me both!" Harry agreed with enthusiasm. "You know, he comes to ask me to build this boiler, and he's got papers all covered with arithmetics and he says the iron has got to be a half inch thick. And I got to telling him what the iron would cost and how heavy it would be to freight it up here and how long I'd have to hammer it to get it bent just so, and you know what he done?"

"What?" Doc asked.

"He changed his arithmetics! That's what he done. He said the metal could be an eighth inch thick. Now, that don't make no sense at all, does it?"

"No more than putting a two-thousand-pound gage on it does," Doc agreed.

"Then when he gets all the iron up here, he give me a little picture of what he wants and I see where it doesn't show how many bolts it needs to hold the lid on, so I asked him, and do you know what he said?"

"Not unless you tell me," Doc answered.

"He said, 'How many have you got?' That's what he said!"

"Haw, haw, haw!" Doc laughed, "How many have you got! Haw, haw, haw!" But then he sobered up a bit, saying, "That Colonel Wellingboor of yours was a dummy all right, but he isn't the dummy that's trying to fire it up today!"

"That's another thing I told the colonel," Harry said, grinning from ear to ear. " 'Course, I made it sound like a joke, but I meant it right down to the marrow of my bones! 'Colonel,' I says, 'I'll build you this here boiler, but I don't want to be nowheres near it when you fires it up!' "

Doc started to leave. He wanted to get right back to the barn and see for himself that the pressure controller was right.

"And, Doc, does you want to know how Colonel Wellingboor decided on the right number of rivets to use?" Harry called after him, chuckling like a maniac.

"No, I does not!" Doc yelled out, adopting Harry's grammar

in his preoccupied state. He hurried back to the barn and went straight to the boiler.

It looked peaceful enough. The pressure controller contraption was in place with one brick holding it down, just as he'd ordered. Shielding his hand with a rag, he gave the dowel a gentle twist and found that it was reasonably loose and was indeed holding back a head of steam.

Doc stepped back and looked the whole thing over. The boiler was just a big egg of a tank with an iron skirt around the bottom to serve as a firebox. Nothing fancy about the firebox. Just two front doors, one above the grate for loading wood and another below the grate for regulating air and removing ashes. Frypan had fitted a tin stovepipe on the exhaust at the back of the firebox and run it out a window that was stuffed with bricks for insulation.

Simplicity itself. And further proof that Colonel Wellingboor didn't know anything about boilers. A decent boiler would have had that hot flue running right up through the middle of the boiler. And a really good one would have had water tubes running right through the flames. Hell! The way Colonel Wellingboor had designed this one, most of the heat was going right out the chimney and maybe the boiler would never get enough heat to build a dangerous pressure.

So much for the boiler. Doc's professional confidence had been restored for the moment and he decided to check on Frypan's condition. "Looks like we're sailing right along, eh, Frypan?" he asked.

"I dunno, Doc, I just don't know. I sure hope so," Frypan answered. "That mob of miners is starting to get pretty wild out there, ain't they?"

"Wild? No such thing. They're about as peaceful as I've ever seen 'em. What ails you, Frypan?"

"Nothing. I'm just scairt they'll come busting in here looking for their feast before I'm ready."

"Well, they won't," Doc said. "They're being sober, sociable, and neighborly today."

"Sober?" Frypan challenged. "Not for long they won't be. They'll drink the saloons dry before noon!"

"Not likely," Doc reassured him. "They ain't that rich. They're still panning gold to pay last winter's bills. Sam Ibsen tells me nearly ever' one of 'em owes him."

Frypan thought it over awhile and said, "That's worse. A sober man's harder to fool than a drunk!"

"Don't be so damn contrary," Doc roared. "Why, if I—"

Doc was cut off in mid-thought by a loud banging on the door. "Open up in there!" someone yelled.

"Oh my Gawd, they've come!" Frypan said, and you could see the pallor of his face in spite of that grey-and-black beard stubble.

"Who's there?" George Gatlin challenged.

"The Dutchman sent me for coffee," someone answered.

"Coffee?" Doc asked. "Why would he send here for coffee?"

"The Dutchman bought up all the flour and salt in town and made me pay part of my hide for it, so I bought up all the coffee," Frypan explained, the color slowly coming back to his face.

"So now you're out to skin the hide off the Dutchman, are you?" Doc asked.

Frypan didn't answer, but went to the door. "What's the Dutchman willing to pay?" he asked.

"He says he needs it pretty bad and he's willing to pay your price," the voice answered.

"My price is, he pays me back the extra twenty dollars he charged me for the salt and flour, and after that he can have all the coffee he wants at the regular price, same as I paid."

This being quickly agreed to, the door was opened a foot or so and several sacks of coffee were exchanged for cash in hand.

When the door was closed and bolted again, Doc clapped a hand on Frypan's shoulder and said, "That's the most civilized thing I've ever seen in these parts. There you stood with the sword of vengeance at your adversary's throat and you let him go! That's—by God, I want to shake your hand, Frypan!" And Doc did just that.

"You're making too much of it, Doc," Frypan admitted. "It's just that I'm gonna need every friend I can get before this day's over. Fact is, there's a little errand you gotta do for me."

"What's that?"

"Well, sir," Frypan said, fishing a wad of paper money out of his back pocket, "there's about a thousand dollars there. Take it over to the Thirsty Saloon and tell Jason the drinks are on me for the next hour. Don't tell him how much money you've got there, just tell him I'll pay for all the drinks he can pour in the next hour."

"You're sure you want to do that?" Doc asked, fixing a quizzical eye on Frypan.

"Doc," Frypan answered with an edge of desperation in his voice, "I want them miners too soused to know deer from rabbit and too grateful to kill me if they do."

Doc concluded that Frypan was a hopeless case. He carried his message over to Jason, offered himself as the first free customer, then went through the crowd spreading the word. The crush on the saloon got so bad the customers were going in and out through the windows as well as the door. Jason was out of glasses after the first wave hit, but everyone had their tin coffee cups with them, so it was no problem. Jason simply sloshed each coffee cup brim-full and asked folks to move on outside and share some with the folks that were having trouble getting in. Then a kind of bucket brigade formed from the bar to the side window, and a steady stream of coffee cups came in empty and went out full. Jason was pouring just as fast as the stuff would pour.

In the fullness of the generous spirit of the moment, some of the miners took it upon themselves to deliver the stuff to Momma Rose's house, The Dutchman's, Sam Ibsen's General Store, the livery stable, and even to those hard-working cooks down in Frypan's barn. Frypan knew he'd unleashed a flood when he saw free booze being delivered to Downwind at the front door and George at the back door at one and the same time. And those people outside were getting a lot noisier than they had been. Frypan had set out to get 'em drunk, and now he wasn't so sure it was a good idea after all. Worry, worry, worry. Worry if they're sober, worry if they're drunk. Everything depended on how things were going inside that boiler, and there was no way to see in there.

Doc came back to the barn shortly after the hour of free drinks was over and handed Frypan one lonely dollar bill, saying, "You gave me too much."

"They're too drunk, ain't they?" Frypan asked.

"Too drunk?" Doz puzzled. "Yep! Most of 'em are. Too drunk to hang you because they can't tie a knot, and too drunk to shoot you because they'd be seeing more than one of you!"

"Lord!" Frypan said. "Do you suppose they might eat this dinner today, then come back tomorra not remembering they had it?"

"Jason and Reverend John are sober," Doc said carelessly, settling his weary bones onto a bench. "They'll testify for you."

Suddenly, a hiss of steam erupted from the boiler. Doc looked at it and jumped to his feet. "Who in hell piled all those bricks on the pressure control?"

"We need the pressure, Doc; that stuff has got to cook!" Frypan said.

"Douse the fire! Douse the fire!" Doc shouted, frantically looking for water.

Then, with a mighty WHOOMP, a piece of leather gasket blew out from under the lid and a cloud of steam belched into the room. "Duck!" Doc shouted, dropping flat on the dirt along with Frypan, George, and Downwind.

"Do you reckon it's done?" Frypan asked when the steam had cleared a bit.

"Oh, it's done all right," Doc answered.

They got up, smothered the fire with dirt, and set about getting the lid off the boiler. Frypan poked around inside as soon as the lid was off. "Needs a little water, but it ain't burnt!" he announced. "By Gawd, it looks good and tastes good, Doc! And them rabbit bones is ready to pull right out."

Right away they set about sorting things out. Frypan set up three large pots: one for soup, one for deer, and one for rabbit. George and Downwind were put to work deboning and dicing the rabbit meat into small chunks. Doc did much the same with the deer meat, except that he left it in chunks that were obviously too big to be rabbit.

Finally, the moment of truth arrived. "It's time we started

serving, Frypan," Doc announced. "We can't keep this stuff hot very long."

"Yeah," Frypan agreed with a sigh of resignation. "It's now or never." He took one last look around and said, "George, shovel them rabbit bones into the nearest stall and cover 'em with straw. And we'll leave the deer bones in plain sight, I reckon."

When George had taken care of the rabbit bones, they lined up their tasks. Frypan would stand at the door and pass the plates to Doc, who would hustle over to the table where George and Downwind would fill them with stew, meat, and pancakes. They would serve rabbit until it was gone unless Frypan called for "venison," meaning that he was faced with some sober or discerning customer who damn well better get the real thing.

Frypan opened the door and banged on a pan, yelling, "Come and get it!" A horde of miners responded like pigs to the trough, and Frypan switched his tune, to, "Line up, line up! Form a line, dammit!"

The line formed, and tin platters began streaming in and out through the door. Frypan tried not to give a damn whether the men liked the stuff or not, but his spirits took a soaring leap as the first few miners to taste the stuff pronounced it the best damned venison they'd ever had! From there on, it was easy. A frantically busy hour, but easy.

When the serving was done and the doors were closed, Frypan, Doc, George and Downwind sat down with the portions they'd saved for themselves.

"Not bad at all," Doc said. "And I think I like the rabbit better than the venison!"

"You're right," Frypan agreed as George and Downwind nodded their approval too. "Maybe I ought to do this again a time or two."

"You do," Doc warned, "and I'm leaving town quicker'n you can say jackrabbit!"

"Don't make no jokes like that, Doc," Frypan said. "Somebody's liable to catch on yet! Reverend John there, he was one of the ones we served with venison, and damn lucky we did! He says to me, 'Frypan, I'm blest if I know where you got all this deer. I haven't seen a deer in a day's ride from here in nigh onto a year.' And I says to him, 'Parson, when a feller trusts in the Lord, he finds manna in the desert, or he feeds a multitude with a few loaves and fishes, or he finds deer where there ain't any.' Just like that, I told him the truth before I stopped to think! Told him we found deer where there ain't any! But that's the Reverend John; he wants to believe the Lord provided the deer and he won't push it no further. But that ain't like the other folks in this town, and they ain't gonna be pleased at being fooled!''

So Frypan pledged not to cook up any more venison feasts in Thirsty, and the others pledged never to break the secret, a bottle of rye whiskey being uncorked to make the pledges official.

CHAPTER 7

CABIN FEVER

WINTER was a special hardship for Thirsty's miners. Except for the mine tunnels Hard Rock Hackett was working, all the miners were working surface dirt. When winter really settled down on Crystal Creek, the dirt froze as hard as rock. And even if a feller was stubborn enough to go on digging, he needed water to sluice the dirt from the gold. It wasn't too often that Crystal Creek froze solid, but the stuff that kept flowing was so close to freezing that you couldn't get but a few minutes' use of it in your diggings before it would freeze, too.

Aside from cutting firewood, fixing up their cabins, and doing a little hunting, the miners had a lot of time on their hands. It was always a test of character. How much sleeping, alone or otherwise, drinking, card playing, or story telling could a man take? Eventually, the old entertainments became boring. And what Doc Crane called "tedium tension" would set in.

It was at such times as these that Bill Astor was likely to dream up a sucker bet for his favorite victim, Lou Clark. No matter how fair the bet might seem at first blush, Bill always set it up with some hidden advantage for himself and Lou always lost. If Bill and Lou had a bet going on whether the sun would come up tomorrow, a sane man would bet on Bill to win, no matter which side of the bet Bill happened to be on. Most people in Lou's shoes would have refused to bet with Bill anymore, but it had become a matter of pride with Lou. Someday, by Jesus, he was going to win against Bill.

Old Losin' Lou, as people started calling him, was a slow learner. Take, for instance, the night that Bill Astor was sitting in the Thirsty Saloon with his fourth or fifth beer of the evening, bragging about how fast he could run. Lou sat there listening to him, and you could damn near see Lou rising to the bait. He watched Bill swilling down that beer, and he cast a thoughtful look at the excess flab on Bill and told himself that Bill was certainly not a runner now, if he ever had been. And he got to peeking at Bill's boots and saw that they were a monstrously heavy style, built for the coldest day of the century at the North Pole. Lou was lean and rugged, and he was wearing a simple pair of work shoes. To his credit, Lou took his time and thought it over very carefully before he challenged Bill to the race.

"Well hell, not just now, Lou," Bill protested. "I'd need a few days to get in shape for a genuine race."

"All that bragging you were just doing on being such a good runner and all; it don't mean nothing then, does it?" Lou needled.

"I'm full of beer just now," Bill said, with a pat on his ample stomach. "It wouldn't be a fair race no way."

"You're the one what was bragging," Lou said.

"Well, just you don't be so damn sure of yourself, Lou Clark! I could still beat you in a short race!"

"Sure you could," Lou mocked.

"You put your money where your mouth is!" Bill said, rising to his feet and prancing about to stretch his legs. "My ten dollars says I can beat you in a race from here to Jake Teller's shanty and back!"

"None of your tricks!" Lou warned. "We draw a line in the street outside and start all even with a clear street in front of us."

"Where's your ten dollars?" Bill asked.

"Let's make it twenty!" Lou said, slapping a gold piece on the table.

"Twenty it is," Bill said, matching the gold piece. Then they went out in the street with the whole saloon patronage following.

Lou drew his line across the street and toed the mark, facing up the street toward Jake Teller's shack, which was just around the bend beyond Momma Rose's place. Bill took his place at the line, and one of the spectators volunteered to serve as starter.

"One . . . two . . . three." Bang! And the great race started on the pistol shot.

Lou promptly shot ahead of Bill, then Bill turned and ran in the opposite direction! The fact is that Jake Teller's shanty wasn't much bigger than a big outhouse and Bill had arranged for Jake to move it down the street, behind the livery stable. By the time Lou reached the place where Jake Teller's shanty used to be, Bill had reached its new location and gotten back to the starting line.

Lou made a lot of indignant noises, but he stood alone. The rest of Thirsty enjoyed the joke too much to deprive Bill of his prize money. And that was just exactly how all of these bets between Bill and Old Losin' Lou had been going. Bill always had some outrageous deceit working for him, but the whole town would side with Bill at pay-up time. Aside from the joke, the people of Thirsty generally felt that a grown man had ought to keep his eyes open and face up to the consequences of whatever he did, including stupid bets.

But it had gotten to the point where Lou figured that Bill was getting too sure of himself. Lou kept a quiet and thoughtful eye on Bill and dreamed of the day he'd find himself one step ahead of Bill.

One day there was a lull in the after-dinner talk over at The Dutchman's and Lou, who was sitting kitty-corner across the table from Bill, saw something worth remembering. Bill was idly looking at his hands, turning them this way and that. Then he paused, palms down, and broke into a wide grin—which he quickly erased by swiping the back of his hand across his mouth, napkin-like. Lou sensed that he had seen the birth of a bet, even though he didn't know what the bet was going to be.

Nor did Lou know just how soon Bill would be ready to spring his bet, but he kept an eye on Bill for several days, hoping for some clue on just how Bill planned to cheat him next. In doing this, Lou discovered two things; Bill made an odd purchase at Sam Ibsen's General Store, and he visited Doc Crane, though he hadn't been complaining of anything. And Bill wasn't generally silent when he had something to complain of.

A day or so later, Bill and Lou were sitting on opposite sides of a poker table in the Thirsty Saloon and Lou was having a run of good luck for a change.

"You're too damn lucky tonight, Lou," Bill said. "I'll have to make you a bet some other which way. It just don't seem natural, me not collecting from you."

"Uh huh," Lou grunted.

Bill drummed his fingers on the table in deep thought. "Come on, Lou, what'll we bet on this time?"

"Let's just play poker," Lou said. "That suits me fine to-night."

Bill drummed his fingers a bit longer, then exclaimed, "That's it. We'll bet on who can grow the longest fingernails in the next three months!"

"Nothing doing," Lou snapped.

"What could be more fair?" Bill coaxed. "We cut all our nails down to the pink tonight. Three months from now, we measure them all from the tips to the pinks, add 'em up, and whichever adds up to the most wins."

"I know and you know that you've got some damn fool way to cheat me on it," Lou said. "I ain't about to swallow your hook again."

"Now Lou, if I had some sort of trick going, don't you think you'd figure it out before three months goes by?"

"You're too damn fond of three months, let's make it two months."

"Then it's a bet?"

"I didn't say that. You'll have to give me a half-inch advantage. If your nails ain't no more'n a half inch longer than mine, I win!"

"What!" Bill shouted. "What for?"

"It's for to make up for whatever it is that you're counting on that I don't know about."

"I won't do no such thing," Bill proclaimed.

"Good," Lou said. "No bet. Let's get on with the poker game."

"A quarter inch," Bill said.

"And two months?" Lou asked.

"I'll go you one better," Bill declared. "Let's make it three months, except that either of us can call a showdown after two months."

Lou thought it over. Knowing Bill, a quarter-inch advantage would somehow not be enough, but this time Lou did know a little more than usual about Bill's plans. And, being able to call a showdown any time between two and three months sounded fair enough. Lou could feel the old betting fever rising in his breast, but still he hesitated.

"Let's put it in writing, sign it, and shake on it," Bill coaxed.

"Yeah, put it in writing," Lou said.

Jason, the bartender, dug out a piece of paper, a rusty pen, and a small pot of ink. Bill flattened out the paper, pulled his sleeves up, dipped the pen, stared at the ceiling a moment, then laboriously printed the terms of the bet as follows:

Bill Astor hereby makes a bet with Lou Clark regarding which will grow the longest nails in 2 or 3 months time. Both parties will cut thar finger nails to mutual satisfaction today. Ether partie can call for final measure after two months. Other else, final measure to be made 3 months from today. All nails to be measured from pink to tip and added for each partie. Bill Astor to win only if his nails add up a quarter inch or more longer than what Lou has.

Bill read it out loud, then signed and dated it and passed it over to Lou. Lou studied it carefully. Reading wasn't his specialty and there were some words he didn't know, but he wasn't going to admit it to Bill. "Looks okay," he said, "but let's cut our fingernails and see if we can agree on how they're cut before I sign it."

"By God, you're a Philadelphia lawyer, you are!" Bill said. "Thinking like a fox all the time, ain'tcha?"

"There ain't no other way to think around you," Lou said.

They got out their penknives and began the nail-cutting ceremony, each being very careful not to go beyond the pink. Finally they compared hands, quibbled a little over this nail or that, each trimming a tiny bit from the disputed nails, and eventually reaching agreement that a fair job had been done. Lou signed the note, which was passed over to Jason for safe keeping, and the race was on.

Lou dropped in at Doc Crane's office early the next morning, rousting him out of bed. "Doc," he said, "you gotta tell me how to grow fingernails."

Doc rubbed his eyes and glared at Lou. "That couldn't wait till a decent time of day, could it?"

"Sorry, Doc, I didn't want nobody to see me here. You know how Bill's always beating me on bets. Just tell me what you told Bill."

"Who says I told Bill anything?" Doc asked.

"I saw him come in here when he had nothing ailing him, and then he wants to bet on how fast he can grow fingernails. That says he asked you about fingernails. Now, you tell me if I'm wrong."

"He didn't say anything about a bet," Doc conceded.

"Thanks, Doc," Lou said with a big, grateful, conspiratorial grin. Then he drew up a chair to whispering distance and asked, "What's the secret?"

"There ain't no particular secret," Doc said. "It's generally believed that eating gelatin helps them to grow and keeps them from getting brittle so's they break. Aside from that, it's just a matter of taking care of them so's they don't get damaged scratching in the dirt and such-like."

"That's all?" Lou asked, considerably disappointed.

"Yep, that's it," Doc confirmed. "There ain't been much medical attention to fingernails because there ain't much goes wrong with them. Sometimes a doctor that knows what he's doing can diagnose an ailment or two by the appearance of the nails, and sometimes a doctor will test nail clippings for arsenic poisoning, but I don't recall that I've ever heard any complaints of nails growing too fast or too slow."

"Where do I get gelatin?" Lou asked.

"Sam Ibsen probably has it over at his store."

"That's if Bill didn't buy it up already," Lou said with a knowing frown.

"See if the Dutchman has some bones you can take home to cook, then. They'll generally have some gristle and tender stuff on them, and that's got a lot of gelatin," Doc said.

"Thanks, Doc," Lou said, and left immediately for The Dutchman's, knowing that his kitchen would be open, getting ready for customers who were still sleeping.

Having made a deal with the Dutchman that guaranteed him all the gristle he could eat, Lou set out on a secret mission to the general store at Smithville to purchase certain things he didn't want Bill to hear about.

A week or so later, Lou went into the Thirsty Saloon and found a place at the poker table where Bill sat. Bill kept his mouth shut until Lou picked up his first hand of cards. "You're gonna play with your gloves on?" he asked.

"They're light gloves," Lou said casually. "I'll manage."

"Now, what's the sense of that?" Bill asked.

"Protects the fingernails. Also keeps 'em from prying eyes," Lou answered.

Bill scoffed, teased, and needled at Lou all evening over those gloves, but Lou enjoyed it as a sure sign that he was one step ahead of Bill. And Bill was seen wearing gloves while eating at The Dutchman's the next day. After that, neither Bill nor Lou would remove their gloves in public for the duration of the bet.

With the winter doldrums and all, the fingernail contest got to be the major topic of conversation in Thirsty. The only other speculation of comparable interest was the question of who had gotten Junie May, one of Momma Rose's girls, in a family way. Momma Rose was stalking the town for a suitable husband for Junie May. And there wasn't anyone who wanted to win that contest, so the boys were all keeping a low profile. Junie May had become a liability for Momma Rose; her condition would make a man think, and thinking wasn't good for Momma Rose's business. Besides which, Momma Rose was gonna have to pounce on a husband candidate pretty soon or just plain send Junie May away. Too many of the boys were staying away from Momma Rose's place because of it.

The boys were all pretending that the Junie May problem didn't concern them, and one of the best ways of doing that was to make a big fuss over something else. Everybody was speculating on what sort of nails were growing under those gloves that Lou and Bill were wearing, and a lot of people got to measuring their own and comparing measurements to see what sort of differences there might be from one person to another and just how much advantage that quarter inch might be for Lou. After all, when you divide a quarter inch among ten fingers, you don't get much more than a gnat's eyelash advantage for each finger. And when all was said and done, there was no getting around the fact that Lou had never won this sort of bet against Bill. Most people were betting that Bill had the usual ace or two up his sleeve.

Those few hardy souls who were betting on Lou took their comfort in two things. First off, they were sitting on the optimistic side of ten-to-one odds, the kind of lure that turned an ordinary man into a gold miner in the first place. Second, Lou had taken all of that ten-to-one money he could cover, and he hadn't been known to be that confident in past bets with Bill.

One night nearly two months after the bet had started, Lou went into the Thirsty Saloon and hadn't no more than gotten to the bar when Cindy cuddled up beside him, wrapped a friendly arm around his waist and kissed him on the cheek, saying, "Howdy, Lou, how's my favorite miner today?"

Lou, not being a lady's man at all, was totally flustered. "Well uh, gosh, Cindy, I reckon I'm as well as ever," he stammered. A moment later he realized that Cindy was squeezing his hand kinda hard for a lady, and he suddenly knew what she was up to. He jerked his hand away, but she clung to the glove and yanked on it.

Lou twisted away and glared at her. "Shame on you! Who put you up to that?"

"Nobody," Cindy said. "Just wanted to see for myself. Why don't you come over to my place and just show them nails to me. I won't tell nobody."

"The heck you won't! You tried to break 'em at first, didn't you?"

"You got little boards tied to every finger, ain'tcha?" Cindy asked.

"Yes, ma'am, I do." Lou sneered. "And I got my gloves pinned to my sleeves in case you're wondering why they didn't come off."

"My goodness, ain't we getting cautious in our old age," Bill Astor said, joining the discussion.

"You the one what put Cindy up to that?" Lou demanded.

"You accusing me?" Bill asked, looking as mean as he knew how to.

"I ain't accusing nobody," Lou said, "but I think I better warn all my good friends here and now to stay clear of my cabin for a time 'cause I got her ringed with bear traps starting today!"

"Bear traps! What for?"

"Prowlers! That's what for. There's been footprints under my windows. Somebody's been trying to spy on me."

"Good Lord, Lou! You ever seen a leg that's been in a bear trap?" Doc Crane asked. "A man could bleed to death if it caught him just right. You don't want to do that to a man just for trying to peek in your window! Whoever's doing it most likely don't mean nothing by it."

"Well, Doc," Lou said, "when I catch him in a bear trap and you patch him up, you can tell him for me that I most likely didn't mean nothing by it neither!"

That pretty much ended the discussion, and the rest of the evening went by fairly peaceably. But it was Bill Astor's turn to be mad the following night. He came into the Thirsty Saloon about two hours after dark, which was late for him in the midwinter season, and went stomping over to a table where Lou was swapping yarns with a couple of other miners.

"Some good-fer-nuthin bastard damn near killed me!" he declared, glaring right at Lou.

"Meaning what?" Lou asked.

"Meaning some good-fer-nuthin bastard snuck up to my cabin after dark whilst I was fixing supper and poured water all over my doorstep, slow and careful-like, so's it froze thick and slick as bear grease. I steps out to go to the outhouse, and damned if my feet don't go flying higher'n my head so's I come slamming down fit to bust every bone God gave me!"

"Get yourself some bear traps like I done," Lou advised.

"I think I damn well know who the bear is," Bill growled.

"Do you suppose it could have been the same good-fer-nuthin

bastard what was prowling my place?" Lou asked, just as poker-faced as a wooden Indian.

"Did you bust any fingernails when you fell?" George Gatlin interrupted.

"Naw, just my right arm," Bill groused, taking a seat at the table.

"Should I fetch Doc Crane?" George asked, trying to make out as if Bill's arm were as important as all those fingernails his money was bet on.

"Hell no!" Bill said. "A few drinks'll take care of it. But I'm gonna set me some traps tomorrow, so's anybody coming to my cabin better give a holler a hundred yards out if he's wanting to get in alive!"

It was just the sort of thing you might expect in the winter doldrums. One damned fool little bet between two fairly peaceable people and what happens? Undeclared war! Cabins ringed with traps and fingernails being guarded like the mother lode.

The prescribed two-month minimum had gone by, but Lou seemed in no hurry to call for the showdown. Bill let it ride, knowing that whoever called for the showdown would look especially foolish losing. But the days crept by and Lou looked so damned calm and unconcerned. That was what Bill couldn't stand; his victim wasn't squirming. In the end, it was Bill who broke first.

"Would you mind telling me, Lou, why in hell you haven't called for a measure?"

"No need," Lou answered. "I can win later as easy as sooner."

"The hell you can!" Bill said. "That quarter-inch advantage I gave you ain't as good tomorrow as it is today. On the very first day of the bet, you was a quarter inch ahead of me. Now, if my nails grow faster'n yours like I say they do, you lose a little bit of that quarter-inch advantage ever' day. Hell, I just put that calling the bet thing in there for a joke; something worthless to dicker with, that's all. It wouldn't be no different than a straight two-month bet if you knew what you was about!"

"Maybe I have faith that my nails grow faster'n your'n and I just want to see how much I can beat you by," Lou answered, just as cool and unperturbed as you please.

Bill glared at Lou awhile, then broke into a crafty grin. "Maybe you ain't so dumb after all. You probably busted some of your nails and now you're just stalling around, hoping I'll bust some of mine. That's it, ain't it? You busted some of your nails!"

"The way I figure it," Lou said, "if the one that calls the bet loses, he's gonna look twice as silly as if the other feller done the calling."

"You never was good at bluffing," Bill said. "I know I've got you beat just as sure as I'm sitting here. Maybe I'd string you along another week or so just for fun, but I smell a thaw in the air, and I don't want to be wearing all these fingernails when it comes time to work the claim again. You're called, Lou. Let's measure up so's I can collect and be done with it!"

So a ruler was brought out, and the gloves came off, and the little wooden splints came off. News of the showdown had flashed up and down the street, bringing dang near the whole populace of Thirsty into the saloon.

"See any busted ones, Bill?" Lou asked, flashing a full set of fingernails that ranged somewhere between a half and three quarters of an inch each.

"Just let's measure up," Bill grumped.

Jason was the only one present who hadn't bet on the outcome, so he did the measuring and adding under the close scrutiny of Lou, Bill, and all those fortunate enough to have gotten to the table before the crowd arrived. He started with Lou's left hand, calling out the result for each finger as he wrote it down. Sam Ibsen off in one corner of the crowd, Doc Crane squeezed up against the wall near the door, and Reverend John pressed against the bar did their own adding as a check on Jason. Among the four of them, they had the adding business to themselves, there being no others in Thirsty who had mastered the mysteries of adding fractions.

After Lou's left hand, Jason measured Bill's left, generating a gasp of amazement when Bill came out an eighth of an inch short of Lou. Jason turned back to Lou's right hand and proceeded to measure it up, interrupted only by Bill's quibbling over thirty-seconds of an inch.

"You cain't measure no thirty-seconds, Jace," he protested. "They ain't no thirty-seconds on that ruler."

"There's sixteeths," Jason said. "When the measure falls between those sixteenths, I give it a thirty-second one way or the other."

"Yeah?" Bill said. "Well, just see to it that it falls the right way!"

Coming back to Bill's right hand, Jason finished the job with all the deliberate, squinting care appropriate to his high office and announced that Lou's right-hand nails had beat Bill's by five thirty-seconds of an inch.

"Five thirty-seconds!" Lou exulted. "That's damn near another eighth, ain't it?"

"A bit more," Jason said. "Both hands together, your nails are one thirty-second more than a quarter inch longer than Bill's."

"And that's on top of the quarter-inch advantage the bet allowed!" Lou declared over the hubbub of the crowd. "Pay up, Bill! Pay up!"

"You ain't won yet. Let's get on with the measuring!" And, so saying, Bill pushed his chair back and started to unlace his boots.

"What in hell are you doing?" Lou shouted.

"We gotta get the toenail measure yet," Bill said.

"Toenails!" Lou screamed, turning a bit purple in the face.

"We bet on which of us would grow the longest nails. The bet is all writ down. You read it and signed it, the same as me."

"We bet on fingernails!" Lou screamed, but he had precious little support from a crowd that had bet ten-to-one in Bill's favor. "Yessir! The old ace in the hole!" they said. "Didn't I tell you?" they said. "Bill always wins against Lou," they said.

"Read us that bet, Jace," Lou demanded, so Jason read it aloud:

"Bill Astor hereby makes a bet with Lou Clark regarding which will grow the longest nails in two or three months' time. Both parties will cut thar fingernails to mutual satisfaction today. Either party can call for final measure after two months. Other else, final measure to be made three months from today. All nails to be measured from pink to tip and added for each party. Bill Astor to win only if his nails add up a quarter inch or more longer than what Lou has.''

"There," Bill said. "It says the bet is on nails, not just fingernails!"

"Then what's all that about cutting fingernails?" Lou demanded. "Why don't it say nothing about cutting toenails?"

"That don't mean nothing," Bill insisted. "It coulda said we'd cut toenails to start and left out the fingernails. What's the difference?"

"It ain't a fair bet, that's the difference!"

"You gonna get your toenails out here for measuring, or are you gonna allow as how I won?" Bill asked, grinning fit to tie Lou in knots.

"I got more'n half an inch of fingernail on you, and by God, I'm gonna beat you, toenails or not!" Lou insisted.

"Since you're so sure," Bill smirked, "why don't we double the bet?"

"Done!" Lou roared. "It's doubled!"

Bill whipped off his left boot and sock, revealing all toes carefully fitted with little wooden splints protecting a set of pampered toenails. Lou sat sullen and motionless as Jason went through the measuring and adding process. "Well?" Bill asked, "you gonna take off a boot, Lou, or do you expect Jason to do that for you?"

Lou undid the laces on his left boot. "Look out for the smell, boys!" Bill warned. "He probably ain't washed his socks all winter!"

But when Lou shucked off his boot and sock, the general shock that hit the saloon wasn't from odor, it was from the sight of all those little wooden splints on Lou's toes. There must have been at least ten people who said, "Well, I'll be damned!" almost in unison.

"Now, ain't you glad we just doubled the bet?" Lou asked with a big grin smeared all over his face.

Bill's face and spirit had gone flat. "You're getting smart in your old age," he said. "I never thought that would happen."

Lou got rid of the splints and Jason worked his way through the measurement, announcing that Lou's left foot had beaten Bill's by a sixteenth of an inch!

"Let's see that right foot of yours, Bill," Lou teased. "That's got to be the world's champeen nail-grower if you're gonna beat me with it!"

"No need, you win. Hell, I don't mind your winning once ever' five years or so," Bill said.

"You sure?" Lou asked. "What if I was to tell you I broke three nails on my right foot yesterday?"

Bill looked up sharply, but read the mockery in Lou's face correctly. "I've seen all the nails I want to see for a while," he said, then jammed his left shoe on and shouldered his way out of the saloon. Lou broke into a big, "Haw, haw, haw!" and winners and losers alike joined in the laugh.

Bill made himself scarce around Thirsty for the next few days, waiting for that laugh to die down. Lou, on the other hand, took every opportunity to enjoy the company of his fellow citizens. One afternoon when Doc Crane was sitting alone in his office, just trying to stay awake next to the comforting heat of a small pot-bellied stove, Lou dropped in on a neighborly visit.

"Just wanted to thank you for your help with my fingernails, Doc," Lou began.

"I didn't do any more for you than I did for Bill," Doc said, "but I don't mind telling you I was really tickled to see the way you beat him!"

"Yessir!" Lou said. "I really shellacked him!"

"Yep," Doc agreed, "you really shellacked him!"

"Doc," Lou said, drawing up a chair to whispering range, "if you can keep it a secret, I can tell you something about growing nails."

"Well, I reckon you're the expert on the subject," Doc said. "I expect I can keep a confidence on it if that's how it has to be."

"It's gotta be a secret," Lou insisted.

"Okay," Doc said, "a secret it is."

"Well, sir," Lou said, "if a feller really wants to grow fingernails and has the time and patience for it, he might just dip his nails in shellack and let 'em dry and dip 'em again and let 'em dry, and hone 'em down along the grain of the natural nail every so often with a fine whetstone in between dippings. Then you might have to stain 'em just a little bit with terbacca juice so's everything matches up, but a patient man can help nature along a good bit, and it don't look no different than the natural thing."

"Is that a fact?" Doc said. "Haw, haw, haw! You really did shellack Bill, didn't you?"

"Yessir, I shellacked him all right. Got the shellack down in Smithville, where I got a pair of oversized boots like I seen Bill buying over to Sam Ibsen's!"

A confidence like that called for a celebration, so Doc dug out a bottle of whiskey kept for medicinal purposes, and they hoisted a toast to Lou's secret weapon.

Later, as Lou was about to leave, he reminded Doc once again not to break the secret. "No sir, Lou, I'll keep that secret tight as a drum. But if I were a betting man, I'd bet everything I've got that you won't be keeping it. That's just one of those things that's too good to keep!"

Doc was right. You could tell that Lou was telling it to this one and that one and so forth. Any time the talk turned to the fingernail-growing contest, all you had to say was, "Lou sure shellacked him," and right away you knew who knew the whole story and who didn't.

CHAPTER 8

A DOG'S DAY

IT started as an ordinary evening at the Thirsty Saloon. Notches and Lucky Martin had been hanging around since supper time, and the miners began drifting in about an hour before dusk. Lucky had a poker game going and things were reasonably sociable and civilized.

In a corner away from the bar and the doorway, Shifty Knots sat on the floor with a mug of beer next to the dog named Shiftless. They were a pair, those two. Shifty might have been known as the town drunk if there weren't so many other serious contenders for the title. Actually, what set Shifty apart was that he'd given up any pretense of working for anything but the next drink. He mooched drinks when he could, and he'd sweep the floor for a drink, but that was about it. Aside from booze, he survived on whatever scraps or garbage the Dutchman might save for him, and these he shared with the dog.

Somewhere along the way Shifty had lost his self-esteem. He couldn't look any other man in the eye, and that had earned him his nickname. When he wanted to mooch a drink, he'd shuffle up to his prospect sort of sideways, and his downcast eyes would be darting from side to side and across the room as he made his plea. It was a pathetic show. He'd been that way since he and a fellow prospector had gotten lost in the desert without enough water. The other fellow died and Shifty barely made it out, only to torment himself with the thought that he hadn't done enough to help his friend. Maybe he should have given his friend more of the water? Who's to say that fifty-fifty is a fair split of the water between two men? Maybe one naturally needs more than another and should have more for an even chance of survival. Whatever the case, Shifty might rather have accepted a merciful end in the desert than the life he now led.

Even the dog seemed to rank higher than Shifty. He never called it "Ole Shiftless" like everyone else. He called it "my dawg," and said it with a touch of pride, the only pride he ever showed in anything. And he often made the supreme sacrifice for his dog, pouring a little beer in his hand for the dog to lap up when the fizzing ceased.

People came and went that evening. Momma Rose's girls were thinning out the ranks by leading them off to other diversions. Lucky and Notches were having a good night, milking a steady stream of dollars from a string of uncomplaining souls who seemed to consider their losses as part of having a good time. What the heck; they won a pot or two before their pile disappeared, didn't they?

Notches was feeling pretty good about the game and it put him in a generous mood. Along about midnight he stood up to stretch his legs and, seeing Shifty sitting in his corner with an empty beer mug, Notches yelled out, "Hey Shifty, here's a bent silver dollar for you!" He rolled the dollar across the floor and it wandered over toward the wall some distance from where Shifty sat.

Shifty watched the progress of the dollar as it rolled across the floor and rocked over onto his knees to crawl after it with his empty beer mug in one hand. "Thanks, Notches," he said. "That's real generous of you. Why, it ain't bent hardly at all!"

That's what Notches was waiting for. He whipped out his gun, drew a quick bead on the dollar, and sent a bullet crashing into it as Shifty reached for it. The dollar spun violently into the wall in a blur of silver. Notches roared with laughter at Shifty's startled pantomime of sudden fear. "Is it bent enough for you now, Shifty?"

Recovering enough to go after the bent dollar, Shifty just mumbled, "A feller shouldn't ought to do that." He picked up the dollar and went straight to the bar.

The poker game was back in session, and the excitement of the moment had faded by the time Shifty headed back to his corner with two beers, one for himself and one for Ole Shiftless. Shifty just couldn't be dollar-wealthy without sharing his good fortune. Now he could share a drink with his dog and wish again that he'd had more to share with his buddy out on the desert.

He set the two mugs down on the floor and settled down beside the dog. Then he saw the gouge in the floor where the bullet had ricocheted before plunging into Old Shiftless's head. Tears sprang to Shifty's eyes as he moved the dog about, seeking any sign of life. Then he stumbled to his feet crying out, "You kilt my dawg! You kilt my dawg!"

Notches was holding a good hand and didn't much appreciate the interruption. "Hesh up!" he barked, without so much as turning his head. "I'll get you another mutt somewheres!" But Shifty came right over beside Notches' chair and took him by the shoulder. Notches slammed his cards down and glared at Shifty, a tactic well calculated to send him cringing back to his corner. Instead, Shifty repeated his bawling accusation as if Notches hadn't understood. "You kilt my dawg!"

"So what?" Notches demanded, spitting the words out and turning his glare up to full venom.

Shifty apparently hadn't considered anything in the nature of reprisal, and he rocked back a step as he considered it a moment before announcing in a soft, almost apologetic tone, "I'm gonna have to kill you, Notches."

Notches doubled up with laughter and everyone else in the saloon joined in. Shifty just stood there and waited for Notches to quit laughing.

Lucky recovered first. "Go on home while you can, Shifty," he said. "You'll feel better tomorrow. We'll get you a new dog."

"No, sir," Shifty insisted. "This here is between me and Notches. He ain't even sorry he kilt my dawg!"

Finally Notches got down to business in a mocking sort of way. "You ain't even got a gun, Shifty," he said. "You gonna borrow one from someone here?"

"I'll have me a gun when I'm ready," Shifty said.

"Good! Glad to hear it," Notches said. "I wuz afraid you wuz gonna throw rocks at me!" That got a good laugh, so Notches pressed on. "Just how soon do you figure to be ready?"

"Day after tomorrow," Shifty said. "I gotta bury my dawg first."

"Right. Don't want no dead dog stinking up the town, do we? Well now, I don't hardly never get up early in the morning lessen it's for something important, so why don't we wait till noon for our shoot-out?"

"Noon's fine," Shifty said.

"Okay. Noon, day after tomorrow, right out front in the street."

Shifty nodded, picked up his dog like a sleeping child, and started for the door. "Hey Shifty! When you get a box for that dog, don't forget to order one for yourself!" someone called after him.

The story was all over town and the surrounding camps before noon the next day. The funeral of Ole Shiftless was better attended than a great many others the town had known. Reverend John had balked at burying Ole Shiftless in the regular cemetery with all the other folks, but he had agreed to burial just outside the cemetery boundary. That suited Shifty just fine since there was no boundary marker and only the surveyors would see the difference.

Those who came to the funeral mostly came to be in on the joke, but they found more than they had expected. Shifty's grief and tears washed out the joke. Most everyone there was reminded of somebody they had lost. Miners with oak-bark calluses on their hands and barbed-wire stubble on leather cheeks stood quietly with tears running down those cheeks while Reverend John delivered the eulogy. Shifty, standing there in his worn clothes, a bit shorter than average and looking older than his years, rose enormously in the eyes of the town that day. He was sober and standing straight. When people tried to talk him out of the shoot-out with Notches, he stood fast; he was a man who had been pushed too far.

After the funeral George Gatlin passed a hat and collected enough money to buy a whopping good dinner at The Dutchman's for Shifty. George took the money over to Shifty's shack right away and called him out.

Shifty opened the door and stood there, squinting in the sunlight.

"Come on down to The Dutchman's," George invited. "Folks want to buy you a first-class dinner."

"Cain't," Shifty said. "I got work to do."

"The work'll still be there when you get back," George insisted, "and you've gotta have something to eat."

"Come on in and take a look at what I'm doing," Shifty invited with an urgent wave of his hand.

George went in and watched while Shifty buckled on a gun belt. "It's gonna have two holsters," Shifty said, "but I gotta finish the second gun and holster."

"What kind of gun is that?" George asked.

"Shotgun," Shifty said. "Double-barreled. I sawed off the barrels and carved the stock into a pistol grip. Sure takes a big holster, don't it?"

"That thing will bust your hand, wrist, and elbow if you ever fire it!"

"Don't matter," Shifty said. "I only gotta fire it the once. Notches is gonna gun me down tomorrow and that don't matter either. But Notches ain't gonna walk away from it neither, and that's what matters."

"Supposing I bring your dinner up here for you?" George asked.

"I'd be much obliged, George. That's real neighborly of you."

"Anything special you'd like?"

"You know me, I'll eat anything!" Shifty said, then had a second thought and added, "Unless you got some more of that venison you helped Frypan cook up last fall. Now that was something! Miss Hoffman, she give me a platter of that. Lordy, I'd like to give old Saint Pete a platter of that at the Pearly Gates! There ain't no way he'd turn me away."

"Reckon we're all out of that," George said, "but I'll do the best I can."

George trotted back to The Dutchman's, bursting with the news of Shifty's artillery. Folks from clear out in Laramie and over to Dodge City would be wishing they could have seen this shoot-out.

Lucky Martin was the only sourpuss in the crowd at The Dutchman's. "Now hold on just a damn minute!" he protested.

"What kind of fair fight is that? These things is done with six-guns, not shotguns!"

"Don't know as I've ever heard of any rules on the guns," Sheriff Jones said. "Anything that'll draw from a holster ought to be fair enough. Notches can use the same kind of guns as Shifty if he wants to. When it comes right down to fair, Notches has drawn on more than his share of men that didn't have a Chinaman's chance against him."

Lucky got a couple of beers and eased into a chair next to Notches at the Thirsty Saloon. "Have a beer," he said, sliding one over to Notches.

"You buying?" Notches asked.

"Yep," Lucky answered, and took a slow sip before getting to the point.

"You know how you put a notch in your gun butt after every shoot-out?" Lucky asked.

"Yeah, what about it?" Notches asked.

"Well, I'm not so sure you're gonna do that for Shifty."

Notches grinned from ear to ear. "The little yellow-bellied bastard left town?"

"No. He's busy getting his guns ready."

"Gonna use two guns, eh? Hell, he oughta save the expense. He couldn't hit me with a dozen guns no more'n he could with one."

"He's gonna use two double-barreled shotguns cut down like pistols."

Notches' face screwed up into an awful grimace. "Gawd!" he said. "Them things'll bust his wrists something awful!"

"Might even hurt you some," Lucky said.

"Yeah," Notches agreed with a thoughtful frown. "They might if he gets 'em out afore I cut him down. Reckon I ought to send him over a couple bottles of whiskey to slow him down?"

"He ain't drinking," Lucky said.

"Damn! All for a no-account dog. If I'da blowed his right hand off he'da called it square for a bottle of red-eye! Now, where's the sense in that?"

"Can't say," Lucky admitted.

"What would you do in my shoes?"

"I might tell folks I don't want to hurt poor old Shifty. Just saddle up, tell folks I'd be back in thirty days' time at noon to settle up with Shifty if he was still feeling foolish. Just ride out and figure Shifty to go back to his old ways before I got back. That's what I might do."

Notches took a long, thoughtful sip of his beer. "Naw," he said finally. "Folks wouldn't let it lay. I betcha ever'body in town has got bets on the shoot-out already. Ain't that so?"

"Just about," Lucky agreed.

"How are they betting?" Notches asked with an eager grin. "You remember that shoot-out when they was giving twenty-to-one odds against the other feller ever getting his gun out? What the hell was that damn fool's name anyhow? I never can remember it."

"Philpot. You ought to remember that."

"Oh, yeah," Notches agreed with a chuckle. "He was the one what got mad when I asked him what kind of pot he filled!"

"It didn't cool him off any when you started telling him what he could fill pots with, either."

"Yeah," Notches said, "I ought to remember that name. I wonder if his momma ever thought his name would get him kilt?"

Lucky didn't answer that. He just sipped his beer and rocked his chair back on two legs, waiting for Notches to get back on the subject of current interest.

"So how's the betting? What are the odds?" Notches finally asked.

"Well, Momma Rose's girls were betting ten to one that you'd kill Shifty if he didn't back out. But that was before they heard about Shifty's guns."

"What then?"

"Except for Junie May, they all wanted to change their bets, but nobody would let 'em."

Notches' face fell flat. "Well, leastways Junie May stuck by me!"

"Naw, she was betting on Shifty from the start."

"She was!" Notches yelped. "Without knowing nothing about the guns and all?"

"Yeah," Lucky shrugged. "Some kind of female notion, I guess."

"How much have you got riding on me?" Notches asked.

"Nothing yet," Lucky answered.

"Why the hell not?" Notches roared. "You don't think a two-legged *nothing* like Shifty can take *me*, do you? Supposing I want to bet on me to win. What odds do I get?"

"Even money."

"Even! Does this damn fool town think Shifty's as likely to get me as the other way around?"

"Yep. Most are thinking that Reverend John is right."

"About what?"

"Well, he's asked Joe Turner to build *two* pine boxes for to-morrow."

"Two, huh?" Notches reflected. "Don't nobody remember that I'm a lot faster'n Shifty?"

"There's a couple of other things that I ain't mentioned yet," Lucky said in the tone of one who's about to break some bad news gently.

Notches gritted his teeth and narrowed his eyes. He didn't really want to hear anything worse than what he had been hearing.

"For one thing," Lucky said, "Shifty's holsters are pivoted and he's sawed the trigger guards off his guns. When he slams his hands down on the gun butts, the barrels come level and all he has to do is squeeze the triggers. He doesn't have to draw."

Notches could feel himself go pale and clammy. "That don't sound legal."

"I argued about that," Lucky said, "but nobody else seemed to care."

The two of them sat and sipped their beer awhile longer. Notches tried to outwait Lucky, but he couldn't stand the suspense. "You said there was a couple of things you hadn't mentioned. Did you spill it all yet, or is there more?"

"Only that Shifty might be able to fire after he's dead," Lucky said.

Notches squinted at Lucky. "You don't usually talk stupid," he said, with an accusing edge on his voice, "but I guess there's a first time for everything, ain't there?"

"Tain't me that says it," Lucky protested with that hopeless gesture of palms upward. "It's Doc Crane. He said that Shifty's so determined to get you that his hands might still be able to fire those guns for a second or so after you'd blow his head off!"

"You don't believe that, do you?" Notches said, spitting in disgust.

"Doc says it happens. Kind of like a chicken running around with its head chopped off. You whack off its head and turn it loose and it runs because that's the last order the legs got from the head."

"Chickens is something different," Notches said.

"Doc says that dead people who clutched at something in their dying moment sometimes keep such a grip on that thing that you've got to pry their fingers loose. He really thinks that you could get shot by a dead man!"

"So far, you've told me that Shifty has four cannon barrels to fire at me, that he don't hardly got to draw, and that he can go on firing after I kill him! You got any more good news, or is that the whole load?"

"That's all of it," Lucky said.

"Well, you was right not to bet right off," Notches said. "I expect you'll get better odds by and by." Notches tried to force a laugh, but it fell sort of flat. So he finished his beer and called for another round.

"Here you are, gents," Jason said, delivering two full mugs of beer to the table. "Anything else I can get you?"

"Not just now, Jace," Notches said, "but maybe you could tell me how you're betting on the shoot-out tomorrow?"

"I never bet on those things, Notches," Jason said. "It's sort of like wishing bad luck on somebody. Tell you what I've been thinking about tomorrow, though."

"What's that?" Notches asked.

"Well," Jason said, not sure what reaction his idea might bring, "you're getting to be a famous man, Notches. No matter what happens tomorrow, you'll be more famous."

"Yeah. I reckon that's so."

"I've been thinking that people shouldn't forget a man like you. Like, supposing you ran into some bad luck tomorrow; there ought to be a fitting memorial."

"Uh huh," Notches agreed somberly.

"If you say so, what I'd like to do is have your gun mounted in a polished walnut frame with a glass front and hang it over the bar, and we'd have your name on it and a sign saying how many notches was in the gun butt and all."

Notches thought about it, then said, "Yeah, that's what ought to be done, unless maybe you want the gun, Lucky?"

"Naw," Lucky said, "Jason's got the right idea there."

"Then you'll do that for me, Jace?" Notches agreed. "You'll put my gun in that fancy case?"

"Yes, sir! I'd be proud to do that for you, Notches," Jason said and went back to the bar thinking he might even do something more for Notches, seeing as how he was getting that gun for free. For a moment, Jason was about to tell Notches that his drinks were on the house until tomorrow, but he thought of several ways that could backfire and he didn't do it. That's what makes a successful man; doing and not doing, the one being just as important as the other.

Reverend John entered the saloon a short time later and went straight to Notches' table. "May I sit a spell with you?" he asked.

"It's a free country," Notches grumped. The reverend drew up a chair.

"I don't hardly never see you in here," Notches said, then added, "That's one of the things I like about this place. Speak your piece."

The reverend nodded. "Notches, I want you to know that the church is always open to you. The Lord is very forgiving, and if you feel a need to make your peace with Him, you'll find Him waiting to receive you."

"Damn you!" Notches exploded, jumping to his feet. "I'm not ready for that damned pine box you're getting built for me, and I don't hanker to hear any of your mush-mouthed ravings! Now you just scoot your tail on out of here afore I commence the shoot-out a mite early."

The reverend grabbed his hat and ran. There was a wild look in Notches' eye that wasn't to be tested.

"The buzzards don't always get what they're circling for," Lucky said. "I still think I'd just ride out for a while and let Shifty get back to his old ways."

"You ain't me!" Notches snapped. "You just tell folks for me that there ain't gonna be but one pine box buried tomorrow, and Shifty's gonna be in it."

"I'll do that," Lucky said. "And, what's more, I'll bet on it!"

That was what Notches most wanted to hear. Lucky was betting on him to win!

It was a high point, though, meaning that everything went downhill from there. True, Lucky was betting on Notches to win, but he was naming odds that were too high to attract many gamblers. He was also making fancy bets that didn't depend on Notches getting out alive.

Notches sat and sulked and drank. He could afford to get drunk this night. Nobody in the whole world was gonna pick a fight with him. They all wanted to see what Shifty was going to do to him tomorrow. It was all Lucky could do to help him stagger back to their cabin that night.

Late the next morning, Notches awoke with a terrible hangover. He hauled his boots on, advising Lucky that he was headed for the Thirsty Saloon.

As he approached the saloon, he heard laughter inside as if a party were going on. It stopped the moment he stepped inside. He stood there a moment, casting a baleful eye over the crowd. It was so quiet he could hear his watch ticking. Bastards! Every one of 'em whooping it up. Celebrating the shoot-out in advance! Notches walked to the bar with each step sounding like a drumbeat in the silence.

"What'll it be, Notches?" Jason asked.

"Whiskey! Make it double."

Jason complied promptly, and Notches asked, "You want to be paid now, or will this afternoon be okay?"

"This afternoon will be fine, Notches," Jason answered. His momma hadn't raised any idiot sons!

Notches downed the whiskey and took another look around the room, which was still death-quiet. "Some folks think I won't be here this afternoon, Jason, and that seems to tickle their funny-bone. But I'm getting a line on who all them folks is and I'm gonna set 'em straight this afternoon. You know what I mean?"

"Yes sir, Notches, I know what you mean," Jason answered. "And I know that you're a man of your word."

Customers finished their drinks and got out of there. Notches watched them go with an angry face that hid his satisfaction at having sent them scurrying like a flock of addled chickens. Notches and Jason had the place to themselves.

"Gimme another double," Notches ordered.

"Sure thing," Jason said, pouring in something close to record time. "Hope it steadies your aim."

"Don't seem like it much matters from what they say about Shifty and them guns of his," Notches answered flatly before downing his drink.

"Aw, you don't believe that," Jason said. "Hell, not five minutes ago you gave that crowd in here the message on what they could expect from you this afternoon!"

"That bunch ain't no friends of mine like you are, Jace," Notches said. "I can tell you the truth, and the truth is I think my luck has done run out!"

"It ain't like you to give up like that," Jason said.

"It ain't a matter of givin' up. That damned fool Shifty has set it up to kill me no matter what I do or what happens to him. I think he's gonna do it. If you think otherwise, you look me right straight in the eye while you say so!"

Jason looked Notches right straight in the eye, then lowered his eyes and said, "Truth is, Notches, you ain't got much of a chance."

"Yeah," Notches agreed. "That's what I thought."

"Mighty brave of you, facing up to it the way you are," Jason said. "There ain't anybody else in town that could take it any better."

"What would you do if you was me?" Notches asked. "Would you cut and run?"

"No. A man can't do that. But I reckon I'd of camped on Shifty's doorstep to talk him out of it."

"Maybe you could do that," Notches said, "but I couldn't. I got a different kind of reputation to pertect."

"That's the way of it, clear back to Socrates' time," Jason said. "Thousands of years ago he refused to obey some fool law he didn't agree with, and a court sentenced him to die by drinking poison."

"He drunk it?"

"Every drop. He could have got out of it by knuckling under, and the people who sentenced him thought he would, but he said the order was according to the laws of his country, and he believed in obeying just laws. He drank the poison."

Notches chuckled. "Sort of made fools of the people what gave the order, didn't he?"

"Sometimes a feller with all the cards stacked against him can still make his point," Jason agreed.

Notches frowned. "I wonder if there ain't some way I could hoo-raw that bunch outside?"

"That would be something, wouldn't it?"

"You got any ideas?" Notches asked.

"Nothing you'd want to try," Jason said.

"Lemme hear it. I don't gotta do it if I don't want to."

"Well, you've heard of how Christ died on the cross?"

"He was the fella that was Baby Jesus at Christmastime, wasn't he?" Notches asked.

"I reckon you know your Bible, all right!" Jason said.

"I know a thing or two that ain't generally knowed around here."

Jason continued, "There was Christ, nailed to the cross and He was God's son. He could of brought down all kinds of fire and brimstone all over those people who treated Him so miserably. But what does He do instead? He looks up to God and says, 'Father, forgive them, for they know not what they do!' "

Notches was awed. "I don't think I could do nothing like that!"

"You could in a sort of a way," Jason said. "If you're sure that Shifty is going to shoot you no matter what you do, you could walk out there with an empty gun, and after it's all over and people see that your gun wasn't even loaded, it'd be like you were saying, 'Shifty, you damned fool, you didn't know what you were doing, but I forgive you.' "

Notches thought it over very carefully. "Gimme another double," he said. Jason poured and left the bottle on the bar.

"If I did that—went out there with an empty gun—Shifty wouldn't never know if he outdrawed me or not, would he?" Notches asked.

"Nobody would," Jason answered.

"And folks would do a whole lot of fussing and fighting over that blood money they been betting against me, wouldn't they?"

"I reckon so. There ain't nobody going to agree on how to settle those bets."

"I'm gonna do it!" Notches said, and gulped another drink.

"You're really something, Notches!" Jason said. "I'm gonna see to it that a stone monument is carved for you. Nobody is ever going to forget you or what you did this day."

"You will?" Notches asked, his eyes just short of tears.

"Let's shake on it," Jason said, extending his hand. Notches took Jason's hand in both of his and shook it as warmly as ever a hand was shaken.

"It's time, ain't it?" Notches said.

"Let them wait. There's no hurry."

"I don't give a damn how long *they* wait," Notches said, "but for me the doing is easier than the waiting." Notches took out his gun, dumped the bullets onto the bar, and put the gun back in its holster. "We're gonna give 'em one hell of a surprise, ain't we?" he asked.

"Them and the whole country," Jason answered.

Out on the porch, Notches hitched up his gun belt and felt for the butt of his six-shooter, getting it in place, just so. It felt just as reassuring empty as if it were loaded.

Lucky Martin came across the porch and whispered, "I'll get

off to the right of Shifty and fire into the air when you're about to draw. You hit him fast while he's distracted!''

"You just stay the hell out of this!'' Notches growled. "I got my own way to handle this, and I ain't gonna thank you if you mess it up!''

Lucky backed off. "Anything you say, Notches,'' he said. "Just wanted to help.''

Then Notches walked straight out to the center of the street and turned right to face Shifty, standing in the bright sunlight down at the far end. Notches grinned and wondered how long Shifty had been standing there. Long enough to make his feet ache and his eyes burn from squinting, he hoped. Miserable little man. He had probably begun to think he'd won on a bluff—that nobody would dare face him.

Hell! With all that talk of sawed-off shotguns, maybe there hadn't been enough thought about the sawed-off Nothing holding those shotguns! Maybe he'd be too scared stiff to make his play. Maybe if a feller came down on him looking real murderous-mean and whipped out an empty six-gun and shouted, "Bang! Bang!'', Shifty would just drop dead with fright.

The more he thought of it, the more certain Notches was that it would go just exactly that way. The evil grin spread clear across his face and he began a slow, deliberate walk toward Shifty. Shifty hesitated, then started to move toward Notches with steps as short and cautious as he could manage.

They got to be fifty feet apart and the crowd tensed for the explosion. Forty feet and the tension was unbearable, and why in God's name was Notches grinning so? Thirty feet, then twenty feet! The crowd was paralyzed! Then fifteen feet! Notches' hand darted for his gun! It cleared the holster and leveled just as Shifty's guns blew a tremendous hole in the silence.

Some wondered at the surprised look on Notches' face and puzzled over whatever he could have been thinking, but most were so pleased at Shifty's survival they were willing to forget Notches as quick as he hit the ground.

Jason had run out the back door of his saloon, come in between the buildings, and then darted out to Notches about as soon as the echoes died. He picked up Notches' gun and went through the motions of emptying its cylinder into the hand that held the six bullets Notches had left on the bar. "Never fired a shot!" he announced, holding the bullets out for inspection.

As Jason confided to Doc Crane some years afterward, it was a kindness to Shifty, not a spite to Notches. Besides, if folks knew about Notches' empty gun and got to quarreling over whether the bets ought to be paid or not, it just wouldn't be a healthy thing for the town.

Doc Crane spent little time on Notches. The damage was such that death was certain. Shifty was something else. Both hands were badly sprained and torn where the kick of the guns had done the inevitable.

The crowd heisted Shifty onto their shoulders and carried him off to the Thirsty Saloon, where Jason was back in business with Notches' gun lying on the liquor shelf, awaiting the promised walnut case and plaque. They plunked Shifty down in the chair that used to be reserved for Notches.

Doc Crane had no choice but to do his doctoring there in the saloon, stitching together some of the gashes left by the shotgun hammers and wrapping both hands nice and neat.

And now that the whole world wanted to buy Shifty a drink, the only drink he wanted was sarsaparilla. He hoisted his first sarsaparilla toast "To my dawg!" and the party went roaring right along.

Reverend John was sitting quietly on the other side of Shifty, opposite Doc, when Doc said, "Where in the world did you ever get the courage to go through with that, Shifty?"

"Well," Shifty laughed, "I prayed a lot!"

"Amen!" Reverend John shouted, leaping to his feet. "Did all of you hear what Mr. Shifty just said? And do you remember how Notches chased me from this very table when I offered him the Lord's peace? There's a lesson in this for all of us. Mr. Shifty turned to the Lord in prayer, and the Lord answered him! Notches scorned the Lord and sorely repents at this very moment!"

Reverend John was set to cut loose on that topic for a spell, but when he paused to catch his breath, Joe Turner interrupted.

"Reverend," he said, "I got a problem getting Notches into that pine box. Problem is he keeps groaning and flopping; he ain't dead yet!"

"Ain't dead yet!" a dozen voices echoed.

Jason turned ghostly white and gulped a shot of whiskey, both being things he hardly ever did. Doc snapped his bag shut, grabbed Joe by the arm, and hustled to the door with George Gatlin right behind him. "Get him over to my office right away!" Doc ordered. "I'll wash up and be ready for him."

As soon as Notches was hauled into Doc's office, George began ripping away clothes while Doc swabbed off blood, searching for the worst of the damage. A few minutes more and his search was done. "Just one big slug, but it's liable to be one too many. It's got to be setting right next to his heart."

"Maybe we ought to let that one alone?" George asked.

"It's got to come out sooner or later," Doc said. "Rinse those long, narrow forceps in alcohol and hand 'em over."

Moments later, Doc was cautiously probing for the slug, grunting and muttering softly to himself as the forceps sank deep into the hole. "There it is. Now, if I can just get a grip on it—" A few more grunts and grimaces, and Doc had worked his forceps back out of the hole with the slug held fast in their grasp. It was followed by an awful rush of blood. Doc hustled to stop it, but it stopped when Notches' heart stopped.

"He's gone," Doc said simply. "We lost that one."

"You did what you could," George said. "Nothing but a miracle could have saved him."

"I'll clean things up," Doc said. "Let the folks outside know how it went."

George went out to the waiting room and passed the word. Everyone traipsed back to the saloon to resume the celebration. Everyone but Doc.

As for Shifty, he wound up a double hero as husband to Junie May. The whole town turned out for the wedding. Reverend John was happy. Momma Rose was happy. Junie May was happy. Shifty was happy. And the boys passed a very generous and grateful hat for their double hero.

CHAPTER 9

THE TRIAL OF DOCTOR CRANE

A couple of months after the shoot-out between Notches and Shifty, there came one of those absolutely perfect days when a man ought to be able to do anything he had a mind to do. Doc saw that it was that kind of day early in the morning and decided to do his duty. He had a duty to keep that promise he'd made to George Gatlin the day he and George and Sam Ibsen were on the way back to Thirsty from the wedding between Downwind and Betty Lee. He'd promised to go fishing with George, and now it was his duty to keep that promise.

George being agreeable, they were soon out on the South Fork trying to coax a few fish out of the water. It went reasonably well, but by mid-afternoon the fish had quit biting and the fishermen had settled on the grassy bank of a large pool, their lines rigged with floats to keep up the pretense of fishing.

Doc had always believed that when a person runs out of things to say, he ought to quit talking. Though he always believed that, he didn't always practice it and was about to pay the price. Doc and George had about exhausted all the possibilities of small talk. It would have been a good time to take a nap, and Doc was on the brink of doing just that when George asked, "You ain't never killed anybody, have you, Doc?" That was how George asked it. More like a statement than a question. If he'd asked it differently, like, "Have you ever killed anyone?", Doc would have given him a simple no, but now he couldn't decline the challenge.

"I might have," Doc answered.

"Wouldn't you know?"

"No. Not for sure."

"How did it happen then?"

"You tell me. You were there."

George thought it over a long time. It was a puzzle. "Beats me. When was it?"

"More like who," Doc said. "It was Notches."

"Notches! You didn't kill him; he got killed in that shoot-out with Shifty!"

"He got shot in that shoot-out with Shifty," Doc corrected. "He might be alive today if he'd had a decent doctor."

"You been chewing on loco weed?" George asked. "Shifty gunned that man down with a pair of cannons. Notches had a cannonball right next to his heart. Nobody could of saved him!"

"Least of all, a doctor that left him lying in the dirt whilst he fiddled around bandaging the other man's hand," Doc said.

"That just shows how near dead Notches was, not that you killed him. You did as much as any man could have!"

"Did I?" Doc asked. "You had sense enough to ask if we ought not leave that bullet alone awhile. I grabbed for that bullet right off, didn't I?"

"Yes, you did. That's what any doctor would've done."

"There's times when a man who knows his job knows not to do it the usual way. The way that bullet sat called for holding off and thinking things out. Given more time, maybe I'd have been able to handle the bleeding better, maybe Notches would've been a little stronger, and, most likely, I'd have remembered that burr on my forceps."

"What burr?"

"There was a sharp little spur down near the tip of the forceps I pulled the bullet out with. Must've gotten banged against something in my travels. I'd noticed it a few days before, but never thought of it again until after Notches died."

"You think the burr made a difference?"

"Not sure. That's what bothers me. Don't you see, I'm a first-rate doctor, I know that! Yet, when it came time to help Notches, I bungled. The doctor that worked on Notches was not a good doctor. Maybe I killed the man!"

"Forget it," George said. "Hell, even if you had killed

Notches, you'd just have been saving the extra people that bastard would've gunned down if he'd lived!''

"It ain't my place nor any doctor's place to judge that," Doc said. "My duty and every doctor's duty is to do the best possible for the injured party."

That was the gist of it. Nothing more was said of it till they were headed home and Doc asked George not to speak of it to anyone else. "It ain't the sort of thing I'd have told just anyone," Doc said. "You tell me you hope to be a doctor someday, George. I want you to know about this sort of thing. You won't find it in schoolbooks."

George thanked him and promised not to breathe a word of it. It was a sincere promise; George honestly thought he could keep his mouth shut when it was important to do so. Don't we all?

Anyway, he almost kept the promise. He only told Cindy. There had been a quiet moment when he felt like he had to say something interesting. Cindy promised to keep it quiet, and she quietly told it to a few dozen other people. After that, she quit talking about it because it seemed as if everybody had already heard of it.

Doc might have been better tuned-in to what was going on if he hadn't been busy with a patient. The stage had picked up a man in the desert and dropped him on Doc's doorstep. The fellow had a broken arm, a bad case of dehydration, and a sunburn like a blowtorch had made it. Doc stayed close to him the better part of three days to get him back to something near normal.

Being busy, Doc didn't pay much attention to what else was going on in town. People wanted to believe that Doc had done Notches in; it made sense. Doc hated the cruel bullying and killing Notches stood for. Saving a murderous bastard like Notches wasn't much different than turning a mad dog loose. For most people, it was comforting to know that Doc, in spite of all his book learning, still had some native common sense.

Lucky Martin must have been one of the last in town to hear of it. The story Lucky heard said that Doc knew Notches was still alive after the shoot-out and had just walked off and left him lying in the dust. Also, the version Lucky heard had Doc whacking sharp spurs into his forceps and wriggling them around next to Notches' heart while he poked at the bullet.

Lucky was filled with a cold anger and determined that Doc would pay. If it had been a hot anger, he might have gone after Doc with a gun. But a cold anger was a thinking anger, and Lucky got to thinking that Doc would be killed several times over if he were to die by legal hanging. Of all the ways a man might die, there would probably be no way more repulsive to Doc than to die by public hanging. Lucky went to Sheriff Jones and insisted that Doc be arrested for the murder of Notches.

Sheriff Jones had heard the story going around town. He drummed his fingers on his desk and glared at Lucky.

"You gotta arrest that man, Sheriff. That's the law! I'm swearing out a complaint and you gotta arrest him."

"I'll arrest him," Sheriff Jones answered in a flat, low voice. "Then I'll release him till the trial comes up. It's legal. And this town needs that man. He does more good every day than Notches did in his whole damned life!"

Doc was peeved something awful when Sheriff Jones told him what folks were saying about him killing Notches. Part of the peeve was over George spilling the beans, but mostly it was the way the story had been twisted that upset him. The arrest didn't bother him much. It seemed like a joke.

When the sheriff left, Doc was still fuming. "What you need is a good lawyer," his patient said when Doc paused to catch his breath.

"Lawyer!" Doc snorted. "Folks in this town must know blamed good and well I wouldn't kill Notches nor anybody else the way that story has it."

"Just the same, I'll stick around awhile," the patient said. "It might be the only way I can pay you."

"You're a lawyer, Mr. Redford?"

"My father was, and I have been. I'm good at it, but always had this fool notion in my mind that I ought to be something else. When do you suppose this thing will come to a trial if it does?"

"The sheriff will let us know," Doc said. "The circuit court doesn't come up this way unless the sheriff sends 'em a note saying there's some business to attend to. Between sending the note and getting an answer, it might be a week before we know."

"The sheriff said Lucky Martin is pushing this thing. Who is Lucky Martin?"

Doc filled Mr. Redford in on the whole story of Notches and Lucky. "Not much chance this Lucky will drop the whole thing then?" Mr. Redford concluded.

"Naw," Doc said. "That ain't his style. Look here, now, you're telling me this murder charge is serious, aren't you?"

"Oh, yes," Mr. Redford answered, nodding gravely.

"Well, don't that beat all," Doc said, shaking his head in the final realization that he actually was being charged with murder.

The way Mr. Redford explained his approach to Doc, there were at least three sets of facts to be considered in a jury trial. One set concerned the legal charges, testimony, and such-like. The second set concerned the nature of the community and the jury. He said he'd come to the third set of facts later.

Sheriff Jones stopped by in the third week of July to announce that Judge Palmer would arrive in Thirsty on the tenth of August to commence the trial of Doctor Edward E. Crane for the murder of the man known as Notches. Mr. Redford's reaction to this news was a puzzle and a worry to Doc. The lawyer just rented himself a horse, said he'd be back in time for the trial, and rode off.

It was a bad time for Doc. Folks would assure him that the trial was nothing and they were as sure as anything that he'd be found innocent. Then, in the next breath, they'd thank him for doing away with Notches! And George Gatlin stopped by nearly every day to apologize again for spilling the beans. Doc managed to keep his exasperation in check and assured George that he himself was the primary culprit, the supreme ass who had first said what should not have been said. George would go away feeling a little better, but it did nothing at all for Doc's spirits. Worst of all was the fear that Mr. Redford might not come back. Doc felt a great need for the sort of comfort and solace that Miss Hoffman might provide if he could bring himself to forgive and trust her once again. But he couldn't do that just for expediency. God, what a mess he was in!

Mr. Redford rode in on the morning of August ninth, no explanation of where he'd been or why. Within a few hours he'd visited the livery stable, the barber, The Dutchman's, and the Thirsty Saloon. Then, having caught up on the local news, he dropped in on Doc Crane.

Doc looked him over a moment, then said, "Well, sir, now I know how a man with a busted leg feels when the doctor finally shows up!"

"You knew I'd be back."

"There's knowing and there's feeling," Doc said. "Maybe I knew you'd come back, but I didn't feel so damn sure of it, sort of like the man with the busted leg knowing the doctor will come but feeling he might come too late."

"Have no fear, my friend," Mr. Redford assured him, "I have been constantly at work on your case, gathering information on the third set of facts."

"You going to let me in on that third set of facts, or is it some mystical lawyer's rite?"

"Has this affair taught you to keep a secret?"

"I reckon it has."

"Then you'll keep it quiet if I tell you what the third set of facts is?"

"Absolutely!"

"I'm going to tell you since, in my professional opinion, your well-being requires that I restore your confidence in my wisdom as applied to your defense. The third set of facts concerns the judge in your case. I have searched out his likes, dislikes, and weaknesses. I discovered all there was to know about Judge Palmer."

"I suppose that's useful information," Doc agreed.

"Absolutely vital!" Mr. Redford said. "It turns out that Judge Palmer is the most unpredictable, cantankerous, spiteful old fool in this circuit or any other."

"Good Lord!" Doc said. "What can we do?"

"Already done, Doc! Judge Palmer won't be coming. You'll have Judge Fuller."

"How did that happen?"

"Beats me, I don't know a thing about it! And, if you know what's good for you, you'll be as surprised as me when Judge Fuller gets off that stage tomorrow."

"Oh, it's that way, is it?"

"Yep! That's the way it is! But we'll get on fine with Judge Fuller."

"Sounds underhanded, deceitful, dishonest, and not very nice," Doc said.

"Judge Palmer is a hanging judge."

"You did right, Mr. Redford, absolutely right!"

When the stage rolled into Thirsty the next day, Sheriff Jones greeted the well-dressed dude who climbed down. He was close to six feet tall, sported a well-clipped Van Dyke beard, and there wasn't a speck of dust or wrinkle on his clothes.

"Judge Palmer, welcome to Thirsty!" Sheriff Jones said, holding out his hand.

"Judge Palmer won't be coming. I'm Judge Fuller," the dude said, accepting the handshake a bit coldly. "You have no newspaper in Thirsty, I take it?"

"No, sir, no newspaper. How did you know that?"

"You would hardly mistake me for anyone else if you had any news of the rest of the country."

Mr. Redford watched the arrival, then came over to introduce himself. "Judge Fuller, this is indeed a pleasure!" he said, shaking hands.

"You know me?" the judge asked, obviously pleased.

"Of course. I make it a point to study your more important cases. Very informative!"

"You are a member of the legal profession, then?"

"Indeed, yes, Your Honor. Thaddeus Redford, Attorney at Law. I represent Doctor Edward E. Crane, who will be appearing before you as the defendant."

"I see," Judge Fuller said, frowning. "We did not expect the doctor would have found a lawyer in such an area. These two men," the judge said, waving toward two riders who had followed the stage, "have come along expecting that one would be prosecutor and the other would represent the defendant. Perhaps you would prefer to be a philosophical observer in this case, Mr. Redford?"

"Well, sir, the doctor and I are old friends, and I have such deep faith in Doctor Crane's innocence that I cannot stand idly by."

"I see." Judge Fuller sighed. "And you have credentials to prove that you are qualified to practice law in this district?"

"Most of my papers were lost in an incident on the desert a short time ago," Mr. Redford explained. "Came near to losing my life with them."

"I'm afraid such credentials are quite necessary, Mr. Redford," the judge said, obviously relieved to see an insurmountable obstacle drift into Mr. Redford's path.

"Suppose I telegraph Governor Tyler for confirmation?" Mr. Redford suggested. "He'll be happy to vouch for me."

"Governor Tyler?" the judge asked, turning sharply toward Mr. Redford at the mention of the name. "You know him?"

"An uncle on my mother's side," Mr. Redford said casually.

"Indeed? A great man, your uncle. And your cousin Ann, how is she?"

"Little Peachy?" Mr. Redford asked, using a nickname known to very few. "Quite well now. Her arm has healed and she's riding again. A very spirited girl."

"Glad to hear it! Well, sir, we shall be pleased to have you represent the defendant here. You will be a credit to your uncle, I'm sure!"

"Do telegraph Uncle Charles," Mr. Redford advised. "He'll set your mind at ease on my qualifications."

"No, quite unnecessary! I wouldn't think of it," Judge Fuller assured him.

At that point one of the lawyers who had followed the stage burst in upon the judge. "Your Honor, the murderer is loose. The sheriff here hasn't locked him up at all!"

"Most irregular." The judge snorted. "How is it that your client is free, Mr. Redford?"

"He's the only doctor these good people have," Mr. Redford explained. "And there isn't a man in town that would expect him to run off."

"Quite irregular," the judge repeated, "but we shall leave it as it is. He's your responsibility, Mr. Redford."

Doc Crane was delighted when he heard what had transpired between Judge Fuller and Mr. Redford. "I sure wouldn't want a circuit lawyer who owed more to the judge than he did to me. Praise the Lord that you're Governor Tyler's nephew!"

"Don't give the Lord all the credit," Mr. Redford said. "I gave Him a lot of help on it!"

Doc paused and fixed a suspicious gaze on Mr. Redford. "You ain't any relation to Governor Tyler at all, are you?" he asked.

"Oh yes," Mr. Redford contradicted. "I'm not all that much of a liar."

"Then I apologize," Doc said.

"Governor Tyler and I both trace our ancestry to Adam and Eve," Mr. Redford continued. "We're related, all right!"

"I swear, you could talk the claws off a grizzly bear if you had a mind to!"

"It's all in knowing your audience," Mr. Redford said with a casual shrug of his shoulders. "Judge Fuller hopes to be Governor Fuller some day. He knows that Governor Tyler doesn't want another term and the job will probably fall to whoever Governor Tyler names."

"You'll get special treatment so long as Judge Fuller doesn't catch you in the lie, and you'll get special treatment if the judge does catch you at it!" Doc said.

"Control, my dear doctor, is not a thing of chance. If Judge Fuller telegraphs the governor, a friend of mine at the capitol will see to it that the reply is entirely harmonious."

"If I did my doctoring the way you do your lawyering—well, there's no way I could."

"Somebody's got to be honest, I guess," Mr. Redford said.

"Eventually, maybe you'll even be honest to yourself about Miss Hoffman."

"Meaning what?" Doc asked, startled that Mr. Redford knew anything about Miss Hoffman.

"Meaning that folks around here say you aren't the sort of person who takes revenge. Yet there you are, sticking pins in Miss Hoffman and pretending you don't know a thing about it."

"I never did no such thing!" Doc protested. "That woman did something awful to me. Had me wishing I was stone-cold dead. If I were a vengeful man, I'd of had her tarred and feathered and run out of town when she came back here. But did I? No siree! Live and let live is my way. She's there and I'm here, and that's the way it is."

"Just sitting there sticking pins in her, aren't you?" Mr. Redford said, grinning.

"Not one mean trick! Not so much as a word, cross or otherwise."

"Just ignoring her, eh?"

"Exactly!"

"You and everybody else. And that's the way it'll stay unless you hang out an olive branch."

"It ain't my doing. If she's having a bad time, it's her own fault."

"You're right, Doctor, absolutely right," Mr. Redford nodded, smiling pleasantly. "You ought to play your cards the same way on broken bones, too. If some damned fool gets a busted arm through their own fault, there's no call for you to do anything about it, is there?"

"It ain't the same thing, and anybody who ain't a lawyer knows it!"

"Think about it, my friend! Somebody's hurting. Think about it." Mr. Redford flashed that pleasant smile again, turned and left.

"Damndest man I ever met," Doc muttered aloud, but he sat down to think about it. And he relived that magnificent, terrible love affair again right through to the back-stabbing end. It was a cruel, bitchy thing she'd done. To hell with her. Let her suffer!

But he sat awhile longer and a little doubt crept in. Was he sticking pins in her? Suppose she was trying to reform? Maybe she deserved a second chance?

Doc churned the thing over in his mind endlessly, alternating between the hard line of the Old Testament and the forgiveness of the New Testament. Finally he muttered, "Revenge—it ain't worth a bucket of warm spit." He got up and rummaged through his bedroom for some clothes in need of laundering.

And there he was, crossing the street in broad daylight, hauling a bundle of laundry over to Miss Hoffman's. Her first customer in weeks, not counting Lucky Martin.

He hesitated a moment in the doorway, then crossed to the counter and jangled the small bell that sat there. Miss Hoffman appeared, sleepy-eyed at first, then startled to see who had rung the bell. She tried to straighten her hair and brush away the wrinkles in her blouse, then stopped self-consciously and said, "You brought laundry?"

"Yes," Doc answered, taking off his hat. "You do laundry?"

"Sure do," she said, forcing a laugh. "I'll have it ready early tomorrow."

"No hurry."

"Regular service," Miss Hoffman insisted. "Any time they aren't ready the next day, there'll be no charge."

"Fine, fine," Doc said, then turned and left. He'd done his Christian duty; he didn't figure on doing any more than that.

"Starch?" she called after him.

"No! Not much call for it hereabouts," he answered, and went on his way, over to Sam Ibsen's for a game of checkers. Sam had most likely seen him trotting down the street with his laundry, but Doc wanted to be sure of it.

But he didn't go back for his laundry the next day. He asked George to fetch it for him as a favor. He didn't want that woman to get the notion that things could ever be as they were. Besides, Doc was feeling nervous and fidgety. Judge Fuller and the lawyers were picking jurors and getting things set up to start the trial the following day. And it didn't help much when Mr. Redford came over for a powwow after the jury selection was done.

"I don't think I'll put you on the stand," Mr. Redford said.

"What!" Doc exclaimed. "Who'd know more about the whole thing than I do?"

"That's irrelevant," Mr. Redford said. "The point is, you're too frank. That other lawyer would have you testifying against yourself."

"If I'm afraid to speak my piece on the stand, most of the folks around here will take it to mean I'm guilty and, like as not, the jury will, too!"

"It's a risk," Mr. Redford admitted, "but someone's been getting the word around town that the prosecuting lawyer is a mean, ambitious scoundrel who'd hang his own grandmother to make his record look good."

"Someone, eh?" Doc asked.

"Yep, someone's been doing that. And I think if folks go in looking for that mean rascal, the prosecutor won't disappoint them. We'll be okay on that score."

"You're one hell of a salesman," Doc admitted. "I suppose anyone who could talk me into taking my laundry over to Miss Hoffman just might be able to turn a jury any way he wanted to."

"That was mighty nice of you, Doc, taking your laundry over there! Other folks are doing the same now. It says a lot about what they think of you."

"It's a small thing. I'm glad you set me right on it," Doc admitted.

"Had to, absolutely had to," Mr. Redford said. "Another day and I'd have had to do my own laundry. I couldn't go over there till you did, you know!"

"Damnation!" Doc exploded. "Is that all you had in mind?"

"A man's got a right to use his talents for small personal things," Mr. Redford insisted. "You lance your own boils, don't you?"

He was one sharp lawyer, all right. Doc held onto that thought as court was convened in Reverend John's church the next day. Surely there wasn't another lawyer like Mr. Redford west of the Mississippi.

The prosecution started out with Jason on the stand, having

him testify to a lot of general stuff about the fatal duel between Notches and Shifty. Doc leaned over to Mr. Redford and whispered, "What do you suppose Jason's so upset about? It ain't like him to sweat so and change colors so much."

"Something's got him worried, all right," Mr. Redford agreed, "but believe you me, if he's your friend, we don't want to touch whatever he's worried about."

The prosecutor had taken Notches' gun and Shifty's two cannons from their display case over the bar at the Thirsty Saloon and was asking Jason to declare whether these were the weapons used in the fatal duel. He was deathly afraid that the prosecutor would produce those cartridges from that same display case and ask if they had been in Notches' gun on that fatal day. And what if the prosecutor asked if they had been in Notches' gun during the shoot-out?

How could he tell the truth about that? So much money had been bet on the shoot-out! The winners would call him a liar, and the losers would want their money back. And Lucky! He'd claim Jason had gotten Notches drunk and sent him out with an empty gun! Jason couldn't tell the truth about those bullets, but he had a real fear of lying under oath. If the dreaded question came and he lied, his tongue might immediately swell up and choke him.

Now the prosecutor reached for the empty shotgun shells that had been in that display case over the bar and asked Jason if they were the very ones that Shifty had blasted Notches with. Jason nodded and waited in horror for the next question. But there was no next question. The prosecutor was too caught up in his own performance to notice Jason's distress.

The prosecutor walked slowly down toward the jury with one of Shifty's cannons in each hand, and it was no mistake that they were leveled at the jury. "Gentlemen of the jury," he intoned, "you are looking at the last thing poor, brave Notches saw in this life. You tell me what chance that heroic man had in this so-called fair fight." Then he waved a careless hand at Mr. Redford and said, "Your witness."

Mr. Redford carefully steered his questions toward other shoot-outs wherein Notches had been the winner. Jason slowly came back to normal and proved to have a good memory for all those hapless victims who had become notches on Notches' gun butt. The prosecutor objected hotly and loudly, but Judge Fuller consistently ruled in favor of the governor's nephew. All told, the jury was reminded that Notches had been a bloody, deadly bully.

The prosecutor called Joe Turner next and played him like an old, mellow, sad violin. "You were out there all alone, trying to do what you could for Mr. Notches?"

"Yessir. Everybody left him there for dead and ran off to the saloon."

"Everybody said he was dead?"

"Yessir."

"Including Doctor Crane?"

"Yessir."

"How did you know he was alive, Joe?" the prosecutor asked, wiping at his eyes as if there were tears there.

"Well, he was a heavy man, Mr. Notches was. I couldn't lift him all alone, so I set the box on its side next to him and tried to roll him inta it. That's when he started moaning and flopping around." Joe choked up and started wiping at his eyes.

The prosecutor ran a hanky across his own face and caught a sideways glance at several teary-eyed jurors. He waited a moment, then pointed a finger at Doc Crane and asked, "Did he believe you when you told him Notches was alive?"

"He asked folks to bring Notches over to his office."

"Didn't even go out there to where Notches lay to see for himself?"

"Nossir."

"Like he knew all along that Notches was alive or maybe just didn't give a damn?"

Mr. Redford objected, Judge Fuller sustained the objection, and the prosecutor turned Joe over to the defense.

"You gave Notches a first-class funeral, did you?" Mr. Redford asked.

"Nossir. Just two dollars' worth. That's all I was paid."

"His friends couldn't raise any more than that?"

"He only had one friend. Two dollars was all he'd go."

"I see. But I've seen a fine stone marker on his grave."

"Oh, Jason put that there later. Payment for Notches' guns, it was."

"Sad way to go," Mr. Redford remarked. "Joe, you've done a lot of undertaking here in Thirsty, haven't you?"

"Yessir."

"Have you ever seen anyone live through being as shot up as Notches was?"

"Nossir."

"When Notches was sending customers to you, he never messed them up that much, did he?"

"Notches generally put 'em down with one shot! He sent 'em to me neat."

"A merciful killer, eh?"

"Merciful!" Joe snorted. "He just didn't want anyone living long enough to shoot back at him!"

The courtroom broke into laughter. The prosecutor objected and was overruled.

"Tell me, Joe," Mr. Redford asked when things had settled down, "What was Doc Crane doing when you got Notches over to his office?"

"Well, he had his table ready and his tools laid out."

"Do you suppose that's why he didn't run out to Notches right away? Maybe he had to get his office ready?"

Joe studied the question awhile, then nodded emphatically. "By thunder, Mr. Redford, that's it! That's what Doc said he was gonna do when he hustled out of the saloon that day—get his office ready."

Then the prosecutor called George Gatlin, and things got a lot more sticky. George squirmed and stalled something fierce, but the prosecutor made him say everything he didn't want to say: that Doc had told him he'd killed Notches. That, after all, was the crux of the case. Doc had accused himself, and how could there be a more reliable witness than that?

Mr. Redford asked only one question. "George, you were there. Do you think Doctor Crane killed Notches?"

"No!" George answered. "Doc's the kind of feller who'd find

some way to blame himself if he couldn't raise Lazarus from the dead. That's all there is to it."

"No further questions," Mr. Redford said and sat down.

"He's on our side," Doc whispered. "Don't you think you could have let him say more?"

"Nope. It's our way of telling the jury we don't think George's testimony amounts to anything."

"Mr. Lucky Martin to the stand," the prosecutor barked.

Lucky Martin, dressed as well as any banker ever was, took the stand and was sworn in. The prosecutor approached him with a toothy grin. Here was the witness that would put Mr. Redford in his place. "Mr. Martin," he began, "you were a good friend of the deceased, Mr. Notches, weren't you?"

"We were the best of friends."

"The defense, in its roundabout way, has insinuated that your friendship might be measured by a two-dollar funeral."

"They have their values, I have mine," Lucky said. "Notches deserved a quiet, respectful funeral, not some painted parade to be attended by a mob of hypocrites!"

"I see." The prosecutor nodded sympathetically, then paced back and forth a bit with head bowed before returning to Lucky. "Mr. Martin, maybe you can help me understand something else. I never knew Mr. Notches, and if I'm to believe the insinuations of the defense, he must have been a terrible man. How could a fine gentleman like yourself be his friend?"

"Folks generally didn't understand what Notches was trying to do," Lucky said. "Those people he faced over a gun barrel were people the sheriff should have faced and didn't. Troublemakers! This town would have been crawling with that troublemaking trash if Notches hadn't served notice that he'd be here waiting for 'em."

"I see, I see." The prosecutor nodded. "Notches gave them fair warning, and those that didn't heed it paid the price?"

"Exactly. Notches kept this town peaceable."

"And the people here didn't understand or appreciate what he was doing for them?"

"No, sir. Not in the least! They thought he enjoyed killing, but it just wasn't so."

"Do you suppose the people would have tried harder to save Notches when he lay bleeding in the street if they'd understood him better?"

"They wouldn't have let Doc Crane pretend poor Notches was dead without really looking at him."

"Objection!" Mr. Redford shouted, and Judge Fuller promptly sustained.

"Mr. Martin," the prosecutor continued, "the defendant, Doctor Crane, has treated a great many gunshot wounds and has never been known to do less than his best for any patient. Do you have any good reason to believe he treated your friend Notches any differently?"

"Yes, I do."

"Such as what, Mr. Martin?"

"Before the shoot-out, Doctor Crane bet fifty dollars that Shifty would kill Notches!"

A gasp swept the courtroom, followed by a mumble of whispers. Doc poked Mr. Redford in the ribs. "I never bet any such thing! Ain't you gonna object?"

"No legal grounds," Mr. Redford whispered back. "Keep your powder dry. We'll get our turn."

"How do you know that, Mr. Martin?" the prosecutor asked.

"I still have his receipt! He knew better than to try collecting on it after the way he bungled things."

"Objection, Your Honor!" Mr. Redford shouted. "High time someone did," Lucky shouted right back, and the judge banged his gavel for order before sustaining the objection.

"May we see the receipt?" the prosecutor asked. Lucky plucked a slip of paper from his vest pocket and handed it over. The prosecutor looked it over with a very smug expression while he rocked back and forth on his toes. "It seems to be torn off on one end," he commented.

"Yes, sir," Lucky said. "The customer has the other half. Don't you, Doc?" he asked, wagging a finger in Doc Crane's direction.

Mr. Redford came forward to look at the betting slip then returned to his seat. "Sure looks like you signed it," he whispered to Doc.

"Forged," Doc insisted. "I never made that bet."

The prosecutor belabored and rehashed the bet as far as he could before turning Lucky over to Mr. Redford. Mr. Redford took his time approaching the witness, smiled disarmingly, then said, "How fortunate that you kept that receipt. Do you always make out receipts on your bets?"

"Not always," Lucky admitted. "Just when there's too many bets to remember."

"Can you tell us just exactly when that bet was made and where you were at the time?"

"Can't say as I can. It probably didn't seem to matter at the time. Never thought Doc would let a man die for fifty dollars!"

"Even you know him better than that, eh?"

"I know what happened," Lucky snapped.

"Sure you do," Mr. Redford agreed condescendingly. "Except you don't know when or where the bet was made or whether there were any witnesses."

"Too many bets were made all in a rush," Lucky insisted. "I made up lots of slips with different kinds of bets written on 'em. A man could pick a bet, make his mark on one end, and give the slip back to me with his cash. I'd write in the amount of cash, sign the other end of the slip, then tear it in half and give him the end I signed. When it got busy, I didn't half-notice who was betting."

"Maybe I can help you," Mr. Redford offered with that same disarming grin. "Most everybody in town is within hollering distance. Why don't we ask any witness to that bet to step forward?"

"Yeah," Lucky agreed, looking around the room.

"How about it, folks?" Mr. Redford called out. "Lucky needs a witness to that bet. Pass the word outside. Who saw Doc Crane make that bet?"

A wave of whispers went across the courtroom and swept outside. Moments passed with no witness coming forward. Mr. Redford pretended disappointment and said, "Isn't it strange,

Lucky? You don't remember the bet because so many people were betting at the same time. Yet there aren't any witnesses."

"They were too busy making their own bets!"

"Sure they were," Mr. Redford said. "It must be so if you say so. But tell me, Mr. Martin, I've heard that you won a lot of money betting on that shoot-out. Is that true?"

"Objection!" the prosecutor yelled. "Mr. Martin isn't on trial here."

"There's a fine point here, Your Honor," Mr. Redford pleaded. "Mr. Martin's accusation concerning a bet that may or may not have been made raises a question of proper conduct which is highly prejudicial against the defendant. It seems proper to inquire as to whether Mr. Martin sets the same standards on his own betting as he would like to impose on the defendant."

"Objection overruled," Judge Fuller announced, and the prosecutor let his mouth hang open in silent protest.

"How about it, Mr. Martin?" Mr. Redford asked again. "Did you win a lot of money betting on the shoot-out in which your best friend was killed?"

"There's a lot of ways to bet. Some folks wanted to bet that one or the other would lose, some folks wanted to bet they'd both get killed, and so forth. And there's different odds on all those things. A man that knows his arithmetic can win no matter who loses."

"It's true then? You won money on the shoot-out?"

"Some."

"About six hundred and twenty dollars?" Mr. Redford asked. Lucky stared in amazement and Mr. Redford added, "I'm a man who knows his arithmetic, too."

Mr. Redford paced the floor a bit then in an imitation of the prosecutor that drew some snickers from the crowd. Finally, he shrugged his shoulders and said, "Well, I'm sure Notches would forgive you. Especially since you spent two dollars of your winnings on his funeral. Tell me something else, Mr. Martin; you testified that Mr. Notches was doing this town a favor, keeping out troublemakers. I wonder if you could tell us how many troublemakers have rushed in since we lost Mr. Notches?"

"Oh, they'll come, don't you worry about that! They'll come."

"In a kind of roundabout way, Mr. Martin, I think you're saying that no troublemakers have taken advantage of this situation yet. Is that true?"

"You might say that."

"I do say it, Mr. Martin! I say that Mr. Notches was just exactly what folks thought he was: a mean and dangerous man who enjoyed killing!"

Lucky opened his mouth to say something, but Mr. Redford cut him off with, "No further questions," and returned to his seat.

Judge Fuller declared noon recess, and Mr. Redford hustled over to Doc Crane's office with his client. Sam Ibsen brought in lunch, and they rehashed the trial for a while.

"How does it look to you, Sam?" Mr. Redford asked.

"You're doing just fine, Mr. Redford. Folks are real tickled the way you're getting under that prosecutor fella's skin."

"How's Doc doing? Do folks figure him for innocent?"

"They will soon's he takes the stand, don't you worry none about that!"

"You see?" Doc burst out. "I've got to testify!"

"Might have to," Mr. Redford conceded. "Wouldn't be necessary if Lucky hadn't come up with that betting receipt."

"It's forged!" Doc insisted. "Folks must have known that soon's you called for witnesses to the bet and there weren't any."

"What folks think can be a chancy thing," Mr. Redford said. "And if Lucky forged the receipt, maybe he'll go a step farther and find someone to back it up with another lie."

"Don't you worry none, Mr. Redford," Sam said. "Those folks on the jury will do what's right!"

"That's exactly what does worry me," Mr. Redford answered. "They're just so determined to do what's right. There isn't one man in this town except Lucky Martin that sees any sense in this trial, but everyone goes along with it because they want to do what's right. If I had my druthers, I'druther have a jury determined not to do any wrong! When folks are determined not to do wrong, they don't start wars, burn witches, lynch other folks, and such. You can't say the same about folks with an itch to do right."

They were halfway to the church to resume the trial when Reverend John intercepted them. "Mr. Redford," he said, "when you get to calling your witnesses, call me first!"

"Sir?" Mr. Redford questioned, searching Reverend John's face. "I'd have to know why."

"Have faith, son," Reverend John said. "What I'll have to say I can't say but once. Call on me, and I'll try to do the Lord's work." And, having said it, Reverend John abruptly turned and left.

Shortly after court was convened, the prosecutor rested his case. Mr. Redford called Reverend John as the first defense witness. The reverend was sworn in and Mr. Redford asked, "I believe you have some important information about this case. Is that true?"

"Yes, brother," the reverend answered. "It's about that bet that Mr. Martin believes Doctor Crane made."

"I see," Mr. Redford said. "And do you know for a fact whether Doctor Crane made that bet or not?"

"I know for a fact that he didn't."

"Who did?"

The reverend closed his eyes and answered, "I did." The courtroom burst into a general babble of voices. "Yes, brother, I confess it. I have sinned," said the reverend.

"You signed Doctor Crane's name to that betting receipt?"

"Doctor Crane ordered some carpentry from me. I copied his signature from that note." By now the courtroom had gone silent and the reverend's quiet words sounded crisp and clear in the farthest corner.

"Why on earth would you do that?" Mr. Redford asked.

"I was angered by Mr. Notches! Angered by his denial of God. Determined that he should be made to rain money upon the church when God struck him down as God surely must!"

"And you couldn't bet in your own name?"

"It was a most un-Christian thing, betting on the life of a man.

Even in my anger, I could not forget that. I was a coward and a hypocrite as well as a sinner, so I used another man's name.''

"And how did you choose to use Doctor Crane's name?"

"The doctor keeps other men's secrets far better than he has kept his own. I meant that he should collect the bet for me, but then, the way it turned out, it would have seemed wrong for him to collect such a bet.'' The reverend lowered his head and moaned, banging a fist against his forehead. "I asked the Lord to strike down Notches for his wickedness," he said. "How could I have thought that he would not strike me down for mine?''

"The defense thanks you for your great courage in coming forward with this, Reverend," Mr. Redford said consolingly.

"No man sins in secret," the reverend declared. "See how the Lord has found me out and brought me to judgment. I repent! I repent to the depth of my soul!''

"Your witness," Mr. Redford announced to the prosecutor as Reverend John paused for breath.

"Yea, brethren, hear me!'' the reverend continued. "See how my sins have built themselves, one upon another. It was wrong to bet upon the life of Mr. Notches! I knew that and tried to hide it with a greater wrong: stealing the good name of Doctor Crane. Oh, how weak is the flesh.''

"Yes, yes," the prosecutor interrupted. "You've told us that. Please sit down, Reverend!''

"Sit down?'' The reverend exploded with tears, his arms waving like windmill blades. "I can't sit down! The Lord has found me out and I must confess to save my soul. My sins must be exposed for every man to see and beware of. God help me! I have done this to myself. Of my own free will have I sinned.''

"That can wait, sir," the prosecutor broke in.

"No," the reverend shouted. "It has come out and must serve the Lord's purpose. This is my cross to bear as Christ bore his! Let me start with you!'' the reverend exclaimed, taking hold of the prosecutor's arm. The prosecutor struggled in vain in his powerful grip.

"Get him out of here," Judge Fuller yelled, and the prosecutor obediently struggled to lead the reverend out of the church.

"Do you attend services on Sunday, sir?" the reverend was asking as the prosecutor worked his way out the door with him. Judge Fuller mopped his brow and waited awhile, listening to the sounds of the reverend's continued harangue coming through the walls. Then he called Sheriff Jones and said, "Sheriff, we need our prosecutor. Please go out there and tell the reverend you need to be saved."

"Your Honor, you do need me here, too, don't you?" the sheriff hedged.

"Duty, Sheriff! Do your duty," the judge ordered.

"Lord love you!" the reverend roared when the sheriff offered himself up. The prosecutor scrambled away, and the court came back to order.

So the ball was back in Mr. Redford's court. He smiled pleasantly at the jury, turned to Judge Fuller and said, "The defense calls Doctor Crane!"

Moments later, sworn in and quietly swearing to himself, Doc sat in the witness seat, casting a wary eye on this strange lawyer of his.

"Doctor Crane, did you ever have occasion to treat Mr. Notches before his shoot-out with Shifty?" Mr. Redford asked.

"Yes, sir," Doc answered. "Three times for boils, once for a fever, and twice for bullets."

"Was Mr. Notches' life in danger on any of those occasions?"

"The fever was bad, and the bleeding from that first bullet was a close thing."

"I see," Mr. Redford nodded. "And how did he get that first bullet?"

"It was a shoot-out with another gambler. Notches belly-shot the other man so's he'd die painfully, but it turned out the man had a derringer Notches didn't know about and he got off another shot before he died. Cut Notches' left-arm artery clean in two; he'd of died that day without he got the right help in a hurry."

"How did you feel about saving Mr. Notches' life?"

"Not too proud, not proud at all. Nossir!"

"Did you consider just letting him die?"

"No. I don't have that choice."

"I see. Now, Doctor Crane, please tell us, in your own words, exactly what all you did to and for Mr. Notches after Shifty shot him."

"Everything exactly?" Doc Crane questioned, searching for some hint that Mr. Redford might not mean exactly what he'd said.

"Yes, Doctor, everything exactly!"

Doc gave him everything exactly. And when he was through, Mr. Redford smiled pleasantly, said, "Thank you, Doctor Crane!" turned to the prosecutor and said, "Your witness, sir!"

The prosecutor was delighted. "Doctor Crane," he said, rubbing his hands together, "you say that Mr. Notches might be alive today if you hadn't pulled the bullet out too soon?"

"Yes, sir."

"And you say your forceps had a burr on them that may have started the bleeding you couldn't stop?"

"Yes, sir."

"Do you claim to have helped Mr. Notches by leaving him for dead in the street until Joe Turner came and told you the poor man was alive?"

"No, sir!"

"Very strange," the prosecutor continued. "Strange that a doctor with so much experience in treating gunshot wounds could bungle so badly. Unless, of course, he meant to."

Doc looked to Mr. Redford for an objection, but Mr. Redford was busy tending to a hangnail.

"Well," the prosecutor said with a hopeless wave of the hands, "I do hope that, if you ever meet Mr. Notches in the hereafter, you'll have the decency to apologize!"

Again Doc looked in vain to Mr. Redford for an objection. What in hell was that man up to?

The prosecutor stalked back and forth in front of Doc, stopping from time to time to scowl at him. "Well, Doctor," he barked sarcastically, "nothing to say?"

Doc thought it over a moment, then wagged a thoughtful finger at the prosecutor and said, "Yessir, I do."

"Oh you do, do you?"

"Yes, sir. Your shoes are too tight. Shoes like that can ruin a man's feet and his disposition."

The prosecutor flushed and stared at his feet as the courtroom broke into laughter. The audience could be heard repeating, "His shoes is too tight!" followed by more laughter and backslapping.

Things calmed down again, and the prosecutor glared at Doc, saying, "I'm sure you'd like to change the subject, Doctor, but the subject is murder."

"Yes, sir," Doc answered, "and them shoes can murder your feet!"

Judge Fuller got some more gavel exercise, the room was roaring with laughter, and the prosecutor angrily yanked his shoes off, flung them aside, and shouted, "Is that good enough for you, Doctor?"

For the first time Doc joined in the laughter. There the prosecutor stood, impeccably dressed from neck to ankles, standing in the most frazzled socks in creation, pink toes leaning out the windows, so to speak. Judge Fuller tried to hide his face with one hand while banging away with his gavel. Realizing his mistake, the prosecutor scrambled after his shoes and jammed his feet back into them.

When the uproar died down to an occasional snicker, the prosecutor spoke again, alternately facing judge, jury, and defendant. "We seem to forget that murder is no laughing matter. The defendant has confessed to such incompetence as seems impossible for a man of such experience unless it were deliberate. I have no further questions of this witness."

Doc Crane returned to his seat next to Mr. Redford as Judge Fuller invited the defense to call its next witness.

"I have no further witnesses, Your Honor," Mr. Redford said. "The defense rests."

After court reconvened, the prosecutor got the first chance to get his last licks in. He leaned long and heavily on Doc's amateurish work on Notches, claiming that it wasn't possible for a man of Doc's experience to make so many mistakes accidentally.

Mr. Redford started his talk in the manner of a man trying to solve a puzzle. He agreed with the honorable prosecutor that it didn't seem possible for a man with Doc's experience to make all those mistakes in dealing with Mr. Notches. Yet anyone who knew Doc knew that he wouldn't do less than his best for any patient, no matter what. A puzzle indeed!

Mr. Redford walked down in front of the jury and leaned on the rail of their pew to commune with them, turning his head this way and that, speaking directly and personally to each of them.

"Perhaps," Mr. Redford said, "the answer to the puzzle has come before us and we haven't seen it. Consider Reverend John's testimony; what was it he'd said? The Lord had found him out! There's a lot of truth in that, isn't there? The Lord knows our sins. Mostly, he leaves those sins as weeds in a wheat field, to be taken care of on some distant judgment day. But, suppose the sin is something that won't wait?

"Reverend John sinned. Not a large sin if you or I had done it, but it was a large sin because the Lord expects so much more of a reverend. And the Lord forced him to judgment right here, today!"

"Amen, brothers, amen," came the sorrowful voice of Reverend John from the doorway.

"And Mr. Notches sinned," Mr. Redford continued. "Again and again he sinned! He was cruel. He was mean. How long was the Lord to hold back judgment on such a man? A year? Five years? Ten years?" Mr. Redford asked each of the jurors in turn, then answered for them. "No! There came a time when the Lord's wrath descended on Mr. Notches! Was the Lord to allow a doctor's skill to cheat His judgment day? Indeed, why did He allow Notches to survive the bullet at all? Perhaps, as Reverend John says, the Lord willed that Notches survive for a time to confound the reverend's sinful wager. But once that purpose was served, one might reasonably expect the Lord to so confound that doctor's skill that he would be of no help to Mr. Notches.

"My friends, we know that's exactly what the Lord did!" Mr. Redford proclaimed, stalking over to where Doc Crane sat. "We know, as God gives us to know," he said, grabbing and holding Doc's hand aloft, "Mr. Notches' fate was sealed by the hand of

God Almighty. The hand of God, fitted as a glove to Doctor Crane, struck Notches down!"

There was general bedlam in the courtroom, through which Mr. Redford could barely be heard announcing, "I rest my case, Your Honor."

Judge Fuller waited for the uproar to fade before commencing to bang his gavel for order and shouting, "The jury will retire to the reverend's quarters to consider their verdict."

"Begging your pardon, Your Honor," Bill Astor, the jury foreman, announced, "our minds is made up."

"How do you find?" Judge Fuller asked.

"We find Doc innocent as a jaybird!"

"That ain't a legal verdict!" the judge roared. "By 'innocent as a jaybird,' do you mean just plain innocent?"

"Yessir," Bill yelled. "Just plain innocent!"

"Done," the judge yelled, banging his gavel down in one last whack that snapped off its head and sent it bouncing across the floor. Doc was carried off to the Thirsty Saloon whilst Mr. Redford got clamped in Reverend John's fervent grip and dragged to a bench to hear more congratulations and praise than he wanted.

CHAPTER 10

THE FARMER'S TOUCH

IT was long past Doc's bedtime before he could break away from his well-wishers. His right arm was worn to a frazzle from more handshakes than he could remember. It was an awesome responsibility carrying around a hand that had been The Hand of God at the end of one's own arm.

Mr. Redford came in shortly after Doc made the mistake of lighting his lamp. "Lordy, what a whing-ding!" Mr. Redford said. "You got any antidote for too much whiskey?"

"Next to abstinence, time's the only antidote and a damn poor second at that," Doc admitted. "I could make my fortune right here in Thirsty tomorrow if I had anything better."

"You got any coffee?"

"Sure. It's been simmering since noon. Like as not, it's pure poison, but it'll take your mind off other things." Doc poured a mug of it and handed it over. "Look here, Mr. Redford," he said, "I ain't been in debt so much to anyone since Ma and Pa as I am to you."

"Yessir, that's a fact," Mr. Redford said matter-of-factly. "I don't expect you'll ever be able to repay me."

"Yes. That's what I was about to say," Doc agreed with a hint of annoyance.

"Let's stop this foolishness, Doc!" Mr. Redford snapped. "I owe you, you owe me, we're sort of even and we'll neither of us ever be able to repay the other! That's how it is. Now, let's shake on it and forget it!"

Doc stuck out his paw and shook on it, warmly and solemnly.

"Just don't ever forget that you shook the hand that was the hand of God," Doc said, and they both had a good laugh.

They had just about recovered from that when there came a tap at the door, followed by the entrance of Cindy. She came in and closed the door, then stood there as if she hadn't quite made up her mind what she wanted to do.

"Come in and close the door, won't you?" Doc invited with more humor than sarcasm. Cindy pointed a hesitant finger at Mr. Redford and said, "I bin trying to remember where I seen you before, an' now I know! You was play-acting that King O'Leery fella in Richmond, Virginia, and I went out and picked a rose and gave it to you after the play."

"King Lear," Mr. Redford corrected. "And it was a peony."

"You remember!"

"Hardly ever forget anything."

"Well," Cindy said, "we had a real fine time that day, didn't we?"

"The best!" Mr. Redford agreed. "Maybe we ought to talk about it tomorrow when I sober up?"

"You'll call on me?"

"Sure will."

"See ya," Cindy chirped, casting a flirtatious eye over her shoulder as she left.

Doc had sat there in quiet amazement during this exchange, but now he had to ask, "Just what are you? Lawyer, play-actor, both, or neither?"

"Sometimes I think I'm an actor, and sometimes I think I'm a lawyer," Mr. Redford answered with a shrug of his shoulders. "Whatever I think I am, I guess that's what I am."

"Good Lord! You mean to tell me I've just been on trial for my life without an honest-to-goodness lawyer?"

"That was your ace in the hole, Doc. If we'd lost, you'd of had a perfect legal right to a new trial. But we won and you can't be tried again, no matter what!"

"You're a professional whatzit, all right," Doc sighed. "And what have you in mind for Cindy? More acting?"

Mr. Redford thought it over. "You know, Doc," he said, "that might not be a bad idea. I'll sleep on it."

Just then the door burst open and Downwind poked his head in. "Doc!" he panted. "Ain't I lucky you're still up!"

"What's up, Downwind?" Doc asked in some alarm. "Who's hurt?"

"Nobody's hurt," Downwind said. "It's just that I fell asleep."

"Oh," Doc said. "Well, that's fine, Downwind. You just go back to sleep and I'll try to do the same."

"Betty Lee and me wanted to ask you and Mr. Redford here out to our place for dinner tomorrow, but we couldn't get a word in edgewise after the trial, so I sent Betty Lee on home with the wagon and stayed behind to make the invite. Then, whilst I wuz waiting for things to cool down, I fell asleep in the hay over to the livery stable."

"I'd be proud to come if the invite's still open," Doc said.

"Kin you be there around noon?"

"That's a tall order, but I'll be there!"

"How about you, Mr. Redford?"

"There's a lady friend expecting me to come calling tomorrow."

"Bring her along."

"You're sure Betty Lee won't mind?"

"Shucks, no. The more the merrier!"

"We'll be there, Downwind. And much obliged."

"Bonanza! I gotta get on home an' tell Betty Lee," Downwind exclaimed. "See you all tomorrow."

"That's enough for one day," Doc proclaimed, blowing out the light. "Find your way to your bunk as best you can, Mr. Redford."

Later, when both had settled down for the night, Doc asked, "You know what Cindy does for a living, Mr. Redford?"

"Reckon so. Why?"

"Just wanted to be sure you knew."

The next morning, when they had breakfast together over at The Dutchman's, Doc was still wondering why anyone like Mr.

Redford would be taking someone like Cindy around in broad daylight. That was Mr. Redford's business, of course, and Doc kept his wondering to himself. Mr. Redford was an odd duck.

Doc headed out toward Downwind's place first. Mr. Redford seemed to have all kinds of errands to run, and Doc wasn't eager to ride along with Cindy anyway. And, on top of that, Doc was still attached to that hand that had been the hand of God, and it was getting shook to numbness everywhere he went. It was a genuine relief to get out on the road away from town.

He had taken his buggy because he liked the shade it gave and because he had the notion that his horse preferred the harness to the saddle. He was in a mellow mood, partly due to his deliverance from Lucky's murder charge and partly in gratitude for not having received the hangover he'd earned the night before.

It occurred to Doc that he could just turn south and ride off to anywhere if he had a mind to. That was the point; he could if he wanted to. He was as free as any bird! It was a mellow thought, all right.

And the prospect of a home-cooked dinner with everything absolutely farm-fresh awaiting him was so pleasant that he began looking for something in everything around himself and seeing exactly what he was looking for—the hand of God. That splendid pine tree — how could it exist without the hand of God? And that sparkling little stream skipping over the rocks: God's work! Even that rugged boulder at the side of the road, a thing of beauty, an immense pearl. So who would ever want to leave? Free or not, who would want to leave this place?

That thought was still with him when he reached Downwind's farm.

"Doc, bless your bones! You came." Downwind greeted him.

"Seems as if I did!" Doc confirmed.

"Lemme take care of your horse," Downwind insisted, grabbing the reins.

"Well now, I'd best take care of my own horse," Doc countered. "I can't just stand around swatting flies."

"I'll make you a deal," Downwind said. "I'll tend your horse and you fetch a bucket of water from the crik."

"You got trouble with your well?" Doc asked.

"Naw, it's the horses. They like crik water better'n well water."

"They do? Why is that?"

"I dunno. They ain't told me that."

"But they told you they prefer creek water?"

"You give 'em a choice, and they'll take the crik water ever' time."

"That's good enough for me," Doc admitted. "I'll get the creek water." So he took up a bucket and headed down past the barn, then down into the grove of black willows lining the creek. As he approached the bank of the pool that Downwind had backed up with a small dam, he heard a splashing sound, so he crept up quietly, hoping to see a beaver or muskrat at work. He wasn't expecting to see a naked lady, but that's what he saw.

Who in tarnation was she? He couldn't tell from her backside, but Betty Lee didn't have red hair like that. And Betty Lee wasn't built willowy like that. And an honorable man wasn't supposed to be peeking at a naked lady taking a bath, was he? Reluctantly, Doc backed off and left in nervous haste. There was an after-image of that lady lingering in his mind's eye and, doctor or not, he was suffering from a thoroughly agitated case of natural instincts.

He hustled up past the barn, found Downwind, and said, "Someone's using your creek!"

"They is?"

"Yes, they is."

"My Lord, I plumb forgot! Betty Lee's friend went down there to cool off."

"Uh huh."

"Wuz she dressed?"

"Naked as a jaybird."

"Well, no harm done, you being a doctor an' all. It ain't as if just any man went down there."

"No. It ain't as if just any man went down there," Doc agreed.

"I sure do admire that horse of yours, Doc. Mighty fine filly!"

"Ain'tcha gonna tell me who she is?" Doc demanded.

"Who?"

"The filly down to the creek!"

"I thought you'd know," Downwind apologized. "That's Miss Hoffman!"

"Miss Hoffman?" Doc repeated in astonishment. How could he not have known her? It must have been the hair; he'd never seen her with her hair down. Of course it was Miss Hoffman, and what a mess that made of his mind! Doc stood there with mouth agape. What in hell was a man to do in real-life checkmate?

"You don't really mind Betty Lee inviting Miss Hoffman to dinner here, do you?" Downwind was asking.

"It's your party," Doc answered.

"That's fine, just fine!" Downwind bubbled. "A man of your caliber—well, I already told Betty Lee that you wouldn't be holding no grudge like some folks would."

The arrival of Mr. Redford with Cindy saved Doc from any further sales talk. Doc did his best to throw himself into all the greeting rituals with Mr. Redford, Cindy, Betty Lee, and Downwind, but his mind was still down by the creek.

Mr. Redford noticed that Doc wasn't quite all there, but mistook the cause. "Hang in there, Doc," he whispered. "There's nothing like today's good eating to take care of yesterday's bad booze."

Then Miss Hoffman came ambling up from the creek looking as fresh as springtime, and Mr. Redford saw that he'd misjudged the problem. "If I were a betting man," he whispered to Doc, "I'd bet you didn't know she'd be here."

"It's an ambush, Mr. Redford," Doc whispered back grimly. "Me and General Custer, we know an ambush when we see it."

"Well," Mr. Redford said, casting a sagacious eye on Miss Hoffman, who was wrapped up in greetings with Cindy and Betty Lee, "the enemy appears to be unarmed."

"You know better'n that," Doc snapped.

" 'Deed I do."

"What's your advice?"

"You're asking?"

"I'm asking."

"Well, sir, this thing between you and Miss Hoffman—"

"There ain't nothing between us!"

"Okay. This thing that ain't between you and Miss Hoffman; you mustn't treat it like a war. That takes all the fun out of it. Make it a game, a contest. That's how it ought to be!"

"Uh huh, a game. A contest," Doc repeated. "I reckon you're right. Sounds civilized!"

"Excellent choice of words, Doctor—civilized. Shall we join the ladies and play the game?"

"Do I have time to dust my mustache first?"

"Sure, sneeze on it. Then we can start to chit-chat by discussing the sneeze you snooze!"

So Doc played the game and enjoyed it tolerably well. The dinner was all he could have wished for. The main table topic was the recent trial, starring the courageous Doctor Crane and his brilliant lawyer Mr. Redford. And, perhaps best of all, Doc could see that Miss Hoffman was thoroughly puzzled by his mood. Better that she should worry about him than otherwise!

After dinner, Downwind took Doc and Mr. Redford on a tour of the farm. Afterward Mr. Redford said, "Now that we've seen Downwind's problems in running this farm, how about us hearing about yours, Doc?"

"You're referring to Miss Hoffman, are you?" Doc asked.

"You know damn well I am!"

"Things like this take time, lots of time," Doc answered.

"Horsefeathers," Mr. Redford shot back. "It takes no more time than a man wants to waste."

"Like you and Cindy, eh?" Doc counterattacked. "Yesterday she was everyone's girl. And today she's yours alone forever. Is that the way you've got it figured?"

It was a good shot. Mr. Redford almost lost his cool, but you had to be watching the color and set of his face to know it. "Cindy and I know where we've been," he answered. "Now we'll go a ways together and see how the road suits us. Maybe it'll work, maybe not."

" 'Maybe' isn't good enough for me on a thing like that," Doc said. "You're a different sort of bird than most, Mr. Redford.

I've got to be sure, and I expect it was the same way with Down-wind and Betty Lee. Ain't that so, Downwind?''

"Betty Lee and me, we were sure all right. But mostly, I wuz sure I wanted her and she wuz sure she wanted me, and we wuz both scared to death that the other didn't feel the same!''

"That's what I mean," Doc said. "You were both sure!''

"Well, yessir and nossir," Downwind interrupted. "Neither of us wuz sure what the other was thinking. Just like you and Miss Hoffman.''

"Meaning what?'' Doc asked impatiently.

"Meaning just what I said. You got no idea why she did that mean thing to you. There ain't nobody in Thirsty except Betty Lee that let her explain that.''

"How in the world could she explain it?'' Doc asked. "And no matter what she said, how could anyone believe her?''

"You just don't want to hear it, do you?'' Downwind demanded.

"No, I reckon I don't!'' Doc answered, getting his back up.

"Well, I do!'' Mr. Redford broke in. "I'm getting more and more curious. What's the story, Downwind?''

"Well, sir,'' Downwind began, "Miss Hoffman had this dress shop in Saint Looey, and the wood stove burned it down and left her way deep in debt. She couldn't get no money to get started again, and along comes Momma Rose and gives her a job running this place of hers because Momma Rose wants to come here to Thirsty to start a new place. It wasn't the kind of thing Miss Hoffman wanted to do, but it was the only thing she could find that would let her pay off her debts and get started in the dress business again. So she took the job and she hated it, but she did the best she could. She got to feeling terribly sorry for her girls and awfully mad at uppity people who treated her and her girls like dirt, 'specially when some of them would come sneaking over at night to visit the girls.

"Then she gets this letter from Momma Rose saying there's this real uppity doctor up in Thirsty who needs a lesson and Momma Rose will square away Miss Hoffman's money problems if she'll come to Thirsty and teach this uppity doctor a lesson. So

Miss Hoffman came and it turned out the trick was on her as much as on the uppity doctor. She got to liking him and thought she could be back in the dress business in Saint Looey before the uppity doctor came calling. And then it all blew up. That's all they was to it," Downwind concluded with a wave of his hand.

"Do you reckon that uppity doctor will ever learn anything by it?" Mr. Redford asked with a sidelong glance at Doc.

"I expect so," Downwind answered, casting an appraising eye in the same direction. "He always tries to do the right thing."

Doc stared back at them awhile, then asked plaintively, "Do you suppose anyone would still like to shake the hand that was the hand of God?"

Downwind and Mr. Redford grinned and stuck out their paws for a handshake. Having completed this ceremony, Doc said, "You boys will have to excuse me awhile, I've got some fence-mending to do."

Watching Doc stride off toward the house, Mr. Redford asked, "Do you suppose anything will come of it?"

"Yessir. They'll get hitched," Downwind assured him.

"You sound mighty sure of that."

"I sent him down to the crik to get a peek at her with her clothes off. He didn't know that's what I sent him down there for, but that's what he got and he ain't never gonna forget it."

"That's diabolical!" Mr. Redford exploded, laughing and slapping Downwind on the back. "You'd make a great lawyer."

"It's farming is what it is," Downwind corrected. "It's just getting critters together and making things grow. Purty soon now, Doc's gonna realize that Miss Hoffman ain't got no way to get back to Thirsty today 'lessen she rides along with him. That ought to keep 'em together long enough to make something happen."

"You son of a gun," Mr. Redford laughed. "Doc's just liable to amputate your future and put a real tight tourniquet on your pride when he finds out what you've been up to."

"He mustn't find out—this here's just between us!"

"He won't find out from Cindy or me, my friend," Mr. Redford assured him. "We're heading south this afternoon and don't expect to ever be back this way."

"Cain't you just stay for the wedding?"

"No. Cindy wants to be a has-been and, considering what she has been, we've got to get a fresh start somewheres else."

Downwind nodded sadly. "We'll sure miss you and Cindy, but we ain't never gonna forget you, and you'll always have our best wishes."

In one way or another, Betty Lee, Miss Hoffman, and Doc repeated the same sentiments at great length, and the afternoon ended with Cindy and Mr. Redford on horseback, riding one on either side of the buggy carrying Doc and Miss Hoffman down as far as the fork in the trail.

They parted company there, Cindy and Mr. Redford heading south and Doc and Miss Lillian Hoffman heading for Thirsty and the wedding Downwind had predicted. It was one of Doc's better decisions, even if it wasn't entirely his own doing.

CHAPTER 11

THE SKINNY FELLER

FOLKS around Thirsty tried hard not to believe what was happening during that last summer, but the truth was getting all too obvious; the gold was running out.

The claims along Crystal Creek were being worked as hard as ever, and the yields were fast declining. Some of the miners had already sold out and left, while those who were still in a claim-buying mood were now getting less gold from two or three claims than they used to get from one. Any newcomer to town was almost sure to be besieged with dazzling offers to buy into the gold business. The claim being offered was always the most promising in the area, and the price was always such that the new owner might recover that sum in the very first week for all anybody knew.

The reasons for the sell-out were varied—the owner had to return east to his ailing parents; the owner had a backache, arthritis, and bursitis; the owner was addicted to Demon Rum and would surely drink himself to death on the enormous profits to be made from the claim; or the owner had received a call to the ministry and would henceforth forsake worldly pursuits. The desperate truth of the matter was to be found in the price Lucky Martin put on any claim used as a poker game stake: five dollars. Less than a year earlier, such claims had gone for five hundred to five thousand dollars!

Even Hard Rock Hackett's mines were petering out. The best veins had simply disappeared. Only luck could find a new vein, but there was a general feeling that luck had run out along with the veins. They were drifting new tunnels this way and that, but no one had that feeling of riding the crest of a lucky streak; no one expected to get lucky. People were beginning to talk about rich strikes in other camps. It seemed as if everybody was mulling over where they wanted to go next, as if the demise of Thirsty were a sure thing.

Sam Ibsen didn't like it. There was no dignity in it, no planning, no control. It was as if Thirsty were a lump of mud about to be obliterated in a storm. As mayor, he called a meeting of prominent citizens. Sam wasn't about to tell anybody they weren't good enough to attend his meeting, though, so anybody who showed up uninvited was automatically considered a prominent citizen.

They met in Reverend John's church on a Sunday afternoon. Sam called the meeting to order and tried to get the talk going along lines of how to bring new industry to Thirsty to keep the town going when the gold quit. "Gold ain't everything," Sam proclaimed. "Lots of other towns thrive on cattle, lumber, rail business, and the like."

"Lumber!" Momma Rose snorted. "I've been in lumber camps, Sam Ibsen, and let me tell you; the scraggly stuff we've got around here ain't timber by a damn sight!"

"And just between you and me, Sam," Doc said, "nobody's going to build a railroad to Thirsty. There ain't nothing beyond here but a solid wall of mountains."

"Aha!" Sam exclaimed. "Suppose we tunnel through that wall? We'd have the best passage in hundreds of miles, wouldn't we?"

"C'mon, Sam, that wall you're talking about is the Continental Divide!" Hard Rock said. "It's too much. Twenty miles, forty miles; who knows? That's why there ain't no such tunnel built already."

"Twenty or forty miles of tunnel, eh?" Sam asked with a crafty smile and sideways look at Hard Rock. "A man ought to have a pretty good chance of finding gold in a tunnel that long. If it hits gold, it's a gold mine; if it doesn't, it's a tunnel."

Hard Rock smiled his impish smile. "If you hit that gold, Sam, drop me a letter. I'll be raising horses back in Ohio."

"Well, then, cattle!" Sam exploded. "What's wrong with cattle?"

"We're on the wrong side of the grassland," Jason said. "If some cattle ranches get going out there, they'd favor a town down toward the nearest railroad."

"Okay," Sam said, "you folks tell me. What can we do that will keep Thirsty going?"

"It ain't in the cards, Sam," said Lucky Martin. "Our people are gold miners. When the gold runs out, they'll go."

"You're damn right they will," Momma Rose agreed. "If I'd known the gold was petering out so fast, I'd of sold out last year. Now it's too late. Come the first sign of winter, you'll see nothing but the backsides of miners heading south. And they won't be coming back."

"There's always hope," Reverend John said. "Perhaps the Lord, in His wisdom, will reveal new veins of gold."

"Yes, He will," Lucky Martin agreed, "but it won't be in Thirsty!"

"Oh, ye of little faith," Reverend John countered.

"Quitters is more like it," Sam snapped. "Why don't we just give the place back to the Indians?"

"Best idea you've had yet," Lucky Martin said.

"It does have a certain style to it," Doc Crane said.

"How are we gonna gift-wrap it, Sam?" Hard Rock asked.

"Some gift," Momma Rose snorted. "What would them savages do with my place?"

"Nothing," Doc said, "and that's better'n what you've done with it."

"Hah!" snapped Momma Rose, shifting her bulk.

"This ain't nothing to make jokes about," Sam insisted. "If we don't do something, Thirsty is done for."

"Sam, it is most surely done for," Lillian Crane, the former Miss Hoffman, said. "The gold is going, and Thirsty with it."

The room was quiet while Sam searched the assembled faces. "Jason, how about you? You gonna just ride off and leave your saloon to rot?"

"Sam," Jason explained, "I follow miners like the Indians

used to follow buffalo. Miners are my favorite customers. There's no misers among 'em. When they're running in luck, they share it. If a miner finds a ten-dollar nugget, he feels like spending fifteen dollars, and if he can he does. And come the best part of the evening, they aren't running home to some wife. Yessir, Sam, when the miners leave, I'll follow."

"Dutchman, how about you?" Sam asked.

"Like Mr. Jason says," the Dutchman explained, "miners iss goot customers. Dey iss not fussy. I go mit dem ven dey go."

"They ain't fussy enough, that's for sure," Frypan yelled.

"Ach," the Dutchman exclaimed, good-naturedly, "ven Frypan go, I vatch vich vay he go und I go anudder vay!"

"So," Sam said, "no gold, no Thirsty. Maybe it is time to give it back to the Indians. We can all ride out together instead of just drifting off one by one."

"That's what we've been trying to tell you," Hard Rock said.

"We can't give other folks' property away without they say so," Sam protested. "It would have to be signed over, deed by deed and claim by claim."

"Sam," Jason said, "I'll post a sign-up sheet in my saloon and I'll bet you that before the week is out more than half the folks around here will sign up to give the place to the Indians this fall."

"Go ahead," Sam said. "Post it!"

As it turned out, the notion of giving Thirsty back to the Indians was an instant success. Most of the miners and townspeople had thought or worried about the dwindling gold supply. Not many were willing to spend another winter in Thirsty if things didn't improve before then. So why not give it back to the Indians? Have a nice, friendly ceremony, a whing-ding of a celebration, and all ride out together in search of another big strike.

Just thinking about that big whing-ding celebration put a lot of people in a celebrating mood. More than fifty miners signed Jason's sheet that first night, and some of 'em proceeded to drink themselves silly right afterward.

Roy Flood, in particular, got carried away by the whole thing and had to be carried away. A couple of friends carried him out to his burro, set him astride it, and pointed the little beast toward

Roy's cabin. It wasn't a proper thing to do to a buddy in that condition, but his friends weren't terribly sober either. And it wasn't as if they were sending him into the world bankrupt. He had a pint of red-eye in his hip pocket and a pint stashed in each of his saddlebags.

Some twenty hours later, Roy came riding back down the main street singing "Clementine" at the top of his lungs. He stopped in front of the Thirsty Saloon, tied his burro to the rail, and went in carrying two leather pouches.

"Drinks for everybody!" he commanded, slamming one of the pouches on the bar and stuffing the other, with some difficulty, into his pants pocket.

"Mind if I look?" Jason asked, moving first to inspect the contents of the pouch.

"Hell no," Roy said. "Feast your eyes!"

Jason loosened the drawstrings, held the pouch by the bottom, and tilted it onto the bar. Out tumbled a stream of golden nuggets of a size that had become rare in Thirsty.

Roy was an instant hero. The booze flowed freely, but Roy had to time his guzzling carefully, what with all the backslapping, handshaking, and questions that came his way.

The news raced up and down the main street and the saloon was soon jammed. A new strike, meaning the glory days of Thirsty weren't over! Only Roy hadn't said any of it. He didn't claim to have found a new bonanza. He said a skinny feller had given him the two pouches, but nobody was fool enough to believe that. Everybody knew that was just Roy's way of ducking the question until he could file his new claim. Meanwhile he was being generous with his newfound wealth, and a lot of miners were hanging on his every babbling word, hoping the liquor would eventually lead him to say more than he meant to.

Of course, there were a few sneaky characters who went out and studied the hoofprints of Roy's burro, then set out to backtrack it. It wasn't easy by lantern light, but the prize would surely be worth it. To Thirsty's credit, there were only three such sneaky characters, all the other sneaky characters being in the saloon partaking of Roy's generosity and waiting for him to give away the location of his strike.

Those who had waited inside the saloon waited in vain for any clue to the strike, and the abundant booze eventually took its toll. People were falling asleep all over the place and out onto the porch. Roy himself had fallen asleep on a chair and had been eased onto the floor by a couple of friends who fell asleep on the floor beside him.

Jason wearily surveyed the mess, then went around blowing out lanterns. It wasn't his habit to let anyone stay in the saloon after closing, but there were just too many of them.

Sometime next morning things and people got to moving again. The three sneaky characters who had tried in vain to backtrack Roy's burro came into town convinced that Roy had gone to a great deal of trouble to be sure he couldn't be backtracked. Those tracks had circled back on themselves in endless loops that covered a hell of a lot of territory without going anywhere. No doubt about it; Roy was hiding something mighty valuable.

When Roy woke up, he was still a hero. A couple dozen miners escorted him across the street to The Dutchman's for breakfast. Roy was still claiming that a skinny feller had given him the gold. Nobody believed that, but everybody allowed as how Roy had a right to keep his secret until he could file his claim. With that in mind, they had decided to help him get sobered up so's they could escort him down to the claims office.

Folks started getting impatient with Roy after breakfast, though. Roy claimed he didn't know just exactly where the gold was. Now that was being just too damned cautious. Not neighborly or friendly either! Most likely he was just holding back, maybe waiting for some relatives or such-like to arrive so's they could hog all the good claims for themselves. Didn't know just exactly where the gold was? Stuff like that ought to be handled with a shovel. How dumb did Roy think folks were around Thirsty?

Roy tried to convince them, but the more he tried, the less they seemed to believe him. Things got so bad that nobody would even accept a free drink from him. In Thirsty that was just one notch removed from being the star of a tar-and-feather parade or getting lynched.

Reverend John came to his rescue with a Bible-swearing cere-mony. He brought Roy right into his church and up to the altar. It was one of those very rare occasions when the church was filled to capacity. The assembled witnesses paid close attention as Rever-end John put the preliminary questions to Roy as to his belief in God Almighty and the certain destruction and eternal damnation that awaited anyone so foolish as to make a falsely sworn state-ment before God on the Holy Bible. Roy gave the proper God-fearing answers to all these preliminaries, then Reverend John had Roy place his right hand on the Bible and answer the big question; did he know where he had gotten the gold?

"I swear before God a skinny feller guv me the gold!" Roy said. "I swear, too, that I don't know where that skinny feller or any more of the gold is. I wuz drunk. I own up to it before God that I wuz drunk. Only God and that skinny feller knows where I went that night."

It seemed plain enough that Roy was telling the truth. Most of the witnesses could see that. There was only one diehard who walked away shaking his head in amazement that Roy would ac-tually lie on the Bible to keep his secret.

Now it was a question of how Roy might remember whatever had happened that night when he met the skinny feller. Most of the miners didn't hold much hope for Roy's memory. They had spent a few nights under the influence of Demon Rum themselves and knew only too well the frustration and futility of trying to re-member what-all foolishness they had been up to at such times.

That evening the Thirsty Saloon was strangely quiet. People were sitting around staring at their beer mugs. Talk was low and listless.

Doc Crane walked in about an hour after dark, cast a puzzled glance over the place, and went up to the bar. "You got a new law against talking in here, Jace?"

"Naw. Folks are just down-in-the-mouth over Roy's lost gold mine. Some think he found the lost Brefogle mine, then turned right around and lost it again."

"The Brefogle? That's hundreds of miles south of here," Doc protested.

"How do you know?" Jason asked.

"Well, that Brefogle feller was way south of here when he was rescued, and he was too far gone to have wandered very far after he found the mine."

"Suppose he did," Jason said. "Then everyone would be looking for it in the wrong place. Maybe that's why it hasn't been found."

Doc shrugged his shoulders. "There's lots of gold around here that'll never be found. We only see the stuff that shows on the surface. Lord only knows how many veins stay hidden."

Jason leaned forward on the bar. "You got any kind of medicine that would help Roy's memory, Doc?"

"Naw. Medicine won't do it. You'd have to mesmerize him to find out where he went that night."

Doc had said it right out loud and several people heard him. They turned toward him and waited to hear more. The others in the saloon noticed the swiveled heads and turned their attention on Doc, too.

"Can you do it, Doc?" Jason asked. "Can you mesmerize him?"

"Maybe. Maybe not," Doc answered. "For one thing, Roy would have to be willing. For another thing, I'm not sure but what it might do him some harm."

"Hell, Roy don't mind that!" one of the miners yelled, then turned to Roy for confirmation. "Do you, Roy?"

"I'm ready for anything, Doc," Roy agreed. "You just do your stuff."

There was no turning back. Doc had seen several demonstrations of Mesmer's hypnotic process but had never personally mesmerized anyone for fear of messing up the patient one way or another. Actually, Doc was eager to give it a try, but professional ethics demanded that he give his victim a fair chance to back out.

"Now, you think twice about this, Roy," he said. "Maybe this mesmerizing won't do you any harm, but it ain't likely to do you any good either."

"Let 'er rip, Doc," Roy said. "I gotta find that skinny feller!"

Fair enough. Professional ethics had been taken care of. Doc looked over his audience and took command. "You folks are going to have to keep real quiet. No coughing, talking, foot shuffling, guzzling, or anything. If you've gotta do any of those things, get 'em out of the way before I begin."

Doc went over to a corner table, sat down with his back to the corner and waved Roy to the seat opposite himself. "You just make yourself comfortable there, Roy," he said, unhooking his watch chain from his vest and holding the watch out like a pendulum on its chain.

"You just watch my watch," he said. "Relax and watch my watch. You are feeling very tired. Very tired. Watch the watch. Relax. Rest. Watch the watch. Sleepy. Very sleepy. Close your eyes. You hear only my voice. My voice is all you hear. When I tell you to open your eyes, you will open them, but you will see nothing. Nothing. Okay now, open your eyes."

Roy opened his eyes. Doc put his watch away, then swung a wicked punch at Roy's nose, stopping it a fraction of an inch short. Roy neither flinched nor blinked. "That's good, Roy. Close your eyes again," he said. "Now, just sit there, Roy, and think back to the night before last. You left the Thirsty Saloon on your burro. Tell me where you went."

"All around," Roy said. "Couldn't go straight. Things was twistin' like I wuz dizzy."

"Or like you were drunk?" Doc asked.

"Yep, just like I wuz drunk."

"Where did you meet the skinny feller?" Doc asked.

"Down by the little crik alongside the road," Roy said.

"Which little creek is that?"

"The one that runs into Crystal Crik."

"There's lots of those," Doc said. "Which little creek is it?"

"The little one alongside the road."

"What road is that?"

"The little one alongside the little crik."

Doc paused with rumpled brow. Finally he said, "Roy, you'd like to go see that skinny feller again, wouldn't you?"

"That would be real nice," Roy answered.

"Yes, that would be nice," Doc agreed. "When you open your eyes, Roy, you will see what's there to see and you will do as I say, but you won't pay any attention to anyone else that might be around. When I tell you to, you will open your eyes, go out to your burro, and ride out to visit the skinny feller."

Doc paused and took a deep breath. "Okay, Roy, open your eyes and go."

Roy opened his eyes, pushed his chair back, stood, turned, and walked out. People quietly backed out of his way. He untethered his burro, climbed aboard, and started down the street toward Crystal Creek. Doc Crane and all the other patrons of the Thirsty Saloon followed on foot.

The burro splashed across the creek and headed south, trailed by the soggy-footed crowd. No one spoke, for these were men trained to the silence of the hunt, and they hunted nothing more seriously than gold. A bright August moon hung in the sky, casting grotesque black shadows of the whole troop.

For half an hour they kept to the main road, then Roy turned his burro to the right and went up a lesser trail, headed toward the dry eastern slope of the ridge that ran parallel to Crystal Creek on the west. It was a seldom-used trail, running along one of those little streams that trickled from a deep cut in the ridge. The trail sloped gently upward for a half hour, then rose steeply, gaining a few hundred feet of altitude in a quarter mile before it leveled off again. Here the creek crossed a high meadow cupped in the rocky embrace of the ridge.

Halfway across the meadow, Roy turned toward the gully cut by the little stream and followed along a gravelly path between the stream and its high bank for a few hundred yards before stopping. "Hello, Skinny Feller," he called out. "I'm back!"

Doc and the others closest behind Roy didn't see the skinny feller for a while, but when they did they understood it all. His bones and those of his burro were half-embedded in the bank of the gully, where they had lain for God-only-knows how long.

Doc asked Roy to get off his burro, walked him back down the gully a few yards, then snapped him out of his trance. Roy looked about in amazement. "Did you do it, Doc? Did you help me find the skinny feller?" Doc allowed as how the mystery of the skinny feller had been solved and led Roy back to the skeleton.

"My Gawd!" Roy said, "I didn't remember him being that skinny! The gold pouches were in that hand he's got stretched out toward us there. I reckon, considering what I'd been drinking, it seemed as if he was giving 'em to me."

"Must have been a flash flood caught him here and buried him," Doc said. "I'm sure there's been lots of prospectors up here in the last few years, so the creek must've just dug him up recently."

Roy and most of the miners elected to stay in the gully till morning to check things out in full. Doc and a few others elected to go back to Thirsty, promising to send Reverend John and Joe Turner, the undertaker, out the next day.

As it turned out, the skinny feller had no more gold to offer, and precious little of it could be found along that nameless little stream. The skinny feller had been there, as nearly as they could tell, at least thirty years, and there was no clue to his name. Joe Turner brought his bones back to Thirsty for burial beneath a wooden cross inscribed, "The Skinny Feller Who Died Rich."

CHAPTER 12

EXODUS

THE rise and fall of hope involved in the skinny feller episode helped seal the fate of Thirsty. Those few who had been dead set against giving it back to Chief Many Tongues and his tribe took it as an omen that things weren't going to get better. The list posted in the Thirsty Saloon soon included the owner of every claim and business in Thirsty except Mayor Sam Ibsen, who walked gravely up to the list one Saturday night and hoisted a beer in his right hand as he signed with his left.

The next day, Mayor Ibsen decided it was time to invite the Indians to the ceremony. Accordingly, he sent George Gatlin off to ask Downwind to invite Chief Many Tongues and his tribe; the exact date was to be chosen by the chief.

Perhaps it should be noted in passing that Downwind hadn't signed the Thirsty give-back list because he had always considered his farm to be Indian land and had been in the habit of paying rent to Chief Many Tongues. There were those in Thirsty who had told him he was a damned fool to give anything to those savages, even though it was plain enough that Downwind's isolated farm could not have survived, much less prospered, without Indian friends.

Downwind accepted Thirsty's decision with sadness. Much as he loved his farm and got along well with the Indians, he was not ready to forsake the company of his own people or to ask the same of Betty Lee. If the people of Thirsty left, he must leave, too.

Chief Many Tongues shared Downwind's sadness. Not that he was going to miss Thirsty or any of the miners. He had known that they would go one day and had patiently awaited that day.

But he was going to miss Downwind, his only trusted link to the white world. Both he and Downwind knew the sadness of trying to bridge the two worlds of the red man and the white man. Now Downwind would go with his people, even as Chief Many Tongues had returned to his.

The chief wanted no part of any celebration or ceremony. Thirsty would be his, with or without a ceremony. Why should he take his people into a drunken town just to please a people who had never welcomed them before?

Downwind agreed that it was a tarnished gift, but suggested that it might be worth the trouble if his people got a white man's deed covering the town and all the gold claims. The chief thought it over and agreed that he would go along with it if a legal deed were part of the deal.

So Downwind conveyed the chief's acceptance to Mayor Ibsen. The morning of the first day after the next full moon had been chosen by the chief for the great celebration.

The fate of Thirsty was sealed. Sam Ibsen began selling off whatever he could. Momma Rose took the next stage out and was gone for two weeks, seeking a new location for her girls. Miners who had all but quit working their claims hung around town waiting for the big day. And Hammerin' Harry Smith was kept busy tending to wagons and horseshoes in preparation for the coming exodus.

The night of the full moon was a wild one in Thirsty. There were those who were determined to drink Thirsty dry as a good deed, so's there wouldn't be any of the white man's firewater left to drive their Indian guests berserk the next day. They performed this good deed with saintly fervor, but the next day found them sporting hangovers, not halos.

Most people spent the early part of the next morning loading their pack mules, wagons, or saddlebags with whatever they considered worth keeping. As noon approached, they began assembling along the main street of Thirsty. Only the Dutchman was still in business, cooking up a farewell feed for the townspeople and the Indians.

Sam Ibsen was in a ferment of activity, trying to cook up some friendly contests to make the occasion more sociable. He had corralled several miners who thought their horses could win a race against Indian ponies, and he'd lined up others who thought they could win in footraces or arm-wrestling contests. The trouble was that most of the miners wanted to see some sort of target-shooting contest, and Sam wasn't so sure that was a good idea. For one thing, it didn't have a peaceful flavor, and for another thing, it would contrast gunpower with primitive bows and arrows in a way that Chief Many Tongues might see as a deliberately intimidating show. Doc and Reverend John sided with Mayor Ibsen against shooting contests, but they were only straws against the wind.

Lucky Martin was chosen to show the Indians some fast and fancy six-gun work. Sheriff Jones chose to demonstrate the use of a rifle, deliberately avoiding any six-gun comparison with Lucky Martin.

The Indians came just before noon, Chief Many Tongues riding in the lead with some fifty mounted braves, while squaws and children trailed behind on foot. All of the braves were armed, but the presence of squaws and children proved peaceful intent.

Mayor Ibsen, along with Reverend John, Downwind, Betty Lee, Doc Crane, and Lillian, went out to meet the chief. The rest of the townspeople kept their distance but, being women-starved, took particular note of the squaws. One of the miners summed it up for all with a hoarse whisper: "Gawd, ain't them the homeliest women you ever laid eyes on!" And, indeed, they were. Chief Many Tongues had allowed none but the homeliest females to come to the celebration. Thus temptations were minimized; the white man had put away his firewater, and the red man had protected his women.

Eager to see Chief Many Tongues in a happy mood, Mayor Ibsen set about turning over the deeds right away. He led the chief up to a seat on a raised platform built for the occasion and had Reverend John deliver a brief benediction. Then Sam launched into a long-winded speech praising the red man, expressing thanks for the years in which the miners and the Indians had been peaceful neighbors, extolling the character of the people of

Thirsty, and such-like, until he sensed that the people had had enough. Then he cut it down to a few last words, lasting perhaps fifteen minutes more. Finally, pulling out a leather pouch that he declared to contain a deed to every claim, business, or other property in the district, he handed the whole bundle over to Chief Many Tongues. The chief took the pouch, walked to the front of the platform, said, "Thank you, everybody," and returned to his seat, generating enthusiastic applause for all that he had not said.

The food serving took place then, giving Mayor Ibsen a chance to discuss the contests with Chief Many Tongues. The chief grinned for the first time. Yes, his ponies would race, his braves would race, his braves would arm-wrestle, and the target contests would be much fun. So the chief called one of his red brothers over and explained things to him, and Mayor Ibsen called for the pony race.

The street was cleared and the course established. The horses would start at the far south end of the street, run past the reviewing stand to Crazy Clem's cabin about a half mile north of town, where each rider would pluck a piece of red cloth from a tree, then double back to the finish line in front of the reviewing stand.

The race got off to a good start, flashed by at a furious pace, and shortly afterward came thundering back with George Gatlin in the lead, closely followed by two Indians. Mayor Ibsen was delighted with such a nice, diplomatic finish. He presented small cash prizes to the three winners while miners up and down the street settled up on larger bets.

Next came the footraces over the same course. Three miners and three Indians were entered. But it was clear even as they went by the reviewing stand on the northward leg that it wasn't a good contest. Three Indians in light moccasins were easily pulling ahead of three miners in heavy boots. When they came back toward the finish line, it was clearly a race only among the three Indians. The three miners bringing up the rear were rewarded with hoots and laughter.

The arm-wrestling evened things up. All the finalists were pick-

and-shovel artists from Hard Rock's mines. You break enough rocks and your arms turn to rock in the process.

Lucky Martin's six-gun display was so good that Mayor Ibsen felt obliged to make disparaging remarks about it to Chief Many Tongues. While Lucky twirled a six-gun in each hand, making them glitter like silver wagon wheels, Mayor Ibsen said, "Any man that doesn't do anything useful with his time can learn to do that." Then Lucky sent a rock flying up the street, fanning the hammer of his gun to send six bullets crashing into the rock. "There's a trick to it," Mayor Ibsen said. "What with all the noise and flying dust, a feller could miss a couple of times and nobody would know it."

Lucky finished his performance by offering to show one of his red brothers how to handle a six-gun. Chief Many Tongues accepted the offer and went down to Lucky while Mayor Ibsen cringed inwardly. The chief was wearing his two six-guns, but Mayor Ibsen held little hope that the chief knew any of the finer points of gunmanship. And Lucky might be just brainless enough to humiliate the chief in front of everyone.

"You are very good with the guns," Chief Many Tongues said. "Perhaps you will teach me."

"Be happy to try, Chief," Lucky said, "but it does take a lot of practice. Don't be discouraged if it doesn't come easy."

Mayor Ibsen beamed. Lucky was on his good behavior this day.

"I learn quick," the chief said.

"Good. But maybe for your first practice you should unload your guns in case something goes wrong."

"Nothing will go wrong," the chief promised.

"Ah, yes," Lucky stalled. He could just imagine this proud savage bungling around, spraying bullets all over the place.

Then, in a beautiful piece of diplomacy, Lucky unloaded his own guns and handed them to the chief. "Try mine," he said.

The chief took Lucky's guns and looked them over with obvious pleasure. "Very pretty," he said.

"They're nickel-plated. And the handles are ivory."

"Ivory," the chief repeated. "From the tusks of the elephant. Have you seen an elephant, Mr. Lucky?"

"No, sir. They're mighty scarce around here," Lucky laughed.

"I have seen elephants," the chief said.

"Uh huh," Lucky said. "I'd like to see one someday. Now, about the guns, if you hold them sort of natural-like and stick your trigger finger out for a pivot, you'll find that you can make 'em swing around that finger so's the finger only presses on the trigger guard, never on the trigger."

"Perhaps like so," the chief said, setting the guns to spinning in flashing arcs much as Lucky had done. Lucky knew immediately that the joke was on him, but he took it well. "I'll bet you're one hell of a good poker player, too," he said.

"I am one hell of a good poker player," the chief agreed, then handed back Lucky's guns. "Mine are not as pretty, but I am more accustomed to them." So saying, he set his own guns to spinning and went beyond what Lucky had done by flicking them high into the air and catching them in one smooth holstering sweep that brought applause from his audience.

"I'd guess you're a pretty good shot, too," Lucky said, hoping he was wrong.

"Throw two stones into the street," the chief said.

Lucky chose two pebbles smaller than plums and tossed them out into the street, then watched them fly out of sight as the chief's bullets, fired from two guns, slammed into them.

When the echoes had died out, Lucky said, "Well, Chief, I reckon I've taught you all I know. Just keep in practice." Lucky tipped his hat, and the chief nodded gravely and went back to the reviewing stand.

"It is as you say," the chief told Mayor Ibsen. "Any man can learn to do it if he has nothing useful to do with his time."

The mayor shrugged his shoulders hopelessly and said, "Chief Many Tongues, I have just the one tongue and it's too many." The chief grinned and clapped him on the back.

Sheriff Jones started the rifle demonstration then. He warmed up by snuffing the flames of lighted candles at two hundred feet or so. Then he had a buddy shoot arrows, which he snapped in two in midair.

Mayor Ibsen didn't like it. The white man's bullets snapping the red man's arrows—it was awfully close to being a direct insult to their Indian guests.

The sheriff swaggered over to the reviewing stand and offered his rifle to the chief. "Would you care to try it, Chief?" he asked.

"I believe some of my braves would like to try," the chief answered. He stood and raised a clenched fist. "Riflemen, ho!"

There was a commotion as a group of Indians jumped on their ponies and threaded their way to the reviewing stand. There were no saddles on these horses, but each had a blanket tied in place, housing a rifle scabbard. The chief directed them to form a line down where the sheriff had stood, and they did it with military precision, standing ten abreast.

"Perhaps your friend will fire the arrows for them?" the chief suggested to the sheriff.

"How many arrows?"

"Five or six," the chief answered.

"Ted!" the sheriff shouted. "Give us six arrows, rapid-fire!"

As the first arrow appeared, the ten braves drew their rifles, aimed, and fired virtually as one. The arrow splintered into fragments in midair—as did the next five.

"Riflemen! Cease and disband!" the chief commanded, and the braves holstered their rifles, turned their ponies, and paraded single-file back to where the rest of the tribe's horses were tethered.

The demonstrations had been a shock to the people of Thirsty. An Indian chief who could use six-guns, and now an Indian cavalry with sharpshooting riflemen! It seemed like there ought to be a law against that sort of thing. And who was selling guns to the Indians? Anybody who'd sell guns to Indians had to be lower than a snake's belly! Still, with everybody moving out of Thirsty, what did it matter? With the white man gone, the Indians would probably make war on each other. Let 'em! Hell, they had to have some entertainment.

So the celebration went on, and the Indians began trading

things they'd brought along for that purpose: snowshoes, furs, moccasins, and wooden bowls. They didn't want money. Tinware, knives, iron tools, glassware, and the like were the stuff they wanted. The trading went along well enough until one of the Indian kids saw a jackknife he just had to have. The knife had four blades, and the miner who owned it was carving a horse head from a block of pine to show how sharp the knife was. One of the braves was bidding on the knife with beaver pelts. He had started at one pelt, but was up to three and the miner was holding out for more.

The boy stood there with big, round, dark eyes fixed on that beautiful knife. And he must have remembered what all of his people knew: that the white man would trade anything for gold. The boy had a small leather pouch on a strap around his neck. He pulled the neck of the pouch open, stepped forward, and tapped the white man on the arm. The man looked down at him and the boy poured five gold nuggets from the pouch into his small, dark hand. Then he turned those big serious eyes on the miner and pointed at the knife.

The miner snapped the knife shut and traded it for the nuggets right away. It had happened too quickly. The other Indians took the boy away at once, but they knew the damage was done. One of them went to warn the chief while the miner with the nuggets was busy showing them to all of his white brothers.

Within a half hour the news was all over Thirsty that there was gold on the Indian land. The celebration had ended, and the celebrants slowly separated into three groups. The chief, Mayor Ibsen, Sheriff Jones, Doc Crane, Lillian Crane, Downwind, and Betty Lee were on the reviewing stand sipping coffee and tea. The rest of the Indians were clustered warily around their horses. Most of the miners were in and around the Thirsty Saloon, chewing over the news of the Indian gold. A few miners thought they could massacre the Indians in town and invade their lands at will, but the majority knew better. Even if they could take the land of Chief Many Tongues, that would bring them up against the Wolf Tribe, a notoriously mean and savage tribe that had plagued

Chief Many Tongues' people for generations. How much gold mining could they do with neighbors like that?

Lucky Martin was appointed to negotiate with Chief Many Tongues. He walked over to the reviewing stand, climbed the steps, and slouched against the rail.

"As you say, Chief, you are one hell of a poker player," Lucky began.

The chief looked at him and grinned, but said nothing.

"Those miners over at the saloon figure they could make your people rich by mining the gold on your lands for equal shares," Lucky continued.

"We would get rich and they would not?" the chief asked.

"Well, yeah, they would get rich, too," Lucky admitted.

"This is good," the chief said, "but there is no gold."

"No gold? You could fool me with the stuff the boy traded for the knife."

"It came from what you call Crystal Creek before the time of Thirsty."

Lucky scratched his head and said, "Well, Chief, I know that's the truth because you wouldn't say it if it weren't so. But, just between us poker players, those miners over at the saloon won't believe it."

"In all the land of my people, there is only one small ledge showing what you call color," the Chief said.

"Good enough!" Lucky said. "Why not let us work it for shares?"

"No. That is no good for my people. There is very little gold and my people do not prize the gold as they do the land. Your people have promised to leave. That is what my people want."

Lucky did some more head scratching. "If those miners leave now, they'll leave convinced there's gold on your land. That's the story they'll spread everywhere they go. And, the way it is with gold stories, it's gonna sound like more gold every time it's told."

"I'm sorry, Chief, but that's exactly what would happen," Doc volunteered.

"Yessir!" Mayor Ibsen agreed. "Gold stories always grow and they never die."

"Downwind, my friend, how say you?" the Chief asked.

"I'm afraid they're right, Chief," Downwind confirmed.

"If your people wish to dig gold on my land," the Chief said, "the price is the full wagon of goods which Mayor Ibsen has loaded from his store."

"Lord! That's a price and a half!" Lucky said.

"As one poker player to another," the chief said, "the price is low if one believes there is much gold there."

"You won't take a share of the gold instead?" Lucky asked.

"I do not say there is enough gold to share," the chief said.

"What-all is in your wagon, Sam?" Lucky asked Mayor Ibsen.

"All kinds of cloth, tinware, knives, tools, guns, food, ammunition; supplies of all kinds," Sam answered.

"We'd have to take the guns and ammunition out, chief," Lucky said. "It ain't legal for us to sell you guns."

"Guns stay!" Chief Many Tongues said. "The land belongs to all of my people. Some want only guns. The trade must have something for all my people!"

"How much do you want for the wagonload, Sam?" Lucky asked.

"Not such a whole lot, considering what-all's there," Sam said. "There ain't nothing in that wagon that ain't first-class. That's the only kind of stuff I buy."

"The price, Sam. Just the price!" Lucky snapped.

"Nothing less'n seven hundred."

"Four hundred."

"Six at least. You know it's worth that!"

"Five hundred! Not a cent more."

"That's robbery. I know what that stuff's worth!"

"Five hundred."

"Aw, hell!" Sam snorted. "You dig up the five hundred and it's yours. But I get a share of the gold that's found!"

"Done," Lucky said, and went back to the saloon.

Less than half an hour later, Lucky was back with five hundred dollars to buy Sam Ibsen's wagonload, which he promptly turned over to Chief Many Tongues.

"Well, Chief, which way to the gold?" Lucky asked.

"The small stream that runs down to Mr. Hard Rock's house is known to you?"

"Sure. Little bitty thing," Lucky said.

"Small," the chief agreed, "but very old. It carves its way deep in the rock on my lands."

"Yeah, okay," Lucky said. "And the gold's along the creek?"

"Where the creek flows between solid walls straight up to the sky, and the walls are most close together—there, at a height of seven men above the creek, there is color on both sides of the wall."

"At a height of seven men? How did anyone ever find it?"

"It is said that my people have been there as long as the creek. Perhaps it was seen when first the waters cut into it."

Lucky ran off to tell the others where the gold was. There was a flurry of activity as miners scrambled for their horses or a place on a wagon. Some moved out right away. Lucky could be seen hustling about, getting things going, but he had no sooner walked his own horse out of the livery stable when Hard Rock Hackett took hold of him for some serious words. Lucky nodded and came back over to the reviewing stand.

"Hey Sam," he yelled. "We need some blasting powder! Where do you keep it?"

"It's in the wagon," Sam said. "You just sold it to Chief Many Tongues."

Lucky's face fell a notch, and he turned to the chief. "Your people never use that stuff. You won't mind if I take it?"

"It belongs to my people," the chief said. "What will you pay for it?"

"I ain't got but one twenty-dollar gold piece left," Lucky pleaded.

"I do not value gold," the chief reminded him. "But you have a rifle and a six-gun."

"Chief, I can't part with this six-gun!"

"The rifle and your ammunition for it will be enough."

"You drive a tough bargain, Chief," Lucky complained, handing over the rifle and digging some cartridges out of his saddlebag.

"Not at all," the chief said. "I have said nothing of rent, even though my people now own all of the houses and lands your people once owned."

"Rent!" Lucky exploded.

"As I say," Chief Many Tongues smiled, "I say nothing of rent."

Lucky left, and the last of the miners followed along with him. Doc, Lillian, Downwind, Betty Lee, Sheriff Jones, and Mayor Ibsen were the last white people left in town. Momma Rose and her girls had headed south.

Chief Many Tongues set his people to work unloading Sam's wagon, a task they tackled with glee. The chief assured his friends on the reviewing stand that he would be patient with the miners and would not object to the white man's continued presence in Thirsty while they continued in pursuit of this last glimmer of their golden hope. Then the chief joined his people, and they rode off carrying all the treasures of Sam's General Store. Downwind and Betty Lee headed back to their farm. Sam Ibsen, bereft of any goods to sell in his store or any customers to sell to, and not rightly having a town to be mayor of anymore, elected to go see if anything drinkable was left in the Thirsty Saloon. Doc Crane and Lillian went along to keep him company. As Doc said, "When all those miners get to picking and blasting away on one claim, my office is going to look like the Civil War started up again! Let's enjoy a quiet moment while we can."

Doc was only partly wrong. There were wounded miners in abundance, but Hard Rock put them up in some of his sheds and sent for the doctor. Lillian went along to assist and they got there in mid-morning. Several very tiring and messy hours followed. All of the suffering miners would survive, but there were a few who would carry souvenir scars the rest of their lives.

When all the bandaging, stitching, and splinting was done, Doc and Lillian had dinner with Hard Rock. But he wouldn't talk about the mining. "You gotta see it," he said with a grin. "You just gotta see it!"

So they went to see it. And they understood why Hard Rock had insisted that they see it. The miners had put a platform between the rock walls high above the creek bed and it was creaking and rocking under the weight of wall-to-wall miners. Everyone was slam-banging away at the rock with hammer and chisel and, since the opposite walls were barely an arm's span apart, each hammer on the back-swing was scarcely missing the miner at the opposite wall. And, even as they watched, one of the miners took a step backward and plunged toward the miners below who were waiting their turn to climb the ladder to the platform. A chorus of shouts and curses turned abruptly to laughter as all involved came off with no broken bones.

"Lord Almighty, ain't that something!" Doc said.

"It's something, all right," Lillian agreed. "Let's not watch any blasting!"

They went back to Hard Rock's place to await more casualties and were never kept waiting too long. A new routine quickly set in on Doc and Lillian; card games morning, noon, and evening except when there was doctoring and nursing to do, which could be at any hour since the men were working day and night in shifts.

And they could see the miners' mood shift as the days wore on. At first the wounded came in with game smiles, making jokes at their injuries. One of them said, "Sew me up quick, Doc. If'n I was drunk, I'd be losing whiskey a dollar a minute!"

Then they got sort of glum, pessimistic, or silent. As Doc remarked to Lillian, "Some of these boys are too down-in-the-mouth to say ouch."

From there it turned to angry. "Damned injuns!" they'd say. "We oughta take 'em by the scruff of the neck and make 'em do the digging."

It didn't help any when Jason, through some magic known only to saloon keepers, restocked his whiskey supply and came in search of his missing customers. The talk around the whiskey keg centered on attacking the Indians to teach 'em a lesson. Lucky Martin, who had settled in close to the whiskey keg with his card game, kept the anti-Indian talk going. It seemed as if the man never slept. The card game ran night and day, and there sat Lucky, repeating every slander ever directed against the Indians and doing his best to convince the miners that they could massacre them before they'd know what had hit them.

Lucky was going downhill—had been for some time in a gradual way that no one had much noticed. Durango was gone, Notches too, and some of Lucky's confidence had gone with them. Nothing much had gone right for him. His hell-raising at Israel Douglass's near-lynching and Doc's murder trial had backfired badly. The world as seen by Lucky had become a bitter and pointless place. Time was when Lucky had been careful about his drinking, but that time was past. A close friend would have noticed the change, but Lucky didn't have any close friends anymore.

Sam Ibsen, who was now almost the sole resident of Thirsty, came out one day to look things over. He had to know whether he ought to restock his store or not, and that depended on whether or not the boys were finding gold. Doc Crane gave him a tour of his little hospital, the miners' camp, and the diggings. The twin tunnels, one on each side of the cliffs above the stream, were now each about fifty feet deep and finding no more or less color than had appeared on the original surface of the cliffs.

"What's all this talk about attacking the Indians?" Sam asked.

"Aw, they're full of loco weed!" Doc said. "Fact is, they're feeling sorry for themselves. They've pounded those tunnels into the cliffs, busted up the rocks with sledges, ground it down in a mill, and what have they got? About five dollars each. Hard Rock buys the gold, and most of their money goes to Jason and Lucky. I think that's why Lucky keeps setting them off against the Indians—so's they won't think about where their money's going."

"Any chance they'll take out after the Indians?"

"Hard to say. I try to talk sense to 'em. So does Reverend John, but they don't listen to him any better out here than they did in town."

"I'll stick around and talk to 'em too."

"I wish you would," Doc said, and went back to his doctoring, leaving Sam to salt some sense into the miners' talk.

Downwind came in that afternoon with a wagonload of farm stuff, stopping first at Hard Rock's hacienda to see what the cook might need. Betty Lee was with him and stopped off to visit Lillian Crane while Downwind took the wagon on out to the diggings to finish selling his goods.

The dinner table at Hard Rock's place was an oasis of civilization that night. Good china and clean glasses sparkled on a linen tablecloth. Lillian and Betty Lee gave the Chinese cook a hand with the serving, adding a downright Bostonian refinement to the ceremony. And all the men folk—who now included Doc, Sam, Reverend John, Downwind (strategically seated by a downwind window), and Hard Rock—took the trouble to come to dinner freshly washed and clean shaven.

They made an effort not to speak of the Many Tongues Mine, as it was being called, and succeeded for the most part. Sam got off on the topic of tall tales and told of a farmer who swore he used to grow corn so tall he had to chop it with an axe and use mules to pull the shucks off the ears. Reverend John allowed as how he knew a fisherman who had lost his watch in Lake Tahoe and, catching a large fish there a month later, had found the watch inside, still ticking! Hard Rock said he'd heard of a similar experience where a fisherman off the coast of Virginia had lost a lantern and, catching a shark a week later, had found the lantern inside, still lit!

"Well," Reverend John said, with just a hint of reproach in his tone, "I suppose a shark could swallow a lantern, but I don't think I can swallow that story!"

Hard Rock grinned and said, "I'll blow out my lantern if you'll stop your watch."

Even Reverend John laughed at that, and when they quieted down again, Betty Lee prodded Downwind into society, asking him if he didn't know some stories of that kind.

"Well, I heard about that there corn that had to be chopped with an axe," he said, "but I thought it was the gospel truth till this very minute."

"Oh, you didn't. Did you?" Betty Lee asked.

"Fer a fact!" Downwind insisted. "There was a traveling man I knew who claimed he stopped at that farmer's house late one night and spent a big part of the night drinking corn likker with the farmer, not having any idea why that farmer had so many jugs o' corn likker settin' all over the house!"

Hard Rock thought that was pretty funny and got everyone else to laughing again except Downwind, who sat there with such a perfectly serious and puzzled expression on his face that all the others went on laughing till they'd almost forgotten what they were laughing about.

Downwind waited patiently for them to quiet down. "And, don't you know, the worst part came when that traveling man went out the back door the next morning and saw them huge cornstalks fer the first time! Pore feller, he knew there weren't no cornstalks that big nowheres, and he near went plumb out of his mind thinking he'd shrunk down to such a size that the farmer's cat might come along any minute and gobble him up fer a mouse."

Again, everyone but Downwind sank into hysterical laughter and, again, it was Downwind's totally serious expression that made it so desperately funny.

" 'Course," Downwind continued finally, "the farmer came running out to see what that pore traveling man was screaming about, and the traveling man looked up to see the farmer standing on the porch of a log house made of cornstalk logs and, right off, the traveling man knew the farmer must be shrunk down tiny, too, and that was more'n he could take, so he just fainted dead away, right there."

Seeing that his audience was too exhausted to interrupt, Downwind went on to say that the farmer had taken the unconscious traveling man to the nearest doctor, which was quite a far piece down the road, and left him there because he had to get back and patch his roof, where a kernel of corn had fallen on it after a flock of crows worked it loose and couldn't fly off with it. And when the traveling man came to in the doctor's office and started in to tell what all had happened to him, the doctor just told him he'd had too much to drink, the way doctors usually do in such cases. So the traveling man went off not believing what he'd seen, and the doctor went off not believing what he'd heard.

"I expect it's always going to be that way," Downwind said. "People that see that corn don't believe what they're seeing, and people that hear about that corn don't believe what they're hearing."

"Ha, ha, ha! C'mon, Downwind! You don't really believe that, do you?" Doc asked.

"Doc," Downwind said, "did you know that ordinary corn is descended from grasses the Indians cross-bred for hundreds of years?"

" 'Pears like I heard that somewhere," Doc admitted good-humoredly.

"If you know that ordinary corn is a whole lot bigger'n what the Indians started with, what makes you so sure somebody ain't made corn a whole lot bigger'n what you've seen?"

Hard Rock was nearly tickled to death by the whole thing, but he held up his hands in surrender and said, "My pa warned me not to argue religion or the size of cornstalks, so I'm gonna leave it lay right there."

Reverend John got them off to talking religion then for a while before they could steer him out of that and into other things. But, most importantly, none of the talk concerned gold prospecting or the future of Thirsty.

They all knew Thirsty was on borrowed time, but, typical of such things, none of them guessed that this would be the last time they would all sit down to a meal or a good, aimless conversation together.

Downwind was up earlier than the others the next day because he had promised to give some of the boys a ride out to the mine in his wagon at daybreak. There wasn't a whole lot of planning to it. Downwind didn't know just who all wanted a ride.

He hitched up the team and rolled his wagon out in clear view. The miners came straggling out and climbed aboard without much comment. When the wagon was about full and no others were in sight, Downwind asked, "Have we got everybody?" There being no disagreement, he started off.

About an hour later they had gotten to the mouth of the narrow canyon where the mine was and could see the working platform that spanned the gap between the two tunnels. About fifty miners were milling around the flats at the mouth of the canyon in obvious expectation of some great event. "Don't go no closer!" several of them warned. "We've set ourselves a granddaddy charge! Both tunnels is gonna blast at once, and they've both got twice as much powder as you'd expect!"

Maybe it wasn't much, but it made Downwind kind of glad to be there. It was an event. Something he could tell his kids someday.

Then, sad to say, Tom Slade stirred in his bedroll a little farther out on the flats. He'd been nipping at a bottle while he worked in the mine tunnel the night before and his head felt a little the worse for it now. He reached for his hat to keep the daylight out of his eyes, but his hat wasn't there. That's when he remembered that he'd set it down in the mine tunnel the night before. And that thought brought him full awake. Aside from the great sentimental value of the hat, there was a gold piece hidden in the sweatband.

Tom jumped to his feet, trotted through the clump of miners waiting for the blast, and ran for the ladder leading up to the platform. They yelled for him to come back, but there was always a lot of yelling in camp and a feller learned to ignore it. He got up to the platform and ran into the tunnel on the left, which suddenly belched a tremendous roar of boiling smoke, flinging Tom straight across the platform into the righthand tunnel. Tom managed to stand again on his one good leg and was promptly caught in the second blast there and flung back across the platform into the first tunnel. It had been the shortest and last day of his life.

They didn't know about the hat and the gold piece hidden in the sweatband, so they didn't know why on earth Tom had run into the mine. But they blamed themselves for not stopping him. In memory, it seemed as if he'd trotted past them plain enough and slow enough so's they could have stopped him. Fact was, they'd have had fifteen seconds to stop him if they'd guessed what he was about to do.

They brought him down and laid him in the shade under a blanket. And Lucky set their guilt to rest some. "It was them damned Indians that killed poor Tom!" he said. "There wouldn't be none of us here and poor Tom would be alive yet if the Indians hadn't suckered us into buying this no-account claim."

It didn't help any when the report came back from the tunnels that the color was fading out in the left tunnel and not looking any better in the other.

"What are we waiting for, boys?" Lucky yelled. "Let's go teach them Indians a thing or two!"

Downwind had seen the whole thing and, much as he disagreed with Lucky, would have held silent if anyone else had tried to tone down Lucky's rabble-rousing. But it looked as if most of the miners were ready to go along with Lucky, and there wasn't a word being said against it.

"Boys," Downwind yelled, "you go after them Indians and there won't be half of you come back alive!"

"Hey now," Lucky answered with a grin, "we got an Indian lover among us!"

"I know them Indians well enough to know you won't catch 'em by surprise," Downwind insisted. "Chief Many Tongues has guards posted day and night, just like an army!"

"What of it?" Lucky asked with contempt. "What's he got? A dozen rifles against a couple hundred of us?"

"He's got at least a hundred rifles, not counting the one you sold him."

The answer startled and stung Lucky enough to shut him up for a moment, then he said, "That bunch of Indians north of Many Tongues—the Wolf Tribe—they'll help us!"

"They ain't but one tribe," Downwind said.

"Well, you're wrong about that!" Lucky proclaimed. "Everybody knows the Wolf Tribe is Many Tongues' mortal enemy."

"The Wolf Tribe is just all the hotheads among his braves! He keeps them to the north and puts his most careful braves on the border with us. It's all one tribe, sort of split into two army groups," Downwind explained.

"There ain't no Indian that smart!" Lucky shouted in high indignation.

"Many Tongues is," Downwind insisted. "Him being their general is just as important as those hundred rifles of his, an' that's a fact!"

Lucky glared at Downwind awhile, then made a low-toned

rasping accusation. "Maybe Many Tongues is that smart! Maybe he's smart enough to sell us a no-account gold claim, then send in an Indian-lovin' white spy to talk us out of giving him what he deserves."

"My being a friend to Chief Many Tongues and his people ain't news to nobody," Downwind said. "And you know dang well, Mr. Lucky, that Chief Many Tongues told you there wasn't enough gold here to bother with before you insisted on buying this claim."

"I'm callin' you a liar!" Lucky shouted, and people scrambled to get out of the line of fire between the two. All except George Gatlin, that is. George stepped gingerly in front of Downwind with his hands palm outward and shoulder-high. "There ain't no need to quarrel," George said. "Downwind is just a farmer anyways, not a gunfighter."

"You stay there, George," Lucky warned, "and I'm going to shoot that Indian-lovin' bastard right through you!"

"Move out, George," Downwind whispered. "A man's got to stand on his own."

George walked sideways out of the line of fire.

"Now you'll see how we handle Indian lovers," Lucky said, looking as lethal as a bullet.

"It doesn't have to be this way," Downwind answered.

"Make your move," Lucky ordered.

"It's your move," Downwind said, and an instant later both moved like triggered mousetraps. Three shots roared out and echoed down the canyon. Lucky staggered back with an astonished look on his face and one hand on the gun he hadn't had time to fire.

Lucky fell forward on his face, "Lordy," Downwind moaned, "I thought he wuz faster'n that!"

"He was fast," George whispered. "But I'd say you were about three times faster."

"I wuz scared, George," Downwind whispered back. "I never would have fired three if I'd thought one was enough."

"Where'd you learn to shoot like that?" George asked, still talking in that hoarse, awe-stricken whisper.

"Chief Many Tongues showed me," Downwind answered. "I showed him farmin' and he showed me shootin'."

It ended the talk about teaching the Indians a lesson. Now the miners believed the Indians had sentries, a general, two divisions, a hundred rifles, fast guns, and anything else Downwind said. And they thanked Downwind for the warning.

They tied Tom Slade and Lucky Martin over Lucky's horse for the return to Thirsty, where Joe Turner, the undertaker, was the last man in business. The miners were packing up their gear and Downwind stayed awhile to offer a wagon ride back. The mine was done; no one was staying.

Breakfast had just ended at Hard Rock's hacienda when the first of the miners arrived. Doc, Lillian, Hard Rock, and Betty Lee came out on the porch to see what was busting loose. One of the miners rode straight to the porch, pointed back at the horse carrying the two bodies, and said, "They wuz a shoot-out between Downwind and Lucky Martin!"

Betty Lee screamed and ran toward the horse, but stopped short in confusion, unable to look or turn away. She sank to her knees, wailing and sobbing as Lillian ran out to her.

"My God," Doc said. "She was waiting to tell Downwind he's going to be a daddy."

The miner who had delivered the message dismounted and cast a puzzled look at Betty Lee, saying, "She's got no call to carry on so. Downwind won that shoot-out!"

"Downwind's okay?" Doc asked.

"Sure is," the miner answered.

"Good," Hard Rock answered, and followed through with a smashing fist to the miner's jaw. "There," Hard Rock said, gazing down at the flattened miner with great satisfaction. "Now he don't have to feel like he owes any apologies!"

Doc ran out to Betty Lee with the good news, and everything eventually got set right. Downwind was the hero of the day, though his admirers still did their admiring from upwind. It was the perfect day to be a hero since it was the last day of Thirsty. All these people going their separate ways would carry this permanent hero image of Downwind with them. The hero image just doesn't keep that way at close range; it gets stale or intolerable in a neighbor.

Some of the miners went straight from the mine down through Thirsty, and on down the trail headed south without looking back or stopping at all. Others stopped at Thirsty for the funerals of Tom Slade and Lucky Martin, which were done together late that same day.

Doc Crane and Lillian were among the last half dozen to leave Thirsty the next day. Doc fussed around endlessly that day, saying good-bye to everyone else, checking over his buggy again and again, searching his offices four and five times—anything to delay the departure. And, when he finally climbed up on the driver's seat next to Lillian, he took one final look back and spotted the sign Reverend John had made for him. That was just too good to leave, so he dug out some tools, went back, and took it down. Then, finally, he was ready to leave. Lillian had been remarkably patient with all the delays, but there were sentimental tears in her eyes that explained why.

A mile or so down the trail, they found Downwind and Betty Lee parked in the shade with their wagon. A couple of placid cows were lying behind the wagon chewing their cud, and noisy crates of hens, ducks, and piglets added a Noah's Ark touch.

From that point on, Betty Lee shared the buggy with Lillian while Doc Crane shared the driver's seat of the wagon with Downwind. With their late start and leisurely pace, they didn't expect to reach Smithville that day, so they camped along the trail before dusk.

With most of the population of Thirsty in Smithville by now, accommodations there wouldn't be any better than a trailside camp anyhow. Besides, the company and the food in their camp was the best anywhere. They ended the evening singing "Oh, Susanna," "Camptown Races," and such. It was a time that would live forever, never to be exactly repeated.

Before they got underway again, Betty Lee and Downwind dug a tin box out of a hiding place in their wagon and set it on the seat of Doc's buggy. "We want you and Lillian to have this," Downwind said. "We figure we owe you, and we'd be right pleased if you'll take it."

"If that's some of Betty Lee's cookies," Doc said, reaching for the box, "you won't be able to pry me loose from it!" But, as he took hold of it, he found that it was remarkably heavy. "What in heaven is it?" he asked, working the lid loose.

"Nuggets," Downwind said, though he hardly needed to. Doc and Lillian were caught speechless by the quart or so of gold nuggets that filled the can like golden corn.

Lillian found her voice first. "It's too much, Betty Lee! A box of cookies would do just fine, not that you owe us anything at all."

"We have enough to share," Betty Lee said, "and Downwind and me, we decided we want to share it with you two."

"That's all they is to it, Doc," Downwind said. "You're just gonna have to take it. An' don't be feeling like it's too much. Folks back in Thirsty was paying me more for eggs than they was paying you fer fixing broken bones. They always knew they wouldn't get eggs from me without they paid the price, but when they came to you with a busted leg, they figured you had to fix it whether you got paid or not."

"Most of 'em paid what they could when they could," Doc said. "And I know for a fact that you didn't always charge either. Lots of my patients remarked on how you'd drop by when they were sick and see to it that they had enough to eat."

"It didn't amount to nothin'," Downwind said. "That farm of ours just grew stuff as quick as magic. We never lost a crop of anything."

Doc picked up a few of the nuggets and looked them over with an experienced eye. "Nuggets this size never were common around Thirsty. Where on earth did you get 'em?"

"You won't neither of you be telling anyone?" Downwind asked.

Doc and Lillian agreed with a shake of their heads.

"I think it was the Lord's way of testing me," Downwind said. "He led me to that valley where there was rich level ground and plenty of water, such that a farming man would know right off that it wasn't meant for anything but farming. But then, when I dug my well for drinking water, I hit an old crik bed with gold nuggets mixed in with the gravel. And when I dug my root cellar, the same thing happened. I don't know how much gold was there, but it was a plain choice between the gold and the farm."

"Sounds more like the devil was testing you," Doc said.

"Yessir," Downwind agreed. "Maybe it was the devil! I decided I was gonna stick with farming, but I started finding excuses for digging holes. I put a cellar under the house, I put a cellar under the barn, I moved the outhouse every month, I dug extra wells, and I saved every speck of gold I found down there. An' when I ran out of excuses to dig holes, it like to drove me crazy for a while. It was along about then that Betty Lee came along, and the gold just didn't matter much after that.

"Shucks, most of the nuggets was so big I couldn't even trade 'em in without everybody guessing where they came from. Then what? I'd of been run off my farm by claim jumpers or maybe Chief Many Tongues woulda tried to help me and there'da been war! Or maybe some big company would have got hold of the place and brought in a dredge to rip my farm off the face of the earth! Maybe I couldn't have done it without Betty Lee, but I learned to leave the gold be."

"Well, if you ever change your mind, you'll still know where the gold is," Lillian said.

"We worried some about that, Betty Lee and me. That's why we made sure we couldn't come back for it."

"You mind telling me how you did that?" Doc asked.

"Easy. We told Chief Many Tongues about the gold before we left. He's seen one gold rush, I don't think he'll ever let another one get started."

"Oh, he wouldn't mind if one or two old friends did just a little gold mining, would he?" Doc asked.

Downwind shook his head. "Doc, you gotta understand the way it is with Chief Many Tongues. With him, the tribe comes first."

"Uh huh," Doc said. "And what comes second?"

"Nothing! There ain't no second! If I know the chief, he'll settle a village on the farm, and it won't be the friendly part of his tribe neither!''

So Doc and Lillian went their way, which included a year back in Boston to update his doctoring skills before heading west again. And Downwind and Betty Lee went their way, which was to California, a promised land that sounded almost too good to be true.

And Thirsty slumbered empty and silent: a brand-new ghost town.

EPILOGUE

A hammering noise broke my reverie, and I found myself still sitting there beside the weed-choked main street of Thirsty on the porch of the deserted and dust-dry Thirsty Saloon. Grandpa had just finished hammering a couple of nails some distance above the doorway that had been Doc Crane's. Now he unwrapped the package he'd brought with him and drew forth a sign with raised gilded letters on a black background that said, "Edward E. Crane, Medical Doctor."

Grandpa stood back to admire the sign. "That's just exactly where she belongs," he said. "Just as solid as the day Reverend John made 'er for me!"

I smiled to see his pleasure, but it was a moment all too brief. He looked up and down the street, then came over and sat down next to me with a sigh. "The clock never turns back," he said. "What was, was, and won't be again. I might best have stayed away and left the memory as it was."

"You are a most welcome visitor, Doctor!" a voice behind us declared, and I damned near jumped out of my skin at the sound.

Grandpa got to his feet as quick as I did, and we turned to face a tall Indian clad in buckskin. He was easily as old as Grandpa and, like Grandpa, looked sort of indestructible.

"Chief Many Tongues!" Grandpa said with obvious pleasure, and stuck out the hand that had been the hand of God to shake hands with the chief. Grandpa introduced me, and the chief assured me that the doctor's grandson was welcome too. We were invited to visit the chief's village, but Grandpa explained that people would come looking for us if we weren't back on schedule. The chief nodded sympathetically, then proceeded to lead Grandpa into a long, involved discussion of Shakespeare.

When it was finally determined that the time for parting had come, Grandpa waved a hand toward the deserted buildings and said, "It'll never be the same as it was, will it?"

"Oh yes," the chief contradicted. "One day the buildings will fall and the trees will grow again. Then it will be the same as it was."